Praise for Amanda Hocking

"Hocking hits all the commercial high notes. . . . She knows how to keep readers turning the pages."

—*The New York Times Book Review*

"*Wake* will please fans and likely win new ones. . . . The well-structured story and strong characters carry readers."

—*Publishers Weekly*

"There is no denying that Amanda Hocking knows how to tell a good story and keep readers coming back for more. More is exactly what they will be looking for once they've turned the last page." —*Kirkus Reviews*

"Filled with mysteries, realistic characters, and lots of action . . . *Wake* is the next great book." —*RT Book Reviews*

"Pure imaginative brilliance! *Wake* is full of thrills, eerie suspense, and mystery . . . Incredibly difficult to put down."

—*The Book Faery*

"Hocking's novel effectively melds myth and contemporary teen life. High school, family, young love, and mythology all combine to create an easy-to-read paranormal suspense story that will have fans eagerly awaiting new installments."

—*Booklist*

"Amanda Hocking has a gift for storytelling that will grip readers and keep them wanting more. . . . Entrancing."

—*Library Thing*

"Explosive with a nice, smooth story, a unique mythology, and lovable characters. I thoroughly enjoyed it."

—*The Teen Bookworm*

"A wonderfully adventurous and dynamic series, full of high intrigue, mythology, paranormal lore, romance, and suspense. I can't wait to be swept away in the new world of the *Watersong*." —*Fallen Angel Reviews*

"Real and vibrant. A brand-new series that reawakens everything we love in underwater mythology, *Wake* by Amanda Hocking will certainly leave you with the desire to pick up more of her titles." —*A Cupcake and a Latte*

"Amanda Hocking has such an easy and elegant way with her language—her stories just seem to flow and her words dance. This is going to be another series that I'll fall for. I absolutely cannot wait to see where she takes us with the next book." —*Into the Hall of Books*

"Great chemistry . . . plus a family history that just makes your heart ache, and you've definitely got a recipe for a fantastic new series. Get your hands on this now!"

—*YA Book Central*

"Amanda Hocking is like a breath of fresh air in the young adult paranormal market." —*That Bookish Girl*

"Amanda Hocking is an author whose storytelling skills keep getting better and better." —*Bewitched Bookworms*

"Amanda Hocking surpasses all expectations."
—*Smart Bookworms*

Also by Amanda Hocking

Switched

Torn

Ascend

Wake

Amanda Hocking

St. Martin's Griffin New York

This is a work of fiction. All of the characters, organizations, and events portrayed in this novel are either products of the author's imagination or are used fictitiously.

www.stmartins.com

The Library of Congress has cataloged the hardcover edition as follows:

Hocking, Amanda.
Wake / Amanda Hocking.—1st ed.
p. cm. — (Watersong ; no. 1)
ISBN 978-1-250-00812-1 (hardcover)
ISBN 978-1-4299-5658-1 (e-book)
1. Sirens (Mythology)—Fiction. 2. Supernatural—Fiction. 3. Sisters—Fiction. 4. Love—Fiction. 5. Seaside resorts—Fiction. I. Title.
PZ7.H65828 Wak 2012
[Fic]—dc23

2012014630

ISBN 978-1-250-00564-9 (trade paperback)

First St. Martin's Griffin Trade Paperback Edition: April 2013

10 9 8 7 6 5 4 3 2 1

For my mom and for Eric—for the ridiculous amount of love and support they give me.

And to Jeff Bryan—for always letting me bounce ideas off him.

PROLOGUE

Ours

Even over the sea, Thea could smell the blood on her. When she breathed in, it filled her with a familiar hunger that haunted her dreams. Except now it disgusted her, leaving a horrible taste in her mouth, because she knew where it came from.

"Is it done?" she asked. She stood on the rocky shore, staring over the sea, her back to her sister.

"You know it is," Penn said. Although Penn was angry, her voice still kept its seductive edge, that alluring texture she could never completely erase. "No thanks to you."

Thea glanced back over her shoulder at Penn. Even in the dull light of the moon, Penn's black hair glistened, and her tanned skin seemed to glow. Fresh from eating, she looked even more beautiful than she had a few hours before.

A few droplets of blood splattered Thea's clothes, but Penn

had mostly been spared from it, except for her right hand. It was stained crimson up to her elbow.

Thea's stomach rolled with both hunger and disgust, and she turned away again.

"Thea." Penn sighed and walked over to her. "You know it had to be done."

Thea didn't say anything for a moment. She just listened to the way the ocean sang to her, the watersong calling for her.

"I know," Thea said finally, hoping her words didn't betray her true feelings. "But the timing is awful. We should've waited."

"I couldn't wait anymore," Penn insisted, and Thea wasn't sure if that was true or not. But Penn had made a decision, and Penn always got what she wanted.

"We don't have much time." Thea gestured to the moon, nearly full above them, then looked over at Penn.

"I know. But I already told you, I've had my eye on someone." Penn smiled widely at her, showing her razor-sharp teeth. "And it won't be long before she's ours."

ONE

Midnight Swim

The engine made a bizarre chugging sound, like a dying robot llama, followed by an ominous *click-click*. Then silence. Gemma turned the key harder, hoping that would somehow breathe life into the old Chevy, but it wouldn't even chug anymore. The llama had died.

"You have got to be kidding me," Gemma said, and cursed under her breath.

She'd worked her butt off to pay for this car. Between the long hours she spent training at the pool and keeping up on her schoolwork, she had little time for a steady job. That had left her stuck babysitting the horrible Tennenmeyer boys. They put gum in her hair and poured bleach on her favorite sweater.

But she'd toughed it out. Gemma had been determined to get a car when she turned sixteen, even if that meant dealing with the Tennenmeyers. Her older sister, Harper, had gotten their father's old car as a hand-me-down. Harper had offered to let Gemma drive it, but she had declined.

Mainly, Gemma needed her own car because neither Harper nor her father readily approved of her late-night swims at Anthemusa Bay. They didn't live far from the bay, but the distance wasn't what bothered her family. It was the late-night part—and that was the thing that Gemma craved most.

Out there, under the stars, the water seemed like it went on forever. The bay met the sea, which in turn met the sky, and it all blended together like she was floating in an eternal loop. There was something magical about the bay at night, something that her family couldn't seem to understand.

Gemma tried the key one more time, but it only elicited the same empty clicking sound from her car. Sighing, she leaned forward and stared out at the moonlit sky through the cracked windshield. It was getting late, and even if she left on foot right now, she wouldn't get back from her swim until almost midnight.

That wouldn't be a huge problem, but her curfew was eleven. Starting off the summer being grounded on top of having a dead car was the last thing she wanted. Her swim would have to wait for another night.

She got out of the car. When she tried to slam the door shut in frustration, it only groaned, and a chunk of rust fell off the bottom.

"This is by far the worst three hundred dollars I ever spent," Gemma muttered.

"Car trouble?" Alex asked from behind her, startling her so much she nearly screamed. "Sorry. I didn't mean to scare you."

She turned around to face him. "No, it's okay," she said, waving it off. "I didn't hear you come out."

Alex had lived next door to them for the past ten years, and there was nothing scary about him. As he got older, he'd tried to smooth out his unruly dark hair, but a lock near the front always stood up, a cowlick he could never tame. It made him look younger than eighteen, and when he smiled, he looked younger still.

There was something innocent about him, and that was probably why Harper had never thought of him as anything more than a friend. Even Gemma had dismissed him as uncrushworthy until recently. She'd seen the subtle changes in him, his youthfulness giving way to broad shoulders and strong arms.

It was that new thing, the new *manliness* he was beginning to grow into, that made her stomach flutter when Alex smiled at her. She still wasn't used to feeling that way around him, so she pushed it down and tried to ignore it.

"The stupid piece of junk won't run." Gemma gestured to the rusty compact and stepped over to where Alex stood on his lawn. "I've only had it for three months, and it's dead already."

"I'm sorry to hear that," Alex said. "Do you need help?"

"You know something about cars?" Gemma raised an eyebrow. She had seen him spend plenty of time playing video games or with his nose stuck in a book, but she'd never once seen him under the hood of a car.

Alex smiled sheepishly and lowered his eyes. He had been blessed with tan skin, which made it easier for him to hide his embarrassment, but Gemma knew him well enough to understand that he blushed at almost anything.

"No," he admitted with a small laugh and motioned back to the driveway where his blue Mercury Cougar sat. "But I do have a car of my own."

He pulled his keys out of his pocket and swung them around his finger. For a moment he managed to look slick before the keys flew off his hand and hit him in the chin. Gemma stifled a laugh as he scrambled to pick them up.

"You okay?"

"Uh, yeah, I'm fine." He rubbed his chin and shrugged it off. "So, do you want a ride?"

"Are you sure? It's pretty late. I don't want to bother you."

"Nah, it's no bother." He stepped back toward his car, waiting for Gemma to follow. "Where are you headed?"

"Just to the bay."

"I should've known." He grinned. "Your nightly swim?"

"It's not *nightly,*" Gemma said, though he wasn't too far off base.

"Come on." Alex walked over to the Cougar and opened his door. "Hop in."

"All right, if you insist."

Gemma didn't like imposing on people, but she didn't want to pass up a chance at swimming. A car ride alone with

Alex wouldn't hurt, either. Usually she only got to spend time with him when he was hanging out with her sister.

"So what is it about these swims that you find so entrancing?" Alex asked after she'd gotten in the car.

"I don't think I'd ever describe them as entrancing." She buckled her seat belt, then leaned back. "I don't know what it is exactly. There's just . . . nothing else like it."

"What do you mean?" Alex asked. He'd started the car but stayed parked in the driveway, watching her as she tried to explain.

"During the day there are so many people at the bay, especially during the summer, but at night . . . it's just you and the water and the stars. And it's dark, so it all feels like one thing, and you're part of it all." She furrowed her brow, but her smile was wistful. "I guess it is kind of entrancing," she admitted. She shook her head, clearing it of the thought. "I don't know. Maybe I'm just a freak who likes swimming at night."

That was when Gemma realized Alex was staring at her, and she glanced over at him. He had a strange expression on his face, almost like he was dumbfounded.

"What?" Gemma asked, beginning to feel embarrassed at the way he looked at her. She fidgeted with her hair, tucking it behind her ears, and shifted in her seat.

"Nothing. Sorry." Alex shook his head and put the car in drive. "You probably want to get out to the water."

"I'm not in a huge rush or anything," Gemma said, but that was sort of a lie. She wanted to get as much time in the water as she could before her curfew.

"Are you still training?" Alex asked. "Or did you stop for summer vacation?"

"Nope, I still train." She rolled down the car window, letting the salty air blow in. "I swim every day at the pool with the coach. He says my times are getting really good."

"At the pool you swim all day, and then you want to sneak out and swim all night?" Alex smirked. "How does that work?"

"It's different." She stuck her arm out the open window, holding it straight like the wing of a plane. "Swimming at the pool, it's all laps and time. It's work. Out in the bay, it's just floating and splashing around."

"But don't you ever get sick of being wet?" Alex asked.

"Nope. That's like asking you, *Don't you ever get sick of breathing air?*"

"As a matter of fact, I do. Sometimes I think, *Wouldn't it be grand if I didn't need to breathe?*"

"Why?" Gemma laughed. "Why would that ever be grand?"

"I don't know." He looked self-conscious for a minute, his smile twisting nervously. "I guess I mostly thought it when I was in gym class and they'd make me run or something. I was always so out of breath."

Alex glanced over at her, as if checking to see if she thought he was a complete loser for that admission. But she only smiled at him in response.

"You should've spent more time swimming with me," Gemma said. "Then you wouldn't have been so out of shape."

"I know, but I'm a geek." He sighed. "At least I'm done with all that gym stuff now that I've graduated."

"Soon you'll be so busy at college, you won't even remember the horrors of high school," Gemma said, her tone turning curiously despondent.

"Yeah, I guess." Alex furrowed his brow.

Gemma leaned closer to the window, hanging her elbow down the side and resting her chin on her hand as she stared out at houses and trees passing by. In their neighborhood, the houses were all cheap and run-down, but as soon as they passed Capri Lane, everything was clean and modern.

Since it was tourist season, all the buildings and trees were lit up brightly. Music from the bars and the sounds of people talking and laughing wafted through the air.

"Are you excited to get away from all this?" Gemma asked with a wry smile and pointed to a drunken couple arguing on the boulevard.

"There is some stuff I'll be glad to get away from," he admitted, but when he looked over at her, his expression softened. "But there will definitely be some things that I miss."

The beach was mostly deserted, other than a few teenagers having a bonfire, and Gemma directed Alex to drive a little farther. The soft sand gave way to more jagged rocks lining the shore, and the paved parking lots were replaced by a forest of bald cypress trees. He parked on a dirt road as close to the water as he could get.

This far away from the tourist attractions, there were no people or trails leading to the water. When Alex cut the lights on the Cougar, they were submerged in darkness. The only light came from the moon above them, and from some light pollution cast off by the town.

"Is this really where you swim?" Alex asked.

"Yeah. It's the best place to do it." She shrugged and opened the door.

"But it's all rocky." Alex got out of the car and scanned the mossy stones that covered the ground. "It seems dangerous."

"That's the point." Gemma grinned. "Nobody else would swim here."

As soon as she got out of the car, she slipped off her sundress, revealing the bathing suit she wore underneath. Her dark hair had been in a ponytail, but she pulled it down and shook it loose. She kicked off her flip-flops and tossed them in the car, along with her dress.

Alex stood next to the car, shoving his hands deep in his pockets, and tried not to look at her. He knew she was wearing a bathing suit, one he'd seen her in a hundred times before. Gemma practically lived in swimwear. But alone with her like this, he felt acutely aware of how she looked in the bikini.

Of the two Fisher sisters, Gemma was definitely the prettier. She had a lithe swimmer's body, petite and slender, but curved in all the right places. Her skin was bronze from the sun, and her dark hair had golden highlights running through it from all the chlorine and sunlight. Her eyes were honey, not that he could really see the color in the dim light, but they sparkled when she smiled at him.

"Aren't you going swimming?" Gemma asked.

"Uh, no." He shook his head and deliberately stared off at the bay to avoid looking at her. "I'm good. I'll wait in the car until you're done."

"No, you drove me all the way down here. You can't just wait in the car. You *have* to come swimming with me."

"Nah, I think I'm okay." He scratched his arm and lowered his eyes. "You go have fun."

"Alex, come on." Gemma pretended to pout. "I bet you've never even gone for a swim in the moonlight. And you're leaving for college at the end of the summer. You have to do this at least once, or you haven't really lived."

"I don't have swim trunks," Alex said, but his resistance was already waning.

"Just wear your boxers."

He thought about protesting further, but Gemma had a point. She was always doing stuff like this, but he'd spent most of his high school career in his bedroom.

Besides, swimming would be better than waiting. And when he thought about it, it was much less creepy *joining* her swimming than watching her from the shore.

"Fine, but I better not cut my feet on any of the rocks," Alex said as he slipped off his shoes.

"I promise to keep you safe and sound." She crossed her hand over her heart to prove it.

"I'll hold you to that."

He pulled his shirt up over his head, and it was exactly as Gemma had imagined. His gangly frame had filled out with toned muscles that she didn't completely understand, since he was a self-professed geek.

When he started to undo his pants, Gemma turned away to be polite. Even though she would see him in his boxers in a few seconds, it felt strange watching him take off his jeans. As if it were dirty.

"So how do we get down to the water?" Alex asked.

"Very carefully."

She went first, stepping delicately onto the rocks, and he knew he wouldn't stand a chance of copying her grace. She moved like a ballerina, stepping on the balls of her feet from one smooth rock to the next until she reached the water.

"There are a few sharp stones when you step in the water," Gemma warned him.

"Thanks for the heads-up," he mumbled and moved with as much caution as he could. Following her path, which she'd made look so easy, proved to be rather treacherous, and he stumbled several times.

"Don't rush it! You'll be fine if you go slow."

"I'm trying."

To his own surprise, he managed to make it to the water without slicing open his foot. Gemma smiled proudly at him as she waded out deeper into the bay.

"Aren't you scared?" Alex asked.

"Of what?" She'd gone far enough into the water to lean back and swim, kicking her legs out in front of her.

"I don't know. Sea monsters or something. The water is so dark. You can't see anything." Alex was now in a little over waist-deep, and truthfully, he didn't want to go any farther.

"There's no sea monsters." Gemma laughed and splashed water at him. To encourage him to have fun, she decided to challenge him. "I'll race you to the rock over there."

"What rock?"

"That one." She pointed to a giant gray spike of a rock that stuck out of the water a few yards from where they swam.

"You'll beat me to it," he said.

"I'll give you a head start," Gemma offered.

"How much?"

"Um . . . five seconds."

"Five seconds?" Alex seemed to weigh this. "I guess maybe I could—" Instead of finishing his thought, he dove into the water, swimming fast.

"I'm already giving you a head start!" Gemma called after him, laughing. "You don't need to cheat!"

Alex swam as furiously as he could, but it wasn't long before Gemma was flying past him. She was unstoppable in the water, and he'd honestly never seen anything faster than her. In the past, he'd gone with Harper to swim meets at the school, and there had rarely been one where Gemma didn't win.

"I won!" Gemma declared when she reached the rock.

"As if there was ever any doubt." Alex swam up next to her and hung on to the rock to support himself. His breath was still short, and he wiped the salty water from his eyes. "That was hardly a fair fight."

"Sorry." She smiled. Gemma wasn't anywhere near as winded as Alex was, but she leaned onto the rock next to him.

"For some reason, I don't think you really mean that," Alex said in mock offense.

His hand slipped off the rock, and when he reached out to steady himself again, he accidentally put his hand over Gemma's. His first instinct was to pull it back in some kind of hasty embarrassment, but the second before he did, he changed his mind.

Alex let his hand linger over hers, both of them cool and wet. Her smile had changed, turning into something fonder, and for a moment neither of them said anything. They hung on to the rock like that for a moment longer, the only sound the water lapping around them.

Gemma would've been content to sit with Alex like that, but light exploded in the cove behind him, distracting her. The small cove was at the mouth of the bay, just before it met the ocean, about a quarter mile from where Gemma and Alex floated.

Alex followed her gaze. A moment later, laughter sounded over the water and he pulled his hand away from hers.

A fire flared inside the cove, the light flickering across the three dancing figures that fanned it. From this far away, it was difficult to get a clear view of what they were doing, but it was obvious who they were by the way they moved. Everyone in town knew of them, even if nobody really seemed to know them personally.

"It's those girls," Alex said—softly, as if the girls would overhear him from the cove.

The three girls were dancing with elegance and grace. Even their shadows, looming on the rock walls around them, seemed sensual in their movements.

"What are they doing out here?" Alex asked.

"I don't know." Gemma shrugged, continuing to stare at them, unabashed. "They've been coming out here more and more. They seem to like hanging out in that cove."

"Huh," Alex said. She looked back at him and saw his brow furrowed in thought.

"I don't even know what they're doing in town."

"Me neither." He looked over his shoulder to watch them again. "Somebody told me they were Canadian movie stars."

"Maybe. But they don't have accents."

"You've heard them talk?" Alex asked, sounding impressed.

"Yeah, I've seen them at Pearl's Diner across from the library. They always order milk shakes."

"Didn't there used to be four of them?"

"Yeah, I think so." Gemma squinted, trying to be sure she was counting right. "Last time I saw them out here, there were four. But now there's only three."

"I wonder where the other one went."

Gemma and Alex were too far away to understand them

clearly, but they were talking and laughing, their voices floating over the bay. One of the girls began singing—her voice as clear as crystal, and so sweet it almost hurt to hear. The melody pulled at Gemma's heart.

Alex's jaw dropped, and he gaped at them. He moved away from the rock, floating slowly toward them, but Gemma barely even noticed. Her focus was on the girls. Or, more accurately, on the one girl who wasn't singing.

Penn. Gemma was sure of it, just by the way Penn moved away from the two girls. Her long black hair hung down behind her, and the wind blew it back. She walked with startling grace and purpose, her eyes straight ahead.

From this distance in the dark, Penn shouldn't have noticed her, but Gemma could feel her eyes boring straight through her, sending chills down her spine.

"Alex," Gemma said in a voice that barely sounded like her own. "I think we should go."

"What?" Alex replied dazedly, and that was when Gemma realized how far he'd swum away from her.

"Alex, come on. I think we're bothering them. We should go."

"Go?" He turned back to her, sounding confused by the idea.

"Alex!" Gemma said, nearly shouting now, but at least that seemed to get through to him. "We need to get back. It's late."

"Oh, right." He shook his head, clearing it, and then swam back toward the shore.

When Gemma was convinced he was back to normal, she followed him.

Penn, Thea, Lexi, and Arista had been in town since the weather started warming up, and people assumed they were the first tourists of the season. But nobody really knew exactly who they were or what they were doing here.

All Gemma knew was that she hated it when they came out here. It disrupted her night swims. She didn't feel comfortable being in the water, not when they were out in the cove, dancing and singing and doing whatever it was they did.

TWO

Capri

The slamming of a car door startled her, and Harper sat up, setting aside her e-reader. She hopped off her bed and pushed back the curtain in time to see Gemma saying good night to Alex before coming in the house.

According to the alarm clock on her bedside table, it was only ten-thirty. She didn't really have anything to bust Gemma on, but Harper still didn't like it.

She sat down on her bed and waited for Gemma to come upstairs. It would take a few minutes, since their father, Brian, was downstairs watching TV. He usually waited up for Gemma, not that she seemed to care. She still went out, even when Brian had to be up at five A.M. for work.

That drove Harper nuts, but she'd long ago given up that fight. Her father had set Gemma's curfew, and if it really bothered him to wait up, he could make it earlier. Or at least that was what he said.

Brian and Gemma talked for a couple minutes, with Harper upstairs listening to their muffled conversation. Then she heard footsteps on the stairs, and before Gemma could make it to her own room, Harper opened her bedroom door and caught her.

"Gemma," Harper whispered.

Gemma stood across the hall from her, her back to Harper and her hand on the bedroom door. Her sundress stuck to her damp skin, and Harper could see the outline of the bikini through the fabric.

With heavy reluctance, Gemma turned to face her older sister. "You know, you don't have to wait up for me. Dad does that."

"I wasn't waiting for you," Harper lied. "I just happened to be up reading."

"Yeah. Okay." Gemma rolled her eyes and crossed her arms over her chest. "So, get on with it. Tell me what I did wrong."

"You didn't do anything wrong," Harper said, her tone softening.

It wasn't like she enjoyed yelling at Gemma all the time. She really didn't. Gemma just had the awful habit of doing stupid things.

"I know," Gemma replied.

"I was only . . ." Harper ran her fingers over the trim on her bedroom door and avoided looking at Gemma in case she had a judgmental gleam in her eye. "What were you doing with Alex?"

"My car wouldn't start, so he took me for a swim at the bay."

"Why did he take you?"

Gemma shrugged. "I don't know. Because he's nice."

"Gemma," Harper groaned.

"What?" Gemma asked. "I didn't do anything."

Harper sighed. "He's too old for you. I know—"

"Harper! Yuck!" Gemma's cheeks reddened, and she lowered her eyes. "Alex is like . . . a brother or something. Don't be gross. And he's your best friend."

"Don't." Harper shook her head. "I've watched the dance you two have been playing the last few months, and I wouldn't care, except he's going away to college soon. I don't want you to get hurt."

"I'm not getting hurt. Nothing is happening," Gemma insisted. "You know, I thought you would be happy. You're always telling me not to go on those night swims alone, and I brought someone with me."

"Alex?" Harper raised an eyebrow, and even Gemma had to admit that Alex probably wouldn't be a very effective bodyguard. "And those night swims aren't safe. You shouldn't be going on them at all."

"I am fine! Nothing happened!"

"Nothing happened *yet,*" Harper countered. "But three people have gone missing in the last two months, Gemma. You have to be careful."

"I am careful!" Gemma balled her hands into fists at her

sides. "And it doesn't matter what you say anyway. Dad says I can go as long as I'm home by eleven, and I am."

"Well, Dad shouldn't be letting you go."

"Is there a problem, girls?" Brian called from the bottom of the stairs.

"No," Harper muttered.

"I'm going to take a shower and go to bed, if that's okay with Harper," Gemma said.

"I don't care what you do." Harper held up her hands and shrugged.

"Thank you." Gemma turned on her heel and slammed the bedroom door behind her.

Harper leaned on her doorframe as her father climbed the stairs. He was a tall man with big strong hands, worn from years of working at the dock. Though in his forties, Brian was rather fit, and other than the few gray streaks in his hair, he didn't look his age.

Stopping in front of Harper's room, her father crossed his arms and looked down at her. "What was that about?"

"I dunno." She shrugged and stared down at her toes, noticing the bright blue nail polish had begun to chip.

"You've got to stop telling her what to do," Brian said quietly.

"I'm not!"

"She's going to make mistakes, just like you do, but she'll be okay, just like you are."

"Why am I the bad guy?" Harper finally lifted her eyes to

look up at her father. "Alex is too old for her, and it's dangerous out there. I'm not being unreasonable."

"But you're not her parent," Brian said. "I am. You have your own life to live. You should be worrying about college this fall. Let me worry about Gemma, okay? I can take care of her."

"I know." She sighed.

"Do you?" Brian asked honestly, looking her in the eyes. "I know I've let you take on too much since your mom . . ." He trailed off, letting it hang in the air. "But that doesn't mean we won't be okay without you."

"I know. I'm sorry, Dad." She forced a smile. "I just worry."

"Well, try not to, and get some sleep tonight, okay?"

"Okay." She nodded.

He leaned down and kissed her on the forehead. "Night, sweetie."

"Night, Dad."

Harper went back into her room, shutting the door behind her. Her father was right, and she knew it, but that didn't change the way she felt. For good or for bad, Gemma had been Harper's responsibility for the past nine years. Or, at the very least, Harper had felt responsible.

She sat down on her bed with a heavy sigh. Leaving them would be impossible.

She should be excited about finally getting out on her own, especially considering how hard she'd worked for it.

Even with working part-time at the library and volunteering at the animal shelter, Harper had managed to get a 4.0 all through high school.

The scholarship she'd been awarded had opened doors for her that her father's budget couldn't. Every college she'd applied to had been eager to have her. She could've gone anywhere, but she'd chosen a state school only forty minutes away from Capri.

Peering out through the curtains, Harper could see the light from Alex's bedroom. She grabbed her phone from her bedside table, meaning to text him, but changed her mind. He'd been her friend for years, and despite the fact that she'd never harbored any romantic feelings for him, his growing flirtation with her younger sister weirded Harper out a bit.

The pipes groaned as Gemma turned on the hot water in the bathroom across the hall. Harper grabbed the blue nail polish so she could touch up her toenails and listened to Gemma sing in the shower, her voice soft like a lullaby.

Harper gave up after one foot and curled up in bed. Within moments of her head hitting the pillow, she was out.

By the time Harper woke up in the morning, her dad was already gone for work, and Gemma was rushing around the kitchen. It never stopped being strange to Harper that, even waking up at seven in the morning, she was the late sleeper in the family.

"I made some hard-boiled eggs this morning," Gemma said through a mouthful of food. Based on the yellow crumbles coming out of her mouth, it looked like Gemma had just finished off an egg. "I cooked up the whole dozen, so you can have some."

"Thanks." Harper yawned as she sat down at the kitchen table.

Gemma stood next to the open dishwasher, quickly downing a glass of orange juice. When she finished, she threw the glass in the dishwasher, next to her dirty plate. She was already dressed in worn jeans and a T-shirt, and her hair had been pulled up into a ponytail.

"I gotta get to swim practice," Gemma said as she hurried by.

"Why so early?" Harper leaned back in her chair so she could watch through the doorway as Gemma slipped on her shoes. "I thought practice didn't start until eight."

"It doesn't. But my car won't start, so I'm biking it there."

"I can give you a ride," Harper offered.

"Nah, I'm fine." Gemma grabbed her gym bag and sifted through it, making sure she had everything she needed. She pulled out her iPod and shoved it in the pocket of her jeans.

"You're not supposed to listen to that when you ride your bike," Harper reminded her. "You can't hear oncoming traffic."

"I'll be fine." Gemma ignored her and tossed the earbuds around her neck.

"It's supposed to rain today," Harper said.

Gemma grabbed a gray sweatshirt from where it hung on the coatrack, and then she held it up for Harper to see. "Got my hoodie." Without waiting for Harper to say any more, Gemma turned around and opened the front door. "See you later!"

"Have a good day!" Harper called after her, but the door had already slammed shut behind Gemma.

Harper sat in the kitchen for a few minutes, allowing herself to wake up before the silence annoyed her into action. She put on the stereo so the house felt less empty. Her father always kept the radio set on the classic rock station, and she spent a lot of mornings with Bruce Springsteen.

When she opened the fridge to get some breakfast, she saw the crumpled brown paper bag that contained her father's lunch. He'd forgotten it. Again. On her own lunch break, she'd have to leave early to take it down to the docks for him.

After she finished eating breakfast, Harper hurried about her morning routine. She cleaned out the fridge, throwing away old leftovers, before starting the dishwasher and taking out the garbage. It was Thursday, and on the brightly colored chore calendar she'd made it said LAUNDRY and BATHROOM in big block letters.

Since laundry took longer, Harper started that first. In the process, she discovered that Gemma must've borrowed one of her tops and spilled a chili dog on it. She'd have to remember to have a talk with her about that later.

The bathroom was always a pain to clean. The shower drain was always filled with a disproportionate amount of Gemma's golden brown hair. Since Harper's hair was darker, coarser, and longer, she'd expect to see more of it, but it was always Gemma's clogging up the pipes.

Harper finished her chores, then got herself cleaned up and ready for work. The rain she'd predicted earlier that morning was coming down, a heavy garden shower, and she had to run out to her car to keep from getting drenched.

Since it was raining, the library where Harper worked was a little busier than normal. Her coworker Marcy called dibs on putting away books and rearranging shelves, leaving Harper to help the library patrons to check out.

They had an automated system, so people could check out books without involving the clerks or the librarian, but some people never got the hang of it. Several other people had questions about late fees or reserving books, and a nice old lady needed help finding "that one book with the fish, or maybe a whale, and the girl who falls in love."

Near lunchtime the rain had let up, and so had what little rush the library had seen. Marcy had deliberately been in the back aisles rearranging books, but she came out of hiding and sat in the chair next to Harper at the front desk.

Even though Marcy was seven years older than Harper and technically her boss, Harper was the more responsible of the two. Marcy loved books. That was why she'd gotten into the field. But she would have been happy to spend the rest of her life without talking to another person. Her jeans had a hole in the knee, and her T-shirt read I LISTEN TO BANDS THAT DON'T EVEN EXIST YET.

"Well, I'm glad that's over," Marcy said, snapping at the bands on a rubber-band ball.

"If people didn't come here, you would be out of a job," Harper pointed out.

"I know." She shrugged and brushed her straight bangs out of her eyes. "Sometimes I think I'm like that guy on *The Twilight Zone*."

"What guy?" Harper asked.

"That guy. Burgess Meredith, I think." Marcy leaned back in her chair, bouncing the rubber-band ball between her hands. "All he wanted to do was read books, and then he finally gets what he wants, and all the people die in this nuclear holocaust."

"He wanted everyone to be blown up?" Harper asked, looking at her friend seriously. "*You* want everyone to be blown up?"

"No, he didn't, and neither do I." Marcy shook her head. "He just wanted to be left alone to read, and then he is. That's where the irony comes in. He breaks his glasses, and he can't read, and he's all upset. So that's why I eat carrots so much."

"*What?*" Harper asked.

"So I have good vision," Marcy said, like it should be super-obvious. "In the event of bombs being dropped, I won't need to worry about my glasses, and I can survive the fallout or zombie apocalypse or what have you."

"Wow. It seems like you really thought that through."

"I have," Marcy admitted. "And everyone should. It's important stuff."

"Clearly." Harper pushed her chair back from the desk. "Hey, since it's slow, do you mind if I go on my lunch break early? I need to run my dad's lunch down to him."

Marcy shrugged. "Yeah, sure. But he's gonna have to learn to remember that on his own soon."

"I know." Harper sighed. "Thanks."

She got up and went back to the small office behind the front desk to retrieve the sack lunch from the mini-fridge. The office was for the librarian, but she was on her honeymoon for the next month, traveling all around the world. That left Marcy in charge, so it really meant Harper was in charge.

"There they go again," Marcy said.

"There who go?" Harper asked as she came back out to find Marcy staring out the large front window.

"Them." Marcy nodded at the window.

Since the rain had stopped, the streets were once again flooded with tourists, but Harper saw exactly who Marcy was talking about.

Penn, Thea, and Lexi strutted down the sidewalk. Penn led the way, her long bronze legs seeming to stretch for a mile below the hem of her short skirt, and her black hair falling down her back like silk. Lexi and Thea followed right behind her. Lexi was blond, her hair literally the color of gold, and Thea had fiery red curls.

Harper had always thought her sister, Gemma, was the

most beautiful girl in Capri. But ever since Penn and her friends had come to town, that wasn't even close to being true.

Penn winked at Bernie McAllister as she walked past him, and he had to grab a bench to steady himself. He was an older man who rarely left the tiny island he lived on just off Anthemusa Bay. Harper knew him because he used to work with her father before he retired, and Bernie had always been fond of Harper and Gemma, giving them candy whenever they visited the docks. He even used to watch Harper and Gemma when they were younger and their dad was busy.

"Oh, that's not nice at all." Marcy frowned as she watched Bernie hang on to the bench. "They nearly gave him a heart attack."

Harper was about to run out across the street to help him when he finally seemed to collect himself. Straightening up, Bernie walked away, presumably to the bait-and-tackle shop down the street.

"Didn't there used to be four of them?" Marcy asked, her attention back on the three girls.

"I think so."

Privately, Harper felt a small sense of relief at knowing there was one fewer. She'd never thought of herself as prejudiced against anyone, even pretty girls, yet she couldn't help feeling that this town and everyone in it would be better if Penn and her friends left.

"I wonder what they're doing here," Marcy said as the girls walked into Pearl's Diner across from the library.

"Same thing everyone else is doing here." Harper tried to sound unfazed by their presence. "It's summer vacation."

"But they're like movie stars or something." Marcy turned back to face Harper now that Penn, Lexi, and Thea had disappeared inside the diner.

"Even movie stars need a vacation." Harper grabbed her purse from underneath the desk. "I'm running out to the docks to see my dad. I'll be back in a little bit."

Harper hurried out to her old Mercury Sable, hoping to get to and from the docks without getting rained on. She'd just hopped in the car and started it when she glanced up. Penn, Lexi, and Thea were sitting in a booth by the window at Pearl's.

The other two girls were sipping their drinks, behaving like normal customers, but Penn stared out the glass, her dark eyes locked on Harper. Her full lips turned up in a smile. A guy might have found that seductive, but Harper found it strangely menacing.

She put the car in drive and sped off so quickly she nearly clipped another driver, and that was very unlike her. As she drove down to the dock, slowing her racing heart, Harper once again thought about how much better it would be if Penn would just leave.

THREE

Pursued

Harper had been hoping to miss him, but lately it seemed that none of her trips to the dock would be complete without running into Daniel. He lived on a boat that he kept docked there, even though it was a small cabin cruiser, not really meant for habitation of longer than a day or two.

Brian worked at the north end of the bay, unloading barges that came in. Because that side of Anthemusa Bay was used for working ships, it was less appealing to tourists, and most of the privately owned boats were moored down closer to the beach. Of course, there were a few locals who still kept boats at the working end of the dock, and Daniel happened to be one of them.

The first time Harper had met him, she'd been on her way to see Brian at the dock. Apparently, Daniel had woken up and decided to pee over the edge of the boat. She just happened to look up at precisely the wrong time and got a full view of his manly parts.

Harper had screamed, and Daniel immediately pulled up his pants. That was when he had jumped down from the boat to introduce himself and apologize profusely. If he hadn't been laughing the entire time, she might have actually accepted his apology.

Today, as Harper walked by his boat—aptly named *The Dirty Gull*—Daniel was standing shirtless on the deck, even though the air was chilled from the wind blowing across the bay.

He had his back to her, so she could see the tattoo that stretched across it. The roots started just above his pants, and the trunk grew upward, over his spine, then twisted to the side. Thick black branches extended out, covering his shoulder and going down his right arm.

She held her hand to the side of her face, saving herself from looking at him. Just because he had pants on and appeared to be pinning his clothes on a line to dry didn't mean he wouldn't drop trou at any moment.

Because of her attempts to shield her vision, Harper didn't see anything. It wasn't until Daniel shouted, "Watch out!" that she looked up, and a sopping-wet something smacked her in the face.

It knocked her off balance, and Harper fell back onto the dock, landing unceremoniously on her butt. Daniel jumped over the railing on the bow and landed on the dock.

Harper immediately ripped the something from her face, still unsure of what it was exactly, except that it was wet and came from Daniel, so she could only assume that it was something horrendous.

"Sorry about that," Daniel said, but he was laughing as he picked up the item from where she'd thrown it aside. "Are you okay?"

"Yes, I'm fine," Harper snapped. He held out his hand to help her up, but she swatted it away and got to her feet. "No thanks to you."

"I really am sorry," Daniel repeated. He kept smiling at her, but he managed to look sheepish about it, so Harper decided to hate him a little less. But only a little.

"What was that?" Harper asked, wiping at her face with the sleeve of her shirt.

"Just a T-shirt." He unballed it and held it out to reveal an ordinary Hanes shirt. "A clean shirt. I was hanging my laundry up to dry, and the wind got ahold of it and blew it out to you."

"You're hanging your clothes up *now*?" Harper gestured at the overcast sky. "That's completely idiotic."

"Well, I was running out of clean clothes." Daniel shrugged and ran a hand through his shaggy hair. Harper could never tell if it was dirty blond or just dirty. "I know some ladies wouldn't mind if I ran around without clothes, but—"

"Yeah, right." Harper made a disgusted sound in her throat, which only made Daniel laugh again.

"Look, I'm sorry," he said. "I really am. I know you don't believe me, but you can let me make it up to you."

"You can make it up to me by not traumatizing me every time I walk by," Harper suggested.

"Traumatize?" Daniel smirked and raised an eyebrow. "It was just a T-shirt, Harper."

"Yeah, it was just a T-shirt *this time.*" Harper glared at him. "You're not even supposed to be living on these boats. Why don't you get a real place, and this won't be a problem?"

"Easier said than done." He sighed and looked away from her then, staring out at the bay. "You're right, though. I'll be more careful."

"That's all I'm asking," she said and started walking away.

"Harper," Daniel said. Against her better judgment, she stopped and looked back at him. "Why don't you let me buy you a coffee sometime?"

"No, thanks," Harper replied quickly, maybe too quickly judging by the wounded expression that flashed across his face. But he erased it just as fast and smiled at her.

"All right." He nodded. "See you later."

Harper turned away from him without saying anything more, leaving him standing alone on the dock. She was actually taken aback by his invitation, but she wasn't tempted. Not even slightly.

Sure, Daniel was kinda cute, in a grungy rock star sorta way, but he was older than her by a couple of years, and he didn't have his life together at all.

Besides that, she'd made a pact with herself that she

wouldn't date until college. She was too focused on getting her life in order, and she didn't have any time to waste on guys. That had been her plan all along, but she really recommitted to it after her dip into the dating world last fall.

Alex had set her up with his friend Luke Benfield, insisting they would be a good match. Even though they went to the same school, Harper had never had any classes with Luke and didn't really know him, but after much prodding from Alex, she finally caved.

The only time she'd really seen Luke around was when he was at Alex's house for a *Halo* party or some other video gaming event. Harper didn't usually partake in those activities, so her interaction with Luke had been minimal before they went on a date.

The date itself went well enough that she'd agreed to go with Luke on a few more. He was nice and funny, albeit in an overtly geeky manner, but in his own way, he was sorta cute. It was when they'd elevated their relationship to kissing that things went sour.

Harper had only kissed one other boy, at a slumber party in the eighth grade on a dare, but even with her limited experience, she was certain that kissing wasn't supposed to go the way it went with Luke.

It was slobbery and far too eager, like he was attempting to devour her face. Then his hands suddenly went crazy, and at first she wasn't sure if he was trying to feel her up or having a seizure. When she was certain it was the former, she decided to stop seeing him.

He was a nice enough guy, but there wasn't any physical chemistry between them. To break it off, Harper had told him that she needed to focus on her schoolwork and her family, so she didn't have time for a relationship. Still, things ended up being awkward between them the next time she ran into him.

That only solidified her views on romance. She didn't have the time or the need for all that drama.

Gemma leaned against the edge of the pool and took off her goggles. Coach Levi stood over her, and she could already tell by his expression that she'd beat her time.

"I did it, right?" Gemma asked, smiling up at him.

"You did it," Coach said.

"I knew it!" She grabbed the edge of the pool and pulled herself up and out of the water. "I could feel it."

"You did great." Coach nodded. "Now just imagine how great you'd do if you didn't waste your energy on those nightly swims."

Gemma groaned and took off her swim cap, letting her hair fall free. She looked around the empty pool. Nobody else on the swim team practiced during the summer, but then again, nobody trained as hard as she did.

They rarely spoke of it, not in real terms, but both Gemma and the coach had their eyes on the Olympics. The games were years away, but she was determined to be in top form by the time they came around. Coach Levi took her to every meet he could, and she won almost every time.

"It's not wasted energy." Gemma stared down at the water that dripped around her feet. "It's something fun I do. I need to relax."

"You do," Coach agreed. He folded his arms across his chest, holding the clipboard to him. "You need to have fun and kick back and be a kid. But you don't need to be swimming at night."

"You wouldn't even know that I was swimming if Harper didn't narc on me," Gemma muttered.

"Your sister is worried about you," Coach said gently. "And I am, too. It's not about training. The bay is dangerous at night. Another kid went missing just the other week."

"I know." Gemma sighed.

She'd already heard about it a dozen times from Harper. A seventeen-year-old boy had been staying at a beach house with his parents. He went out to meet some friends for a bonfire, and he never came back.

That story in itself didn't sound that bad, but Harper was quick to remind Gemma of the two other boys who had gone missing in the last couple of months. They left one night, and simply didn't come home.

It was usually after Harper told these stories that she'd run to Brian and start demanding that he keep Gemma home. Brian didn't, though. Even after everything that had happened with their mom—or maybe because of it—he felt it was more important that the girls have the chance to live their lives.

"You've just got to be careful," Coach told her. "It's not worth throwing this all away for some stupid mistake."

"I know," Gemma said, this time with more conviction. After all the hard work and sacrifice, she wasn't about to let any of this slip away from her.

"Okay," Coach said. "But Gemma, that really was a great time today. You should be proud."

"Thanks. I'll do even better tomorrow."

"Don't push yourself too hard," Coach said, but he smiled at her.

"All right." She smiled back and pointed to the locker room behind her. "I'm gonna hit the showers now."

"Try to do something fun tonight that doesn't involve water, okay? Expand your horizons beyond the aquatic. It'll be good for you."

"Yes, sir." Gemma saluted him as she walked backward to the lockers, and he laughed.

She showered quickly, mostly just rinsing the chlorine from her hair. All the time in the water should've left her with crazy dry skin, but she used baby oil every time she dried off. It was the only thing that prevented her from turning into an alligator.

After she'd gotten dressed, she went out to unlock her bike. The rain had come back, pouring down twice as hard as it had earlier. Gemma flipped the hood up over her head, regretting her decision to ride the bike to practice, when a horn honked behind her.

"Do you need a lift?" Harper asked, rolling down the car window to yell out at her sister.

"What about my bike?" Gemma asked.

"You can get it tomorrow."

Gemma thought about it for a second before running over and hopping in her sister's car. She tossed her gym bag in the backseat and buckled up.

"I was on my way home from work, and I thought I'd swing by and see if you needed a ride," Harper said as she pulled away from the gymnasium. Practice lasted only a couple of hours, but Gemma would usually grab lunch and then hit the weight room. She wasn't buff, but she needed her body in peak physical condition.

"Thanks." Gemma turned the vents so the heat would blow directly on her. "The rain gets pretty cold."

"How was practice today?"

"Good." Gemma shrugged. "I beat my best time."

"Really?" Harper sounded genuinely excited and smiled over at her. "That's amazing! Congratulations!"

"Thank you." She leaned back in the seat. "Do you know what's going on tonight?"

"With what?" Harper asked. "Dad's making a pizza for supper, and I was thinking of going over to Marcy's to watch this documentary called *Hot Coffee*. What did you have planned?"

"I don't know. Nothing. I think I might stay in tonight."

"You mean like stay in *in*?" Harper asked. "No midnight swims?"

"Nope."

"Oh." Harper paused, surprised. "That'll be nice. Dad will like that."

"I guess."

"I can stay home if you want," Harper offered. "I could rent movies to watch together."

"Nah, that's okay." Gemma stared out the car window as Harper drove them home. "I was thinking after supper I might see if Alex wanted to come over to play *Red Dead Redemption.*"

"Oh." Harper exhaled deeply, but she didn't say anything.

She wasn't thrilled about their friendship, but she'd already said her piece on it. Besides that, it was better if Gemma was at home playing video games with the boy next door than running around all over town in the middle of the night.

"There are only three," Gemma said, pulling Harper from her thoughts.

"What?" Harper looked over to see Penn, Thea, and Lexi walking down the street.

It was pouring rain, but they didn't have any jackets on and didn't seem to mind. If it had been anybody else, she would've offered them a ride, but she purposely sped up as she drove past them.

"There's only three." Gemma turned to her sister. "What happened to the fourth one?"

"I don't know." Harper shook her head. "Maybe she's sick."

"Nah, I don't think so." Gemma rested her head on the seat and leaned back. "What was her name?"

"Arista, I think," Harper said. She'd heard their names from Marcy, who'd heard them from Pearl, who usually was pretty accurate when it came to town gossip.

"Arista," Gemma repeated. "What a stupid name."

"I'm sure plenty of people think our names are stupid," Harper pointed out. "It's not nice to make fun of something people can't control."

"I'm not making fun of her. I'm just saying." Gemma turned around to watch the diminishing figures of the three girls. "Do you think they killed her?"

"Don't say things like that," Harper said, although the idea had actually crossed her mind. "That's how rumors get started."

"I'm not spreading a rumor." Gemma rolled her eyes. "I'm asking you what you think."

"Of course I don't think they killed her." Harper hoped she sounded more convinced than she felt. "She's probably sick or she went back home or something. I'm sure everything is fine."

"But there is something off with those girls," Gemma said reflectively, more to herself than to Harper. "There's something not quite right."

"They're just pretty girls. That's all."

"But nobody knows where they came from," Gemma insisted.

"It's tourist season. Nobody knows where anybody's from." Harper rounded a corner and turned to her sister, meaning to admonish her for feeding the gossip.

"Watch out!" Gemma screamed, and Harper slammed on the brakes just in time to stop herself from driving over Penn and Thea.

For a minute neither Harper nor Gemma said anything, not that Harper could hear anything over the pounding of her own heart. Penn and Thea just stood directly in front of the Sable, staring through the windshield at them.

When Lexi knocked on the window next to Gemma, they yelped in surprise. Gemma glanced back at Harper, as if unsure what to do.

"Roll down the window," Harper said hurriedly, and Gemma complied. She leaned forward and forced a smile at Lexi. "Sorry about that. We didn't see you there."

"It's no problem." Lexi smiled broadly, oblivious to the rain pouring down her blond hair. "We were just looking for directions."

"Directions?" Harper asked.

"Yeah, we got a little lost, and we wanted to go back to the bay." Lexi leaned her slender arms on the car and looked down at Gemma. "You know how to get down to the bay, don't you? We always see you there."

"Uh, yeah." Gemma pointed straight ahead of them. "Just go three blocks down, then make a right onto Seaside Avenue. That'll take you right there."

"Thanks," Lexi said. "Will you be down at the bay tonight?"

"No," Gemma and Harper said in unison, and Gemma shot her sister a look before going on, "It's no fun to swim in all this rain."

"Why not? The water's still wet." Lexi laughed at her own joke, but Gemma didn't say anything. "Oh, well. I'm sure we'll be seeing you around anyway. We'll keep an eye out for you."

She winked at Gemma, then straightened up and stepped back from the car. Gemma rolled up the window, but Penn and Thea were slow to move out from in front of the car. For a moment Harper was afraid that she'd have to throw her car in reverse to get away from them.

When they finally stepped out of the way, Harper had to fight the urge to floor it away from them. Instead she offered them a small wave, but Gemma stayed rigid in her seat, refusing to acknowledge the girls.

"That was bizarre," Harper said as they drove away and her heart began to slow.

"And creepy," Gemma added. When Harper didn't say anything, Gemma glared over at her. "Oh, come on. You have to admit that it was creepy. Why else wouldn't you have offered them a ride home?"

Harper gripped the steering wheel and floundered for an excuse. "They seemed to enjoy the water."

"Whatever." Gemma rolled her eyes. "They came out of

nowhere. You saw that! They were behind us, and then suddenly they were in front of us. They're, like . . . supernatural."

"They took a shortcut," Harper argued lamely as she pulled into the driveway next to her father's beat-up Ford F-150.

"Harper!" Gemma groaned. "Can you stop being logical for a second and admit that those girls give you the creeps?"

"There's nothing to admit," Harper lied. She turned off the engine and changed the subject. "Are you going to have Dad look at your car?"

"Tomorrow, when it's not raining." Gemma grabbed her gym bag from the backseat. She hopped out of the car and ran into the house, and Harper hurried behind her.

As soon as they'd pulled in the driveway, Harper had had the strangest feeling that they were being followed, and she couldn't shake it.

When she went inside, she locked the front door behind her, and listened to Gemma and Brian chat about the day.

The house already smelled like pizza, thanks to Brian's homemade sauce. But despite the cozy atmosphere, Harper couldn't help herself. She peered through the peephole in the door and scanned the street around them, but saw nothing. It took about fifteen minutes for her to settle into being home, and she still couldn't convince herself that they weren't being watched.

FOUR

Mother

Sorry, honey, but this is an all-day project," Brian said with his head under the hood of Gemma's Chevy. Black—presumably oil or other car fluids—smudged his arms and stained his old work shirt.

"I understand," Harper said. She hadn't expected a different answer from him, but that didn't stop her from asking. "Maybe another time."

Brian didn't look up at her. All his attention seemed to be focused on the engine, but he always managed to find something to occupy his time on Saturdays so he wouldn't have to go with Harper and Gemma.

"Okay." Harper sighed and twisted her own car keys in her hand. "I guess we'll get going, then."

The screen door slammed, and Harper glanced back at Gemma, who'd just stepped outside. Gemma wore dark oversized sunglasses, but her lips were pressed into a thin line, so Harper knew she was glaring at their father.

"He's not coming, is he?" Gemma asked, crossing her arms over her chest.

"Not today," Harper said gently, trying to calm her sister.

"Sorry, babe." Brian pulled his head out from under the hood and gestured to the bright sun shining overhead. "I want to get this looked at while the weather holds."

"Whatever," Gemma scoffed and stalked off to Harper's car.

"Gemma!" Harper called after her, but Gemma just shook her head.

"Let her go," Brian told Harper.

Gemma got in the car, slamming the door loudly. Harper knew she was upset, and she even understood it, but that didn't mean Gemma should act so rude.

"Sorry, Dad." Harper smiled wanly at him. "She's . . ." She waved her hands in the air, unsure exactly how to describe Gemma.

"No, it's okay." Brian squinted up at the sun for a moment, then turned back to the car. He had a wrench in one of his hands, and he tapped it absently against the car. "She's right. I know it, and you know it. But I . . ."

He didn't say anything, and his shoulders slacked. His expression tightened, hardening as he tried to hold his emotions in. Harper hated to see her father like that and wished she could say something to make it better.

"I understand, Dad," Harper insisted. "I really do." She reached out, touching him on the shoulder, before being interrupted by the loud blast of her car horn.

"She's waiting for us, Harper!" Gemma shouted from the car.

"Sorry." Harper stepped backward, going to her car. "I gotta go. We'll be back later."

"Take your time," Brian said. He bent over the engine, keeping his back to Harper. "Have fun."

Harper wanted to say more to her dad, but with the way Gemma was acting, she didn't want to push it. Gemma was impatient to begin with, but when she was upset on top of that, she could be downright impossible.

"You are so rude," Harper said as soon as she got in the car.

"*I'm* rude?" Gemma asked in disbelief. "I'm not the one who's bailing out on Mom."

"Shh!" Harper started the car and turned on the stereo, hoping to drown out Gemma so Brian couldn't hear. "He's staying back to work on *your* car."

"No, he's not." Gemma shook her head. She leaned back in the seat, her arms crossed firmly over her chest. "He could work on my car any other day. He's staying back the same reason he stays back every Saturday."

"You don't know what this is like for him."

As they pulled away from the house, Harper looked up in her rearview mirror. Brian was standing in the driveway, appearing uncharacteristically lost.

"And he doesn't know what it's like for us," Gemma countered. "The point is that it is hard for all of us, but we make it work."

"Everybody deals with things in their own way," Harper said. "We can't force him to visit her. I don't even know why it's bothering you so much today. It's been over a year since he's seen her."

"I don't know," Gemma admitted. "Sometimes it just gets to me. Maybe today it was because he was using *me* as an excuse not to see Mom."

"You mean because he's fixing your car?"

"Yeah."

"She'll still be happy to see us." Harper glanced over at Gemma and tried to smile at her, but Gemma was staring out the window. "It doesn't matter if anybody else comes or not. We're doing the best we can by her, and she knows it."

Every Saturday that the weather permitted, Harper and Gemma made the twenty-minute drive to the group home up in Briar Ridge. It was the closest group home specializing in traumatic brain injury, and that was where their mother had lived for the past seven years.

One day nine years ago, Nathalie had been driving Harper to a pizza party when a drunk driver sideswiped them. Harper had been left with a long scar running down her thigh, but her mother had ended up in a coma for nearly six months.

Harper had been convinced she would die, but Gemma had never given up hope. When Nathalie finally came out of it, she barely remembered how to speak or do basic self-care. She stayed in the hospital for a long time, relearning how to do everything. Over time, some of her memories came back.

But she was never quite the same. Her motor skills were very poor, and her ability to remember and reason were drastically impaired. Nathalie had always been caring and loving, but after the accident, she struggled to empathize with anyone.

After a brief but chaotic stint keeping her at home, Brian eventually had to move Nathalie into the group home.

From the outside, the home looked like an ordinary rambler. It was nice without being overly so, and even on the inside it wasn't that different. Nathalie shared the home with two other roommates, and the home had twenty-four-hour staffing.

As soon as Harper pulled into the driveway, Nathalie burst out the front door, running toward them. That was a good sign. Sometimes when they came she would just sit in her room, crying quietly the entire time.

"My girls are here!" Nathalie clapped her hands together, barely containing herself as they got out of the car. "I told them you were coming today!"

Nathalie threw her arms around Harper, squeezing her so tightly it hurt. When Gemma came around the car, Nathalie pulled her into the embrace, holding them uncomfortably close.

"I'm so glad my girls are here," Nathalie murmured. "It's been so long since I've seen you."

"We're glad to see you, too," Gemma said, once she'd pulled herself free from Nathalie's hug. "But we were here just last week."

"Were you really?" Nathalie narrowed her eyes and looked over the girls, as if she didn't quite believe them.

"Yes, we visit you every Saturday," Harper reminded her.

Nathalie's brow furrowed in confusion, and Harper held her breath, wondering if she'd done the right thing by correcting her mom. When she was confused or frustrated, Nathalie's temper had a tendency to get the best of her.

"You look really nice today," Gemma said, rushing to change the subject.

"Do I?" Nathalie looked down at her Justin Bieber T-shirt and smiled. "I do love Justin."

While Harper had taken more after their father, Gemma had gotten her looks from Nathalie. She was slender and beautiful, looking more like a model than a mother. She kept her brown hair long, covering the scars etched on her scalp from the accident. A few locks had been put in narrow braids, and a strand in her bangs had been strung with hot pink beads.

"You both look so good!" Nathalie admired her daughters and touched Gemma's bare arm. "You're so tan! How do you get so tan?"

"I spend a lot of time in the water," Gemma said.

"Right, right, right." Nathalie closed her eyes and rubbed her temple. "You're a swimmer."

"I am." Gemma smiled and nodded, proud of her mother

for remembering something she'd told her a thousand times before.

"Well, come in!" Nathalie erased the pained expression from her face and gestured toward the house. "I told them you were coming today, so they let me make cookies! We should eat them while they're still warm."

She looped her arm around Gemma's shoulders, walking with her into the house. The staff greeted them, and by now they knew more about Gemma's and Harper's lives than Nathalie did.

Not that Nathalie didn't try to learn about her daughters. She just couldn't remember.

Nathalie claimed she'd made the cookies, but the Chips Ahoy! wrapper sat right next to the plate that she'd dumped them on. She did that a lot, for reasons Harper didn't completely understand. Nathalie would lie about little things, making claims that Harper and Gemma knew weren't true.

At first they'd called her on it. Harper would calmly explain why they knew it wasn't true, but Nathalie would get irate when caught in a lie. She'd once thrown a glass at Gemma. It missed her but had shattered against the wall and cut Gemma's ankle.

So now they simply smiled and ate the cookies when Nathalie talked about how she'd made them. She grabbed the plate of cookies and led the girls back to her bedroom.

"It's so much better in here," Nathalie said, shutting the door behind them. "Without people watching over us."

Nathalie sat back on her narrow twin bed, and Gemma

sat next to her. Harper stayed standing, never feeling quite comfortable in her mother's room.

Posters covered the wall—mostly of Justin Bieber, Nathalie's current favorite—but there was also a poster for the last Harry Potter movie and one of a puppy cuddling with a duck. Stuffed animals littered the bed, and the clothes overflowing the hamper had more color and glitter than the average adult wardrobe.

"Do you guys want to listen to music?" Nathalie asked. Before either of them could answer, she jumped off the bed and went over to her stereo. "I just got some new CDs. What do you like to listen to? I have everything."

"Whatever you want is fine," Gemma said. "We came here to visit you."

"You guys can pick something." Nathalie smiled, but there was something sad about it. "They won't let me listen to it too loud, but we can still listen to it softly."

"Justin Bieber?" Harper suggested, not because she wanted to hear it, but because she knew it was something Nathalie would have.

"He's the best, isn't he?" Nathalie actually squealed when she hit play and music came out of the speakers.

She hopped on the bed next to Gemma, making the cookies bounce off the plate. Gemma picked them up, arranging them the same way her mother had had them, but Nathalie didn't even notice.

"So, Mom, how are things going?" Harper asked.

"Same old." Nathalie shrugged. "I wish I lived with you guys."

"I know," Harper said. "But you know it's best for you here."

"Maybe you can come visit," Gemma said. It was an offer she'd been making for years, but Nathalie hadn't been home in a very long time.

"I don't want to visit." She pouted, sticking out her bottom lip and pulling at the hem of her T-shirt. "I bet you guys have fun all the time. Nobody ever tells you what to do."

"Harper tells me what to do all the time." Gemma laughed. "And of course there's Dad."

"Oh. Right," Nathalie said. "I forgot about him." Her forehead pinched in concentration. "What's his name again?"

"Brian." Harper smiled to hide the hurt and swallowed hard. "Dad's name is Brian."

"I thought it was Justin." She waved her hand, brushing off the subject. "Did you guys want to go to the concert with me if I can get tickets?"

"I don't think so," Harper said. "We've got a lot going on."

The conversation went on that way for a while. Nathalie asked about the girls' lives, and they told her things they'd told her a hundred times before. When they left, Harper felt the same way she always did—drained but relieved.

She loved her mother, just as Gemma loved her mother, and they were both glad they saw her. But Harper couldn't help wondering what any of them got out of this.

FIVE

Stargazing

The garbage can smelled like a dead animal. Gemma wrinkled her nose and tried to avoid gagging as she tossed the bag in the can behind her house. She had no idea what her father or Harper had thrown away, but it was pretty rank.

Waving her hand in front of her face, she stepped away. Gemma breathed in the fresh night air as deeply as she could.

She glanced over at the neighbors' house. Lately she found herself glancing over at it more and more, as if subconsciously looking for Alex. This time she was in luck. In the glow from her backyard light, she saw Alex sprawled out on his lawn, staring up at the sky.

"What are you doing?" Gemma asked, walking into Alex's backyard without waiting to be invited.

"Looking at constellations," Alex said, but she'd already known the answer before she'd asked. For as long as she'd known him, he'd spent more time with his head in the stars than here on the ground.

He lay on his back, his fingers latched behind his head, an old blanket beneath him. The Batman T-shirt was actually a bit small for him, a leftover from before his recent growth spurt. The muscles in his arms and his broad shoulders pulled at the fabric. The T-shirt had pulled up a bit, so she could see a hint of his belly above his jeans, and Gemma quickly looked away and pretended she hadn't noticed.

"Mind if I join you?"

"Uh, no. Of course not." Alex quickly scooted over, making room for her on the blanket.

"Thanks."

The blanket wasn't very big, so when Gemma sat down, she was right next to him. As she lay back, her head bumped his elbow. To avoid that, Alex moved his arm so it was in between them. Now his arm was pressed against hers, and she tried not to think about how warm his skin felt.

"So . . . what exactly are you looking at?" Gemma asked.

"I've shown you the constellations before," Alex said, and he had, many times. But most of those times had been when she was younger and she hadn't hung on his words like she did now.

"I was just wondering if there was anything in particular you were watching."

"No. Not really. I just love the stars."

"Is that what you're going to college for?"

"Stars?" Alex asked. "Kind of, I guess. I mean, it's not like I'll be an astronaut or anything."

"Why not?" She tilted her head so she could look over at him.

"I don't know." He shifted on the blanket, and his hand brushed against Gemma's. "Going into outer space is an awesome dream, yeah, but I'd rather stay on the ground and make a difference. I want to study and track the weather and the atmosphere. It could save lives if people knew about storms sooner."

"You'd rather be down here watching the sky instead of up in it because you can help people?" Gemma asked.

She stared at him, surprised by how much he'd grown up. Not just in the strong line of his jaw, or the trail of dark hair she'd seen on his belly. But something had changed *inside* him. At some point he'd stopped being the boy who obsessed over video games and had become somebody concerned with the world around him.

"Yeah." He shrugged and turned to face her. They lay on the blanket staring at each other for a minute, and then Alex smirked. "What? Why are you looking at me like that?"

"I'm not looking at you like anything," Gemma said, but she quickly looked away, afraid that he might see something in her expression.

"You think it's weird, right?" Alex asked, still watching her. "You think I'm a geek for wanting to watch weather patterns."

"No, that's not what I'm thinking at all." She smiled out of embarrassment over what she was really thinking. "I mean, you *are* a geek. But that's not what I was thinking."

"I am a geek," Alex agreed, and Gemma laughed. Then, apparently without thinking, he said, "You're really pretty."

The instant he said it, he turned away from her rigidly.

"I'm sorry. I can't believe I just said that. I don't know why I said that," Alex said in one rushed breath. "I'm sorry."

Gemma lay there for a minute, staring up at the stars while Alex squirmed in embarrassment next to her. She didn't say anything at first, because she wasn't sure what to say or what to make of his random admission.

"Did you . . . you just called me pretty," Gemma said finally, her tone questioning.

"Yeah, I didn't . . ." Alex sat up, as if trying to put some distance between them. "I don't know why I said that. It just slipped out."

"It just slipped out?" Gemma said teasingly and sat up next to him.

He leaned forward, resting his arms on his knees, and kept his back to her. "Yeah." He sighed. "You laughed, and I just thought you looked really pretty, and for some reason, it just . . . I just said it. It was like I forgot how to control my mouth or something."

"Wait." She smiled, the kind of smile she couldn't contain. "You think I'm pretty?"

"Well, yeah." He sighed again and rubbed his arm. "Of

course I do. I mean, you are *very* pretty. You know that." He looked up at the sky and cursed under his breath. "I don't know why I just told you that."

"It's okay." Gemma moved closer to him, sitting next to him but slightly behind him, so her shoulder pressed up against his. "I think you're pretty, too."

"You think I'm pretty?" Alex smiled and turned to look at her, so his face was right in front of hers.

"Yep," she assured him with a grin.

"I'm a guy. Guys aren't pretty."

"You are." Her smile softened, giving way to a slightly nervous and hopeful look.

Alex's dark eyes searched her face, and he paled. He looked downright terrified, and even though the moment felt perfect, Gemma was starting to think he wouldn't take it.

Then he leaned in and his lips pressed softly against hers. The kiss was small and sweet, almost innocent, but it felt like fireworks inside her.

"Sorry," Alex said when he stopped kissing her and looked away.

"Why are you apologizing?" Gemma asked.

"I don't know." He laughed. He shook his head and looked back at her, smiling at him. "I'm not sorry."

"Me neither."

Alex leaned in to kiss her again, but before he could, Brian yelled from the house behind them.

"Gemma!"

That was all it took to ruin the moment. Alex jumped away from Gemma like he'd been shocked.

Gemma got up more slowly than he had, offering him an apologetic smile. "Sorry."

"Yeah, no, it's okay." Alex rubbed the back of his head and refused to even look in the direction of Gemma or her father.

"I'll see you later?" Gemma asked.

"Yeah, yeah, of course." He nodded quickly.

Gemma hurried back over to her house, where her father stood at the back door, holding it open. When she went inside, Brian stood outside for a minute longer, watching Alex as he awkwardly tried to fold the blanket.

"Dad!" Gemma shouted at him.

Brian waited a beat before coming in. He closed the back door behind him and locked it, then flipped off the outside light. When he came into the kitchen, Gemma was pacing and chewing her fingernails.

"You don't have to check up on me, you know."

"You went out fifteen minutes ago to take out the garbage." Brian leaned against the counter. "I was simply making sure you hadn't been kidnapped or attacked by rabid raccoons."

"Well, I wasn't." Gemma stopped moving and took a deep breath.

"Do you want to tell me what was going on out there?"

Her eyes widened. "No!"

"Look, Gemma, I know you're sixteen, and you're going

to start dating." He shifted his weight from one foot to the other. "And Alex isn't a bad kid, exactly. But he's older, and you're too young for certain things—"

"Dad, we just kissed. Okay?" Gemma's face pinched with discomfort over discussing the topic with her father.

"So you're . . . seeing him now?" Brian asked carefully.

"I don't know." She shrugged. "We just kissed."

"And that's all you should do," Brian said. "He's leaving in a couple months, and you're too young to really commit to anything. Plus you have your swimming to focus on."

"Dad, please," Gemma said. "Let me figure this out on my own. Okay?"

"Okay," he said reluctantly. "But if he touches you, I'll kill him. And if he hurts you, I'll kill him."

"I know."

"Does he know that?" Brian gestured toward Alex's house next door. "Because I can go over and tell him that myself."

"No, Dad!" Gemma held up her hands. "I've got it. Now, if you don't mind, I'm going to go to bed so I can get up early tomorrow to swim."

"Tomorrow's Sunday. The pool's closed."

"I'll go out to the bay. I skipped tonight, and I want to be in the water."

Brian nodded, letting the conversation go, and Gemma hurried up to her room. The light shone from beneath Harper's bedroom door, signaling she was still up, probably reading a book. Gemma snuck into her own room quietly, so as not to alert her sister.

From her bedroom window, Harper might have been able to see Gemma and Alex kiss, or she might've overheard Gemma and her dad talking about it. And the last thing Gemma wanted to do was rehash it with Harper, especially when she had no idea how she felt about it herself.

Gemma flopped back on the bed. Plastic stars were stuck to her ceiling, and only a couple of them still managed a dim glow. She stared at them, smiling because they reminded her of Alex.

Harper had been the one to put the stars up when Gemma had been eight and suffered from serious night terrors. Alex had helped, though, mapping out the constellations with as much accuracy as he could manage.

It was so weird thinking of him now. Gemma had been used to having him around as a nerdy friend of her sister's. But now when she thought of him, her heart beat faster and a warm feeling grew from her belly.

Her lips still tingled from his kiss, and she wondered when she'd be able to kiss him again. She stayed up late, replaying their moments under the stars over and over in her head. When she finally fell asleep, she did so with a smile on her face.

The alarm next to her bed jolted her awake in the morning. The sun was just starting to rise, shining bright orange through her curtains. The snooze button was tempting, but she'd already missed a full day of swimming, so she really had to make up for it.

By the time Gemma was up and ready, the whole town of

Capri was bathed in warm sunlight. Both Harper and her dad were still asleep, and she left them a note on the fridge reminding them she'd gone to Anthemusa Bay.

She blasted Lady Gaga on her iPod and hopped on her bike. It was still early, so the rest of the town was asleep. Gemma liked it better that way, when the streets weren't filled to the brim with tourists.

The trip to the bay seemed to go more quickly than normal. Pedaling seemed easier. Gemma felt like she was floating on a cloud. One simple kiss from Alex had somehow made the whole world lighter.

Since she rode her bike, she couldn't swim at the spot with the cypress trees like she usually did. Her bike couldn't make it up the path, and there was no place for her to lock it up. Instead, she went down to the docks near where her father worked.

Technically, people weren't supposed to swim there, since it was dangerous, with all the boats, but she didn't plan to actually swim there. After she locked up her bike, she would dive in and swim out where it was safer. Nobody was really out this early to catch her anyway.

Gemma parked her bike next to a post on the dock. Once she'd stripped down to her bathing suit, she shoved her jean shorts, tank top, and flip-flops in the backpack she'd brought with her. She looped the bike chain through the backpack's straps and secured it with the bike, locking everything up tightly.

She ran to the end of the dock and dove in. The morning

air still had a chill to it, and the water was a tad icy, but Gemma didn't mind. It didn't really matter what the temperature was or what the water was like. Gemma never felt more at home than when she was in the water.

She spent as much time swimming as she could, but by late morning the bay had started to get crowded. It was shaping up to be a beautiful warm day, so the beach was full. The water closer to the dock had filled up with boats heading out to sea, and Gemma knew she had to head back in or risk getting run over with a propeller.

The ladder at the end of the dock was missing a few rungs, so she struggled to pull herself up. She was just about to hoist herself over the end of the dock when somebody stuck a hand in her face. The nails were long and manicured, painted bloodred, and the skin smelled of coconuts.

With salty water dripping down her face, Gemma looked up to see Penn standing right in front of her, her hand outstretched toward Gemma.

"Need a hand?" Penn asked, smiling in a way that reminded Gemma of a hungry animal.

SIX

Cornered

Penn was the closest to Gemma, but the other two girls stood right behind her. Gemma had never been this near to Penn before, and her beauty was even more intimidating up close. Penn was flawless. She looked like an airbrushed model on the cover of *Maxim*.

"Did you need help?" Penn asked more clearly, as if she thought Gemma were deaf since she hadn't done anything except gape at her.

"No, I'm okay." Gemma shook her head.

"Suit yourself." Penn shrugged and moved back so Gemma could climb up.

Gemma had hoped for something more graceful since she'd declined help, but with the top rung on the ladder missing, all she managed was a flop onto the dock. Gemma was acutely aware that she probably looked like a fish flapping about, and she got to her feet as quickly as she could.

"We've seen you swimming out there a lot," Penn said.

Gemma had heard her speak once before, and it still surprised her how Penn sounded. Her voice was that sexy baby-talk that usually drove Gemma nuts, but something silky underneath it made Penn's words strangely beautiful and enticing.

In fact, just hearing Penn talk washed away some of the negative feelings Gemma had about the three girls. They still freaked her out, but her fear had lessened.

"I'm sorry." Penn smiled at her, revealing bright white teeth that seemed abnormally sharp. "You probably have no idea who we are. I'm Penn, and these are my friends, Lexi and Thea."

"Hi." Lexi wagged her fingers at Gemma. Her blond hair glinted like gold in the sunlight, and her eyes were the same aqua shade as the ocean.

"Hey," Thea said. Even though she smiled, she seemed annoyed even to be talking to Gemma. She stared off at the ocean and ran her hand through her red waves of hair.

"And you're Gemma, right?" Penn asked when Gemma didn't say anything.

"Yep, I am." Gemma nodded.

"We've seen you around, and we like your style," Penn went on.

"Thanks?" Gemma questioned, uncertain what to make of that.

She wrapped her arms around herself, feeling naked around the three girls. Gemma knew she was pretty, and sometimes when she was dolled up she thought she was downright hot. But standing next to Penn, Lexi, and Thea, she felt clumsy and unattractive.

Water dripped off her body and onto the wooden planks beneath her feet, and all she could think about was getting to her clothes and putting them on.

"We love going swimming out in the ocean at night," Penn said. "There's something truly exhilarating about it."

"It's *amazing*," Lexi chimed in, sounding a little too enthusiastic about it. Penn shot Lexi a look, and Lexi lowered her eyes.

"Um . . . yeah." Even though Gemma agreed with them, she was afraid to admit it. It felt like Penn was setting some sort of trap she didn't understand.

"We'd love it if you joined us for a swim," Penn said, smiling wider.

"I . . . I don't think so. Sorry." Gemma couldn't really think of an excuse to give them, but there was no way she would accept an invitation to join them doing anything.

"How about an afternoon swim, then?" Penn asked. "We were thinking of taking a dive right now. Weren't we?"

"I've got my bikini under my dress," Lexi said and gestured to the slinky sundress she wore.

"Well, I just got out," Gemma said. "And I'm about to get dressed."

She pointed to her bike, and then, seeing her chance to escape, walked over to it. Gemma had expected them to give up once she'd turned them down, but apparently that was wishful thinking. Penn followed her down the dock.

"I know you to love swim, and I'd really love it if you joined us," Penn said. "If today doesn't work, then let me know when you can."

"I don't know." Gemma fumbled with her bike lock. Penn stood behind her, casting a shadow over her as Gemma crouched next to the bike. "I've got a lot of training to do."

"You can't train all the time," Penn said. "All work and no play makes Jack a dull boy."

"I play," Gemma insisted.

Finally managing to unlock her bag, she grabbed it and stood up. Her urge to get dressed had gone away, though. All she wanted to do was throw the bag over her shoulder, hop on the bike, and ride far away from Penn and her hungry smile.

"You really need to go swimming with us." Penn's voice was like silk, but it was clearly a command. Her dark eyes locked on Gemma's, burning with an intensity that took her breath away.

A splash from behind them momentarily broke Penn's concentration, but the distraction was long enough for Gemma to catch her breath and look away.

Daniel stood on the dock a little way down from them, water dripping down his bare chest and long swim trunks. Gemma knew him from when she visited her father on the docks, but she hadn't found a reason to resent him the way Harper had.

"Is there something wrong?" Daniel asked, wiping the water from his face. Without waiting for them to answer, he started walking to where Penn, Lexi, and Thea had Gemma surrounded.

"Everything's just fine," Lexi said brightly and smiled at him. "You can go about your business."

"I don't think so." Daniel kept walking, ignoring Lexi. When he got close enough, he shouldered Lexi out of the way and looked down at Gemma. "Are you okay?"

"We said she was fine," Penn said icily.

"I didn't ask you." Daniel cast her a glare before he turned back to Gemma and softened his gaze. Gemma stood dripping wet, clutching her bag to her chest. "Come on. Why don't you come on my boat and dry off?"

"Go about your business," Lexi said again, but she sounded more confused than angry. Like she didn't understand how he could ignore her.

Daniel gestured for Gemma to come with him. As Gemma hurried over to him, she couldn't shake the feeling that Penn wanted to rip Daniel's head off, in a very literal sense. Once they slipped away from the girls, Daniel put his arm around her. Not a romantic gesture, but like he meant to protect her.

As they walked over to his boat, Gemma felt Penn's eyes burning into her back. Lexi called after her, saying that they'd see her again, and something about her voice felt like a song.

Gemma almost turned around to go back to them after she heard Lexi, but Daniel's arm around her kept her from it.

Once they got to the boat, Daniel helped Gemma onto it. Since Penn, Lexi, and Thea were still standing on the dock watching them, he suggested they go down into the cabin. Gemma didn't normally get onto boats with older guys she barely knew, but given the circumstances, she felt like he was the safer bet.

His boat was rather small, so the living quarters were pretty cramped. A twin bed across from a small table with cushioned benches on either side. A kitchenette with a mini-fridge and tiny sink. A bathroom and some storage nooks at the other end, and that was about it.

The bed was unmade, and clothes were strewn over it. Dirty dishes were in the sink, and a few empty soda cans and beer bottles were sitting on the counter and table. A stack of books and magazines rested next to the bed.

"Have a seat." Daniel gestured to the bed, since the benches next to the table were mostly covered in clothes and books.

"Are you sure?" Gemma asked. "I'm wet."

"Nah, it's fine. It's a boat. Everything's always wet." He grabbed a couple of towels and tossed one to her. "There you go."

"Thank you." She ran the towel through her hair and sat back on his bed. "And I don't mean just for this. Thank you for . . . well, rescuing me, I guess."

"It was no problem." Daniel shrugged and leaned against his kitchen table. He wiped a towel over his chest, then ran a hand through his short hair, messing it up and spraying salt water. "You looked so terrified."

"I wasn't *terrified*," Gemma said defensively.

"I wouldn't blame you if you were." He leaned farther back, looking out one of the cabin windows behind him. "Those girls give me the creeps."

"That's what I said!" Gemma shouted, excited to hear someone agree with her. "My sister told me that I was being mean."

"Harper?" Daniel looked back at Gemma. "She likes those girls?"

"I don't think she *likes* them, exactly." Gemma shook her head. "She thinks I should be respectful of everyone."

"Well, that is a good philosophy." He reached over and opened the mini-fridge. "Want a soda?"

"Sure."

After Daniel grabbed two cans of grape soda, he handed one to Gemma and kept one for himself. He sat on the table and crossed his legs underneath him. Gemma wrapped her towel around her shoulders and opened the soda.

She looked around the cabin, checking out his bare furnishings. "How long have you lived here?"

"Too long," he said after taking a long swallow of his soda.

"I think I'd like to live on a boat someday. But like a houseboat."

"I would definitely recommend living on something larger, if you can." Daniel gestured to the tight space. "And it can be a bit rough staying out here when the sea gets choppy. I've been out here so long, though, I doubt I could even sleep on land. I need the water to rock me to sleep."

"That would be nice." She smiled wistfully as she imagined sleeping on the bay. "Did you always love the ocean?"

"Uh . . . I don't know." Daniel crinkled his brow as if he hadn't thought of it before. "I guess I've always liked it."

"How did you end up living on a boat, then?"

"It's not very romantic," he warned her. "My grandpa died and left me this boat. I got evicted from my apartment and needed a place to crash. And here we are."

"Gemma!" Someone shouted from outside the boat, and Daniel and Gemma exchanged a confused look. "Gemma!"

"Is that your sister?" Daniel asked.

"I think so." Gemma set down her can and headed out to the deck to see what Harper was carrying on about.

Harper stood on the dock next to Gemma's bike holding the bike chain in her hand. Her dark hair was in a ponytail, which swung back and forth as she looked around frantically.

"Gemma!" Harper yelled again, the tremor in her voice betraying her fear.

Gemma went over to the railing and looked down at her sister. "Harper?"

"Gemma!" Harper turned to face her, relief washing over her until she saw Daniel standing on the boat behind her. "Gemma! What are you doing?"

"I was just drying off," Gemma said. "Why are you freaking out so bad?"

"I came to see if you were coming home for lunch, and I found your bike chain unhooked on the dock, like something happened when you were locking it up, and I couldn't find you, and now you're on *his* boat!" Harper stomped toward Daniel's boat, clenching the bike chain in her fist. "What were you doing?"

"Drying off," Gemma repeated, growing annoyed with her sister for making a scene.

"Why?" Harper demanded and pointed at Daniel. "He is bad news!"

"Thanks," Daniel said wryly, and Harper glared at him.

"Look, I'll get on my bike, and we'll go home, and you can be a total spaz there," Gemma said.

"I am not being a spaz!" Harper shouted, then stopped and took a deep breath. "But you're right. We *will* talk about this at home."

"Yay." Gemma sighed. She took the towel from around her shoulders and handed it back to Daniel. "Thanks."

"No problem. And sorry if I got you in trouble."

"Ditto," Gemma said, offering him a small, apologetic smile.

Gemma threw her backpack onto the dock, then hopped over the railing after it. She took her chain from Harper, grabbed her bag, and went down to her bike to put her clothes on before she rode home.

"You are a disgusting pervert," Harper snarled at Daniel and pointed her finger at him. "Gemma is only sixteen years old, and even though you have some sort of Peter Pan complex, you are still a twenty-year-old man. You are too old to be messing around with her."

"Oh, please." Daniel rolled his eyes. "She's just a kid. I wasn't hitting on her."

"That is *not* what it looks like from here." Harper crossed her arms. "I should report you for living on this stupid boat and for your abhorrent behavior hanging around with underage girls."

"Do what you gotta do, but I'm not a creep." He leaned against the railing and looked down at Harper. "Those girls were hassling your sister, and I stepped in to get her away from them."

"What girls?" Harper asked.

"Those girls." Daniel waved vaguely. "I think the head one is named Penn or something."

"The really pretty girls?" Harper tensed up.

She hadn't thought Daniel had done anything to Gemma, not really, but at the mention of Penn, her stomach tightened.

"I guess." Daniel shrugged.

"They were messing with Gemma?" She glanced back at Gemma, who was pulling on her tank top and appeared unharmed. "How?"

"I don't know exactly." He shook his head. "But they had her surrounded, and she looked scared. I just don't trust them, and I didn't want them around her. I asked her on my boat to hide out until they left, and you showed up like ten minutes later. That's all that happened."

"Oh." Harper felt bad for yelling at him now, but she

didn't want to let on. "Well. Thank you for looking out for my sister. But you shouldn't have her on your boat."

"I hadn't planned on making a habit out of it."

"Good." Harper shifted her weight, still trying to look indignant. "I think she's seeing someone anyway."

"Harper, I already told you, I'm not into your sister." Daniel smirked. "But if I didn't know any better, I would say you were jealous."

"Oh, please." Harper wrinkled her nose. "Don't be disgusting."

Daniel laughed at her protests, and for some reason, Harper began to blush.

Gemma sped past her on her bike, shouting a good-bye to Daniel as she did. With her sister gone, Harper didn't really have any reason to wait around on the dock, but she stayed behind for a moment, trying to think of something to snap at Daniel for. When she couldn't come up with anything, she turned and left, acutely aware that he was watching her walk away.

SEVEN

Picnic

Capri had been founded by Thomas Thermopolis in southeastern Maryland on June 14, 1802, so every fourteenth of June the town held a celebration in his honor. Most of the stores in town closed for it, as they would for any other major holiday. It had become nothing more than a big picnic with a few rides and concessions, but everybody turned out, both the townies and the tourists alike.

Alex had invited Gemma to go with him, and she didn't know exactly what that meant. Since he had invited just *her* and not Harper, too, she was inclined to think it meant something, but she was too afraid to ask.

The car ride was awkward, almost comically so. Neither of them really said anything, aside from Alex stammering out a few comments about how he hoped they would have fun.

When they parked, he ran around the car to open the door for her, and that was actually when Gemma started to relax. He'd never opened the door for her before. Something had definitely changed.

The Founder's Day Picnic took place in the park in the center of town. A couple rides were set up, like the Tilt-A-Whirl and the Zipper. The midway cut through the center, lined with the usual carnival games. Picnic tables and blankets were spread out over the rest of the area, broken up by a few food and drink stands.

"Did you want to play a game?" Alex asked Gemma as they walked down the midway. He gestured to the ring toss next to them. "I could win you a goldfish."

"I don't think that'd be fair to the goldfish," Gemma said. "I've had about a dozen of them, and they all seem to die within days of me getting them."

"Oh, yeah." Alex smiled crookedly. "I remember you making your dad bury them out in the backyard."

"They were my pets, and they deserved a proper burial."

"I better be careful around you." Alex stepped back from her cautiously, giving her a wide berth. "You're a goldfish mass murderer. I don't know what you're capable of."

"Stop!" Gemma laughed. "I didn't kill them on purpose! I was little. I think I overfed them. Out of love, though."

"That's even scarier," he teased. "Do you plan to kill me with kindness?"

"Maybe." She narrowed her eyes at him and tried to look menacing, making him laugh.

Alex walked close to her again. His hand brushed against hers, and Gemma took the opportunity to slip her fingers through his. He didn't comment on it, but he gave her hand the slightest squeeze. Warm tingles swirled inside her, and Gemma tried not to smile too widely at the effect from that simple touch.

"So goldfish are out," Alex said. "What about teddy bears? Would stuffed animals be safe around you?"

"Probably," she allowed. "But you don't need to win me anything."

"You want to walk around for a while?" Alex asked, looking down at her.

"Yeah." She nodded, and he smiled.

"Okay. But if you want anything, just say the word, and I'm on it. I'll win you anything your heart desires."

Gemma didn't want him to win her anything because that meant he would have to stop to play a game and let go of her hand. She was content to walk around all day with him. Just being with him delighted her in a way she hadn't thought possible.

They'd walked a little farther down the midway when they came across Bernie McAllister. He stood in front of the game where the object was to pop balloons with a dart to win a prize. Despite the heat, he wore a sweater, and he squinted at the balloons below his gray eyebrows.

"Mr. McAllister." Gemma smiled and stopped when they got close to him. "What brings you here to the mainland?"

"Oh, you know," he said, his voice lilting with a faded British accent. He pointed to the balloons with his plastic darts. "I've been coming to the Founder's Day Picnic for fifty-four years and winning cheap junk from these games. I wasn't about to miss this one."

"I see." Gemma laughed.

"And what about you, Miss Fisher?" Bernie asked, looking at Alex and then back at her. "Does your father know you're out with a boy?"

"Yeah, he knows," Gemma assured him and squeezed Alex's hand.

"He better." Bernie gave them a stern look until Alex lowered his eyes. "I still remember when you were this big"—he held his hand up to his knee—"and you thought boys were gross." He paused to appraise her and smile. "You kids grow up so fast."

"Sorry. I didn't mean to."

"It's how it goes." He waved his hand, brushing off her apology. "How is your father? Is he here?"

"No, he's at home today." Gemma's smile faltered. Her father rarely came out to stuff like this anymore, not since her mom's car accident. "He's doing good, though."

"Good. Your father's a fine man, a real hard worker." Bernie nodded. "It's been too long since I've seen him."

"I'll tell him you said that," Gemma said. "Maybe he'll head out to the island and visit you."

"I would like that." Bernie held her eyes when he smiled, his own eyes filmy with cataracts and a little sad. Then he shook his head and turned back to the game. "Anyway, I should let you kids get back to your fun."

"All right, good luck at your game," Gemma said as she and Alex started walking away. "It was nice seeing you."

When they'd gotten far enough away from him, Alex asked her, "That was Bernie from Bernie's Island, right?"

"Sure was."

Bernie lived on a small island a few miles off Anthemusa Bay. The only thing on it was the log cabin and boathouse that Bernie had built fifty-some years ago for himself and his wife. His wife had died shortly after that, but Bernie stayed there just the same.

Since the only person who lived on the island was Bernie, the people of Capri had taken to referring to it as Bernie's Island. That wasn't the official name, but that was how everyone knew of it.

After Gemma's mother's car accident, her dad had a tough time. He used to take Gemma and Harper out to Bernie's Island, and Bernie would watch them while her dad went off to deal with things on his own.

Bernie was always kind to them, and not in a creepy-old-man way. He was funny, and he let the girls have free run of the island. That was when Gemma had really developed her love of the water. She spent long summer afternoons out at the bay, swimming around the island.

In fact, if it wasn't for Bernie and his island, she might not have become the swimmer she was today.

"What's going on with Alex and your sister?" Marcy asked, and Harper lifted her head to see Gemma and Alex holding hands as they walked down the midway.

"I don't know." Harper shrugged.

She and Marcy were playing beanbag toss next to a picnic table, until Marcy had gotten distracted.

"You don't know?" Marcy turned back to Harper.

"No, Gemma's being really vague on details." Harper threw her beanbag at the goal, intent on continuing the game even if Marcy was hung up on something else. "I know they kissed the other day because Dad saw them, but when I asked Gemma about it, she wouldn't tell me anything. I think they might be dating."

"Your sister is dating your best friend, and you don't know what's going on?" Marcy asked.

"Gemma never wants to tell me about her boyfriends." Harper sighed. Gemma had had all of two of them before, but she was always secretive about her crushes. "And I haven't really asked Alex about it. I feel a little weird bringing it up."

"Because you have a thing for him," Marcy said.

"For the millionth time, I don't like Alex that way." Harper rolled her eyes. "It's your turn, by the way."

"Don't change the subject."

"I'm not." Harper sat back on the picnic table behind them, since Marcy clearly didn't plan on playing until they discussed things. "I've never had anything other than platonic feelings for Alex. He's geeky and awkward and just a friend."

"Guys and girls can't be friends," Marcy insisted. "You really need to watch *When Harry Met Sally*."

"Brothers and sisters can be just friends, and Alex is like a brother to me," Harper explained. "Which is the only reason why this is weird for me. Because a guy that's like my brother is dating my actual sister."

"That's gross."

"Thanks. Can we get back to the game now?" Harper asked.

"No, this game is boring, and I'm starving." Marcy had a beanbag in her hand, and she gave it a half-assed toss to the side. "Let's get some cheese curds."

"You're the one who wanted to play this," Harper said as she got off the picnic table.

"I know. But I didn't realize how boring it was."

Marcy walked through the park, pushing people if they were in her way. Harper followed more slowly behind her, glancing back over her shoulder to see if she could catch a glimpse of Gemma and Alex together.

Originally, Gemma was going to go with Marcy and Harper to the picnic, but this morning Alex had called over to invite her to go with him. That was when Harper had tried to talk to Gemma about him, but Gemma had refused to give her any details.

Harper was so busy looking for them that she wasn't paying attention to where she was going, and she bumped right into someone, knocking an ice-cream cone out of his hand and smashing it all over his shirt.

"Oh, my gosh, I'm so sorry," Harper said hurriedly, trying to wipe the chocolate ice cream off his T-shirt.

"You really do hate me, don't you?" Daniel asked, and Harper realized with dismay that he was the one she'd covered in ice cream. "I mean, destroying someone's ice-cream cone? That's vicious."

Her cheeks reddened. "I didn't see you there. Honestly." She wiped at his shirt more frantically, as if she could prevent it from staining if she rubbed hard enough.

"Oh, now I see your plan, and it's far more devious than I thought." Daniel smirked. "You were looking for an excuse to grope me."

"I was not!" Harper instantly stopped touching him and took a step back.

"Good. Because you need to buy me dinner first."

"I was only . . ." She gestured to his shirt and sighed. "I am sorry."

"I'm covered in chocolate. Why don't you apologize while we go get some napkins?" Daniel suggested.

Harper went with him over to a concession stand, where he grabbed a stack of napkins. Taking a handful from him, she walked to a drinking fountain, and Daniel followed her.

"I am sorry," Harper repeated. She wet her napkins under the fountain as he wiped at his shirt.

"I didn't actually mean for you to keep apologizing. I know it was an accident."

"I know, but . . ." She shook her head. "I didn't even

properly thank you for helping out my sister, and then I attacked you with your own ice cream."

"That's true. You are a menace and must be stopped."

"I know you're teasing, but I feel bad."

"No, I'm dead serious. I should report you for your abhorrent behavior," Daniel said with a straight face, telling her the same thing she'd told him the day before.

"Now you're making me feel worse." Harper looked down at her shoes and balled up the wet napkins in her hands.

"That's my plan," Daniel said. "I like to guilt pretty girls into going out with me."

"Smooth." Harper narrowed her eyes at him, unsure if he was kidding or not.

"That's what the ladies tell me." He grinned at her, and his hazel eyes had a gleam to them.

"I'm sure they do," she said skeptically.

"You do owe me an ice cream, you know."

"Oh, right, of course." She dug in her pocket for some money. "How much was that? I can give you the cash for it."

"No, no." He waved his hand, stopping her when she pulled out a few crumpled-up dollar bills. "I don't want your money. I want you to have an ice cream *with* me."

"I, uh . . ." Harper fumbled for a reason not to.

"I see how it is." His eyes flashed with something that might've been hurt, but he lowered them before she could be sure. His smile disappeared, though, and he shoved his hands in his pockets.

"No, no, it's not that I don't want to," Harper said quickly, and she was surprised to find that she meant it.

Between his being gracious in the face of her verbal assaults and helping out her sister, Daniel had begun to grow on her. And that was precisely why she couldn't take him up on his offer.

Despite his charms, he still lived on a boat, and from the scruff on his chin, it looked like he hadn't shaved in a few days. He was immature and probably lazy, and she was leaving for school in a couple of months. She didn't need to get mixed up with a slacker on a boat just because he was kinda funny and cute in a grungy sorta way.

"My friend is waiting for me, somewhere," Harper continued to explain and gestured vaguely out at the crowd. Marcy was probably somewhere eating cheese curds. "I was following her when I bumped into you. She doesn't even know where I'm at. So . . . I should go find her."

"I understand." Daniel nodded, and his smile had returned. "I'll take an IOU, then."

"An IOU?" She raised an eyebrow. "For ice cream?"

"Or any meal of equal value." He squinted, thinking about what that would be. "Maybe a smoothie. Or a large coffee. But not like a full meal with fries and a salad." He snapped his fingers as he thought of something. "Soup! A cup of soup would work, too."

"So I owe you one food offering that's equal to ice cream?" Harper asked.

"Yes. And the repayment can happen at your earliest convenience," Daniel said. "Tomorrow or the next day or even next week. Whenever works for you."

"Okay. That sounds like a . . . deal."

"Good," he said as she started walking away from him. "I'll hold you to it. You know that, right?"

"Yes, I do," Harper said, and part of her actually hoped he would.

She weaved her way through the picnic, and it didn't take her long to find Marcy. She was sitting at a picnic table with Gemma and Alex, which would've been nice if Alex's friend Luke Benfield hadn't joined them.

Harper actually slowed down when she saw Luke. And not just because things were weird between them. Whenever Luke and Alex got together, they tended to go into computer-geek mode, talking only in tech terms that Harper didn't understand.

"So when are you gonna make an honest woman out of Gemma here and win her a prize?" Marcy was asking Alex when Harper reached the table.

"Um . . ." Alex's cheeks darkened a little at the question, and he rubbed his hands together nervously.

"I told him *not* to win me a prize," Gemma cut in, rescuing him from embarrassment. "I'm a modern girl. I can win my own prizes."

"You probably stand a better chance since you're the athlete," Marcy said, popping a cheese curd in her mouth. "Alex looks like he throws like a girl."

Luke chuckled at that, as if he stood any chance of throwing better than Alex. He twisted the huge Green Lantern ring he wore on his finger and laughed so hard he snorted a little.

"Like you can talk, Marcy," Harper said and sat down on the bench next to her, across from Luke. "I saw the way you tossed a beanbag. Alex could probably kick your butt."

Gemma gave her a grateful smile for coming to Alex's aid. Harper noticed that she'd put her hand on his leg, giving it a reassuring squeeze.

"Where were you, by the way?" Marcy looked over at Harper, unfazed by her comments. "You just disappeared."

"I ran into someone I know." Harper evaded the question and turned her attention to Gemma and Alex. "How is the picnic treating you guys?"

"Good," Luke said. "Except I should've worn more sunscreen." His pale skin seemed to reflect the light, and the red curls on his head were frizzing out. "I'm not used to this much sun."

"Do you live in a dungeon, Luke?" Marcy asked. "I'm only asking since you're skinny and pale, and it looks like your parents might keep you chained in a basement."

"No." Luke scowled, then pointed to the Canadian flag on her shirt. "I thought Canadians were supposed to be nice."

"I'm not Canadian," Marcy corrected him. "I'm just wearing this shirt to express my anti-patriotism."

"You really are a charming girl, you know that, Marcy?" Alex said.

Marcy shrugged. "I do what I can."

Since the park was filled with pretty much everybody in

town, it had been buzzing with the sounds of talking and music. But somewhat abruptly, the area around the picnic tables seemed to grow quiet, as if everyone were speaking in hushed tones and whispers.

Harper looked around to see what had happened and instantly saw the reason for the silence. The crowd had parted, making way for Penn, Lexi, and Thea, who were heading straight for Harper and Gemma.

Penn wore a dress so low-cut her chest was all but popping out. When she stopped at the end of the picnic table, she put her hands on her hips and smiled down at them.

"How are you guys doing?" she asked, surveying the table.

"Great," Luke said eagerly, oblivious to the tension that hung over them. "I'm, uh, I'm having a great time. You guys look great. I mean, you look like you're having a great time."

"Why, thank you." Penn looked at him, licking her lips hungrily as she smiled.

"You're not so bad yourself," Lexi added.

She reached over and tugged one of his curls, pulling it like a spring so it would bounce back. Luke looked down and giggled in way that was reminiscent of a schoolgirl.

"Is there something you want?" Gemma asked.

Harper noticed that when Penn's dark eyes latched onto Gemma's, her sister lifted her chin higher, as if defying her in her some way. Then Harper saw something that made her blood run cold—Penn's eyes changed, shifting from near-black to an odd golden color, reminding Harper of a bird.

Her weird bird eyes stayed locked on Gemma, but Gemma's expression didn't change, as if she didn't notice the startling shift in Penn's eyes.

As suddenly as they changed, Penn's eyes went back to their normal soulless color. Harper blinked and glanced around, but nobody else seemed to notice the change. They all just stared at Penn as if mesmerized, and Harper wondered if it'd just been her imagination.

"Nope." Penn raised one of her shoulders, managing a seductive shrug. "I just wanted to stop and say hi. We don't know many people here in town yet, and we're always looking to make new friends."

Thea didn't look like she wanted to make new friends, though. She stood off to the side, a bit back from Penn and Lexi. She twirled her long red hair around her finger, and wouldn't look at anyone at the table.

"You already have friends," Harper said to Penn and nodded to Lexi and Thea.

"You can always have more, though, right?" Penn asked, and Lexi winked at Luke, making him giggle again. "And we could definitely use a friend like Gemma."

Harper was about to ask Penn exactly what she meant by that, wondering what on earth they could possibly want with her little sister, but Marcy cut her off.

"Wait," Marcy said through a mouthful of cheese curds. "Didn't there used to be a fourth one?" She gulped down her food and stared up at them. "What did you guys do with her? Did you eat her? And then throw her up afterward, because obviously, you guys are bulimic."

Penn shot her a glare so fierce it actually made Marcy cringe. She lowered her eyes and pulled her cheese curds closer to her, as if she thought that Penn might steal them from her.

"So have you guys been on the rides yet?" Harper asked, in an attempt to keep Penn from slaughtering Marcy. After that look, Harper thought it would be better if she kept the conversation banal instead of confronting Penn about her interest in Gemma.

Penn's icy expression instantly melted, and her saccharine smile returned. Harper noticed that Penn's teeth were unusually sharp. In fact, if Harper didn't know better, she'd say that her incisors had actually grown and gotten more pointed than they had been a few seconds ago.

"No, we just got here," Penn explained in her silky babytalk. "We haven't had a chance to check anything out yet."

As she spoke, some of the unease Harper had been feeling when she noticed her smile vanished. Marcy even seemed to relax a bit and braved looking up at Penn again.

"I'd really *love* to win a teddy bear," Lexi said, her voice going singsong as she spoke.

Both Alex and Luke looked at her, and Luke's mouth fell open, like he was in awe.

Harper had her arms on the table in front of her, and she leaned forward. She couldn't explain it, but she found herself hanging on her every word, as if Lexi were the most fascinating person she'd ever heard. Even the people around them seemed to move in closer, crowding around to get closer to Lexi.

"What do you think?" Lexi tilted her head and looked down at Luke. "Could you win me a teddy bear?"

"Yeah!" Luke shouted in excitement and got to his feet so quickly he nearly fell over the bench. "I mean, yes. I'd love to win you a bear."

"Yay!" Lexi smiled and looped her arm through his.

People parted for them again as Lexi and Luke walked through the crowd toward the midway. Thea followed them, but Penn stayed behind, smiling down at the table. Alex stared after Lexi, watching until she disappeared in the crowd, and Gemma would've noticed, if she hadn't been busy doing the same thing.

"Well, I'll leave you to enjoy the rest of the afternoon," Penn said. It sounded as if Penn were speaking to everyone at the table, but she was only looking at Gemma. "I'll see you around."

"Have a fun time," Alex mumbled, his words coming out a little dazed. Penn laughed, then turned and walked away.

"That was weird," Harper said once Penn had left.

She shook her head, clearing away this fog she didn't understand. It almost felt as if she'd been dreaming, like Penn had never even really been there.

"I do think they killed her." Marcy narrowed her eyes and nodded to herself. "There's just something about those girls I don't trust."

EIGHT

The Cove

As soon as the sun went down, Gemma hopped on her bike and rode out to the bay. She'd hadn't been able to train at the pool with Coach Levi since Friday, and that made her especially anxious to get in the water. For the past couple of days she'd avoided going out late, as Harper wanted, so Gemma felt like she'd earned a night swim.

Even though she'd had a wonderful day at the picnic with Alex, she couldn't wait to swim. Actually, the day was better than wonderful. It was . . . magical, in its own way.

They'd spent some of the afternoon hanging out with Harper and Marcy, and that had gone well—surprisingly, since Gemma wasn't sure how Harper would react to her seeing Alex. Apparently Harper was mostly okay with it.

Eventually Alex and Gemma had gone off on their own again, and that was better. He did little things that made her heart flutter. He fumbled over his words when he tried to impress her, and he smiled at her in a way she'd never seen him smile before.

She thought she'd known him long enough to recognize all his smiles, but not this one. This one was small, almost like a smirk, but it went to his eyes.

When Alex dropped her off at home at eight, he walked her to the door. She knew Harper and her dad were inside, and he knew it, too, so she thought he wouldn't kiss her. But he did. Not too long or too deeply, but there was something nice about that. The way he kissed her was almost respectful and careful.

Gemma had kissed only two boys before Alex, and one had been in the first grade during a game of Truth or Dare. Her only *real* kiss had been with her boyfriend of three weeks, and he'd kissed her with such ferocity she thought she'd have bruises on her face.

Alex's kisses were the opposite of that. They were sweet and perfect and made her heart tingle whenever she thought of them.

She didn't know how she hadn't noticed before how amazing Alex was. If she'd only realized it sooner, there were months and months that they could've been together, time she could've spent stealing his wonderful kisses.

At the bay, she rode her bike down to the dock, the same way she always did, since it was the best place to park. When she passed Daniel's boat, *The Dirty Gull,* she heard Led Zeppelin playing loudly.

If it'd been quiet, she might've stopped by to thank him

again for helping her out yesterday, but she didn't want to disturb him.

It had made her feel bad when Harper yelled at Daniel, and Gemma still didn't understand what her sister had against him. Sure, Daniel seemed like a slacker. Just because he didn't have his life together didn't mean he wasn't a really nice guy.

Whenever Gemma went down to bring her dad lunch, Daniel always said hi to her, and he'd once helped her put her chain back on when it slipped off her bike.

At the end of the dock, Gemma secured her bike and stripped down to her bathing suit. She jumped in the water and swam out in the bay.

More people were hanging out on the beach and in their boats than normal for this time of night, leftovers from the earlier celebration. She'd have to swim out farther, closer to the cove by the mouth of the ocean, to get away from them.

In a way, that was better. She needed to do a long-distance swim to make up for her days without serious training.

Once she was far enough out that she couldn't hear the people on the beach anymore, she rolled onto her back and floated on the water, letting the gentle waves rock her. Gemma stared up at the night sky, marveling at the beauty of it. She completely understood why Alex loved the stars so much.

Harper didn't like swimming as much as Gemma did, but Gemma doubted that anyone liked it as much as she did. The times Harper had gone swimming with her, she had gotten scared when Gemma would float like this. Harper was convinced that the tide would take her out and Gemma would be lost at sea forever.

Gemma had never really believed that would happen, but even if it did, the idea had never frightened her. In reality, being swept off in the ocean had actually been more of a dream of hers than a fear.

"Gemma." Her name floated through the air, like a song.

At first she thought she was hearing things, maybe the sound of somebody's stereo on the beach mixing with the crashing of the waves. But then she heard it again, only louder this time.

"Gemma." Someone was singing her name.

Treading water, she looked around for the source of the voice, but it was pretty easy to spot. Gemma had been letting the current take her, and she hadn't realized how close she'd gotten to the cove. It was only about twenty feet from her, and it glowed from a fire burning in its center.

Even though she hadn't been paying much attention when she was swimming out here, she was sure the fire hadn't been lit a few moments ago. And Penn, Lexi, and Thea definitely hadn't been out there.

Gemma had seen enough of them lately, and if she'd had any inkling that they'd be here, she never would've come out this far and risked running into them.

Thea was crouched right next to the fire, her shadow looming behind her. Penn twirled around, dancing in a slow, graceful circle to music that only she could hear. And Lexi stood right at the edge of the shore, so close that the water was splashing up on her feet.

Lexi was the one calling her name, but she wasn't just saying it. She sang it in a way that Gemma had never heard anyone sing before. It was beauty and magic. It sounded like how Alex's kisses felt, only better.

"Gemma," Lexi sang again. *"Come now, weary traveler, I'll lead you through the waves. Worry not, poor voyager, for my voice is the way."*

Gemma stayed transfixed in the water, completely hypnotized by Lexi's song. It was as if Lexi had somehow put a spell on her, and any unease Gemma had felt about the girls melted away. All she could feel was the beauty and the warmth of her lyrics, crystal and clear running through her.

"Gemma," Penn called out. Her sultry voice wasn't nearly as sweet as Lexi's, but there was something enticing about it just the same. She stopped dancing and stood next to Lexi. "Why don't you join us? We're having so much fun up here. You'd love it."

"Okay," Gemma heard herself saying.

Somewhere way back in her mind warning bells went off, but they were all but obliterated when Lexi started singing again. When Gemma swam toward the three girls, the fear was entirely blocked out. Joining them didn't even feel like a choice. Her body moved toward them, seemingly on its own.

When she reached the shore, Lexi held out her hand and helped her onto the land, into the cove. The only way into the cove was through the bay. It had no connections or openings to the land, yet somehow all three of the girls were perfectly dry.

"Here." Penn had been dancing with a shawl around her, made of some kind of gauzy gold substance, and she wrapped it over Gemma's shoulders. "To keep you warm."

"I'm not cold," Gemma said, and that was true enough. The night was warm to begin with, and the fire inside the cove made it warmer still.

"It feels better with it on, though, doesn't it?" Lexi asked, her voice a soft purring in Gemma's ear.

Lexi put her arm around her, and something about the touch made the hair on the back of Gemma's neck stand up. Instinctively Gemma pulled away from her, but then Lexi began singing again, and Gemma melted beneath her arm.

"Come join us." Penn kept her eyes on Gemma and stepped backward toward the fire.

"Are you guys having a party?" Gemma asked.

Gemma didn't move, so Lexi took her hand and pulled her over to the fire. She led her over to a large rock next to Thea and pushed her gently, so Gemma would sit down. Thea stared at her, the flames reflecting in her eyes as if it were coming directly from them.

"We're having a celebration." Lexi laughed and knelt down next to Gemma.

"What are you celebrating?" Gemma asked, looking over at Penn. She stood on the other side of the fire, across from Gemma, and smiled down at her.

"A feast," Penn answered, and both Lexi and Thea laughed in a way that reminded Gemma of how a crow cackled.

"A feast?" Gemma looked around the cove but saw no signs of any food. "Of what?"

"Don't worry about it," Lexi instructed her.

"You'll have plenty of time to eat later," Thea said with a sly smile.

That was the most Gemma had ever heard Thea speak, and she realized there was something wrong with her voice. Thea's had a rasp to it, like Kathleen Turner's husky whisper. It wasn't unattractive, but it wasn't quite right.

It had a tone to it that was the opposite of Lexi's and Penn's. If Lexi's and Penn's voices were like honey, Thea's was like jagged teeth. It was prickly and somewhat frightening.

"I'm not hungry," Gemma said, causing the girls to erupt in laughter again.

"You're a truly beautiful girl," Lexi commented once she'd stopped laughing. She leaned in closer to her, resting her hand on Gemma's leg, and stared up at her. "You know that, right?"

"I guess." Gemma pulled the shawl more tightly around her, relieved to have it covering her. She didn't know how to take Lexi's compliment, but it left her feeling both flattered and disturbed.

"You're a big fish in a small pond, aren't you?" Penn paced on the other side of the fire, keeping her eyes on Gemma.

"How do you mean?" Gemma asked.

"You're gorgeous, smart, ambitious, fearless," Penn explained. "And this is just a seaside attraction. A small town that would dry up if it weren't for loud tourists wreaking havoc on it every summer."

"It's nice in the off-season." Gemma's defense of Capri sounded lame even to her own ears.

"I doubt that." Penn smirked. "But even if it is, you're still more than this bay will ever be. I've seen you out in that water. You swim with strength and grace and unbridled determination."

"Thank you," Gemma said. "I've been training a lot. I want to go to the Olympics."

"The Olympics are nothing compared to what you can do," Penn scoffed. "You have a natural aptitude that is almost impossible to come by. And believe me, I know. We've searched."

That struck Gemma as odd, alarmingly so. To calm her, Lexi began singing again. It was little more than humming this time, but it was enough to keep Gemma sitting on the rock. Her concerns remained, though, even if she didn't run away.

"Why did you invite me out here?" Gemma asked. "And why'd you want me to swim with you so badly yesterday?"

"I just told you," Penn said. "You are something rare and special."

"But . . ." Gemma furrowed her brow, knowing there was something off about this that she couldn't pinpoint. "You're way hotter than I am. You're more of everything you said I was. What do you need me for?"

"Don't be silly." Penn waved her hand. "And don't worry about any of that."

"Don't worry about anything," Lexi added, and as soon as she'd said it, Gemma felt her worries slipping away, as if she'd never even had them.

"We wanted you to come here and have fun." Penn smiled at Gemma. "We wanted to get to know each other."

"What did you want to know?" Gemma asked.

"Everything!" Penn spread her arms widely. "Tell us everything!"

"Everything?" Gemma looked at Lexi uncertainly.

"Yeah, like what you're doing with that dolt you hang around with," Thea said from beside her, and Gemma snapped around to look at her. "He's way beneath you."

"Dolt?" Gemma bristled when she realized that Thea meant Alex. "Alex is a really fantastic guy. He's sweet and funny and nice to me."

"When you look like us, every guy is nice to you," Thea countered with an even stare. "You realize it doesn't mean anything. Guys are shallow, and that's all."

"You don't know Alex." Gemma shook her head. "He is the most genuine person I know."

"Why don't we talk about boys another day?" Penn interjected. "They're too much drama for tonight. Lexi, why don't you lighten the mood?"

"Oh, right." Lexi reached down the front of her dress and pulled out a small copper flask. "Let's have a drink."

"Sorry, I don't drink."

"Penn told me you weren't afraid of anything," Thea said, provoking her. "And now you're scared of a little drink?"

"I'm not scared," Gemma snapped. "But I'll get kicked off the swim team if I get caught drinking. I've worked too hard for that to throw it away."

"You won't get caught," Penn assured her.

"You guys go ahead and drink," Gemma said. "It's more for you."

"Gemma," Lexi said, her voice a song again. She held out the flask, but Gemma hesitated to take it. *"Drink."*

Then Gemma didn't have a choice. She couldn't even think about another option. Her body moved automatically, taking the flask from Lexi, unscrewing the top, and putting it to her lips. It all happened the same way that she took a breath. Motions without thought or reason or control.

The liquid was thick, and it tasted bitter and salty on her tongue. It burned going down her throat, almost as badly as the time she ate too much wasabi. When she swallowed, she nearly gagged. It felt too heavy and hot to get down, but she forced it.

"That's horrible!" Gemma coughed and wiped her mouth. "What was that?"

"My special cocktail," Penn said with a smile.

Gemma held the flask away from her, not wanting the stuff anywhere near her. Thea snatched it from her hands, moving quickly, as if Gemma would try to stop her. She threw her head back and swallowed it down in a few big gulps. Just watching Thea drink it like that made Gemma gag for real this time.

Penn shrieked. She ran over to Thea and smacked her

across the face, sending the flask flying. Dark burgundy liquid splattered all over the walls of the cove, but the waste didn't seem to bother Penn.

"That's not for you! You know better!"

"I *needed* it!" Thea snarled.

She wiped her mouth, then licked her hand, making sure she got every drop she could. For a second Gemma was afraid Thea might crawl over and lick the liquid off the dirt.

"What was that?" Gemma asked, her words already coming out in a slur.

The cove suddenly pitched to the side, and Gemma grabbed on to Lexi to keep from falling over. Everything swayed around her. She heard Penn talking, but her voice sounded like it was coming from underwater.

"That's not . . ." Gemma struggled to talk. "What did you do?"

"You'll be all right," Lexi said. She got up and tried to put her arm around Gemma, maybe meaning to comfort her, but Gemma pushed her off.

She stood up and nearly tipped forward into the fire, but Penn caught her. Gemma tried to fight her off, but she didn't have the strength anymore. All her energy had left her body, and she couldn't keep her eyes open. The world was fading to black around her.

"You'll thank me for this later," Penn was saying in her ear, and that was the last thing Gemma heard.

NINE

Lost

"Where's your sister?" Brian threw open Harper's bedroom door, banging the doorknob into the plaster.

"What?" Harper rubbed her eyes and rolled over in bed to face her father. "What are you talking about? What time is it?"

"I just got up for work, and Gemma isn't here."

"Did you check her room?" Harper asked, slowly becoming alert.

"No, Harper, I thought I'd check your room first," Brian snapped.

"Sorry, Dad, I just woke up." She sat up and swung her feet over the edge of the bed. "She went out swimming last night. She probably just lost track of time."

"Until five in the morning?" Brian asked, the worry in his voice unmistakable.

But Harper knew he'd been through this once before.

When she and her mother had gotten in the car accident. They'd left for a few hours in the evening, and Brian didn't hear anything from them until the hospital called the next morning saying his wife was in a coma.

"She's fine," Harper said, hoping to ease her dad's fears. "I'm sure she just got sidetracked. You know Gemma."

"Yes, I do, and that's why I'm worried."

"Don't. Gemma's fine." Harper ran her hand through her sleep-disheveled hair and tried to calm Brian. "I'm sure she's with Alex or napping on the beach or something."

"You think telling me she's out with Alex will make me feel better?" Brian asked, but he actually did seem to calm a little. Being out with a boy was a much more favorable alternative to being hurt or dead.

"She's fine," Harper repeated. "Get ready for work. I'll go track her down."

Brian shook his head. "Harper, I can't go to work when my daughter is missing."

"She's not missing," Harper insisted. "She just stayed out too late. It's not a big deal."

"I'll drive around and look for her," Brian said and started to leave her room.

"Dad, you can't miss work. You already missed too much when you sliced open your arm in February. You can't lose your job."

"But . . ." Brian trailed off, knowing she was right.

"I'm sure Gemma is okay," Harper said. "She'll probably be home any second. You go to work. Give me a chance to look for her, and if I can't find her in the next two hours, I'll come get you. Okay?"

He stood indecisively in Harper's doorway, looking pale and gaunt. Brian clearly wanted to go track down his daughter, but he knew Harper was probably right. He couldn't risk his job and being able to support his family just because Gemma stayed out too late.

"All right." He pursed his lips. "See if you can find her. But if you haven't heard from her by seven, you come get me. Okay?"

"Yes, of course." Harper nodded. "I'll call you as soon as I find her."

Once he turned and left her room, Harper let her own panic set in. She didn't want Brian to worry unnecessarily, but that didn't mean she wasn't scared herself. It wasn't like Gemma to stay out past curfew. Gemma liked to push the rules, but she rarely broke them.

Harper went over to her window and pulled back the curtains, looking out at Alex's house. His car was in the driveway, so that meant he wasn't out with Gemma. Harper grabbed her cell phone off her nightstand and dialed his number anyway.

"Hello?" Alex answered groggily after the fifth ring.

"Is Gemma with you?" Harper blurted out and paced her bedroom.

"What?" Alex asked, and his voice suddenly became clearer. "Harper? What's going on?"

"Nothing." She took a deep breath and stifled the urgency

in her words. She didn't need to scare him, too. "I just wanted to know if Gemma was with you."

"No," Alex said. Through her bedroom window, Harper saw the light turn on in his room next door. "I haven't seen or talked to her since I dropped her off at your house last night. Is she okay?"

Harper held the phone away from her mouth and swore under her breath. Alex would never keep Gemma out all night, and she should've known that.

If Gemma had been with him, he would've insisted that she get home right on time. Not just because it was the right thing to do, but because he was afraid of incurring the wrath of Harper and Brian.

"Yeah, no, I mean, I'm sure she's fine," Harper replied quickly. "But I have to go, okay, Alex?"

"What? No, it's not okay. Where's Gemma?"

"I don't know. That's why I have to go. I'm going to look for her. I mean, I know she's fine, but I have to find her."

"I'll go with you," Alex offered. "I'll put on some pants and meet you outside."

"No, don't." She shook her head, even though he couldn't see it. "You stay here in case she comes back. You can keep an eye on the house."

"Are you sure?"

"Yeah, I'm sure." Harper sighed. "Watch out for her, and if she contacts you, let me know, okay?"

"Yeah, I can do that. And you tell her to call me as soon as you find her."

"Will do."

Harper hung up the phone without waiting for him to say anything more. She knew where she had to look, and it twisted her stomach in knots. Gemma had gone out to the bay last night, alone, and she hadn't returned.

Still in her pajamas, Harper slipped on her flip-flops and ran down the stairs. She moved fast in the hope that she wouldn't have time to think about all the horrible things that could've happened to Gemma. Drowning. Kidnapping. Murder. Hell, even a shark attack was possible.

"Did you find her?" Brian shouted from the bathroom. He'd heard Harper flying downstairs.

"Not yet!" Harper yelled back up to him and grabbed her car keys off the rack by the door. "I'm going out now. I'll call you later!" She jogged out to her car.

As she sped through town, Harper looked around as much as she could. Gemma could've just as easily gotten hurt on the way to or from the bay. But somehow Harper knew that wasn't what had happened. The terrified pit in her stomach insisted that it was something else, something worse.

Since Gemma had ridden her bike last night, Harper went down to the docks where Gemma usually parked it. She raced down the worn wooden planks, praying the bike wasn't there. If it was gone, it meant Gemma had left, that she'd gone somewhere else.

As soon as she saw the bike, all locked up with Gemma's backpack, her heart dropped. Gemma was still out in that water, as she had been for the past eight or nine hours.

Unless . . .

Harper whirled around and found *The Dirty Gull* moored in the same spot as always, just a few feet down from where Gemma had locked up her bike.

"Daniel!" Harper shouted and ran over to his boat. "Daniel!" She reached out for the railing and tried to climb up. "Daniel!"

"Harper?" Daniel called. He opened the cabin door and stepped out, buttoning up the pair of jeans he'd just pulled on.

Harper was trying to pull herself up over the railing, but the boat was too far away from the dock. Her foot slipped off the edge, and one of her flip-flops fell off and splashed into the water. She would've fallen in right after it if Daniel hadn't come over and grabbed her arm.

He wrapped a strong arm around her shoulders and lifted her up, pulling her over the railing. To do that, he had to press her against his bare chest. Harper was cold from her panic and the morning air, and his skin felt warm against her.

"What are you doing here?" Daniel asked when he released her.

"Is Gemma here?" Harper asked, but by the confused expression on his face, she already knew the answer.

"No." He shook his head, and his brow furrowed with worry. "Why would she be here?"

"She didn't come home last night. And . . ." Harper pointed at the bike chained to the dock. "Her bike's still here, and she has swim practice in two hours. Gemma *never* misses practice." A shudder ran over her body, and her stomach lurched. "Something's wrong."

"I'll help you find her," Daniel said. "Let me go grab a shirt and shoes."

"No." She shook her head. "I don't have time to wait."

"You're obviously crazy with worry." He gestured to her as she stood trembling on his boat. "You need someone with a clearer head. I'm going with you."

Harper thought about arguing with that, but she just nodded. The urge to panic was all but taking over, and it was hard for her to keep from sobbing. She did need somebody less frantic to help her.

Daniel went belowdecks and came back up a minute later. A minute that felt like hours to Harper. Hours she spent staring out at the dark sea around them, wondering if Gemma's body was floating out in it somewhere.

"Okay," he said as he pulled a T-shirt over his head. "Let's go."

He jumped onto the dock first, then took Harper's hand to help her off the boat. When he'd fished her flip-flip out of the water, she'd protested, but Daniel insisted that it would slow her down if she had to hobble around without it.

"Where do you want to look?" Daniel asked as they walked up the dock, back toward land.

"I think we need to check the shore." She swallowed hard, realizing what she was suggesting. "She may have washed up . . ."

"Is there a certain part that she likes more?" Daniel asked. "Maybe somewhere she would have gone to rest if she got too tired for the ride home?"

"I don't know." Harper shook her head and shrugged. "I thought she might've gone to your boat, since she trusts you. But . . . I don't know. I have no idea what she could've been doing out all night on the water.

"Well, I do have ideas." She sniffled and rubbed her forehead. "The only things I can think of aren't pretty, though. She has no good reason to be out here. Gemma would only stay if something bad happened or if somebody hurt her."

"Hey." Daniel touched her arm, causing Harper to look up at him. "We'll find her, okay? Just think about places she would go if everything was all right. What does Gemma do out here? Where does she go?"

"I don't know!" Harper repeated, exasperated and terrified. She looked away from him and out at the bay, trying to think. "She loves coming out here to swim at night. She likes to go out past that rock over there."

She pointed to a huge rock in the water on the other side of the bay. Harper and Gemma had had a few races to that rock, with Gemma always coming out the winner.

"She likes the other side of the bay more?" Daniel asked.

"Kind of," Harper admitted. "Tourists and boats don't go out there because of all the rocks, and she likes how deserted it is."

"So if she was going to take a break, it would be over there."

"Yes!" She nodded excitedly, realizing what that meant. "When she drives, she parks over there, by the cypress trees."

It would be faster to drive over there than to walk, so Harper ran back out to her car, with Daniel close behind. To get around the bay, Harper drove as fast as she could, which meant running a few stop signs and cutting across the grass.

Once she got to the beach, she was grateful that Daniel had rescued her flip-flop. The shore was covered in sharp rocks, and it would've been nearly impossible to navigate barefoot. Or at least it would've been for her. Harper knew the rocks would not have intimidated Gemma.

She made it out to the edge of the shore, past the trees, so she could have a clear view of the coastline all the way down to the cove. Daniel came up behind her and pointed to a blob of black a ways down.

"What's that?" he asked, but Harper didn't wait to answer.

She went so fast she tripped on the rocks a few times and fell once, tearing open her knee. Daniel followed her as quickly as he could, but he moved at a more cautious pace.

When she was close enough that she could tell for sure, Harper started calling out Gemma's name. She could see it was her sister, lying on her back and tangled in something that resembled a gold fishing net. But Gemma didn't respond.

TEN

Hangover

Gemma!" Harper screamed and collapsed next to her sister, ignoring the rocks stinging her skin. "Gemma, wake up!"

"Is she alive?" Daniel asked, standing behind Harper and staring down at Gemma.

It really didn't look good. Gemma's skin was drained of color, so she looked almost blue. Bruises and scratches covered her arms, and blood had dried on her temple. Her lips were chapped and dry, and seaweed entangled her hair.

And then, even though Harper didn't really think she would, Gemma groaned and turned her head to the side.

"Gemma." Harper brushed back the hair from Gemma's forehead, and her eyes fluttered open.

"Harper?" Gemma asked, her voice coming out in a croak.

"Oh, thank God." Harper let out a deep breath, and relieved tears filled her eyes. "What happened to you?"

"I don't know."

Wincing as she moved, Gemma tried to stand, but the rocks were too uneven. When she started to stumble, Daniel put his arm underneath her legs and scooped her up. Gemma shifted and tried to hang on to him for support, but her arms were too tangled up in the mesh wrapped around her.

"Let's get her back to the car," Harper suggested, and Daniel nodded.

Once the realization that Gemma was alive had settled in, Harper wanted to sob and scream at her. But Gemma still seemed so weak and out of it that she didn't want to interrogate her.

Harper had parked as close as she could get, which meant that she'd parked on the unruly beach grass lining the shore. Daniel set Gemma down on her feet once they got to the car, and she managed to stand up on her own. The mesh was pretty tangled around her, and Harper and Daniel intervened to help her get it off.

"What is this?" Harper asked. "Did you get caught in a fishermen's net? Is that what happened to you?"

"This isn't a net." Daniel shook his head. Once they'd gotten Gemma free from it, he ran it through his hands, admiring the strange texture of it. "At least not any net I've ever seen."

"No, it's not a net." Gemma put her hand on the car to steady herself and leaned against it. "It's a shawl or something."

"A shawl?" Harper asked. "Where did you get a shawl?"

Gemma grimaced, hesitating before she reluctantly admitted, "Penn."

"Penn?" Harper was nearly shrieking. "What the hell were you doing with Penn?"

"You really should stay away from those girls," Daniel said solemnly. "They are . . . there's something off about them."

"Believe me, I know," Gemma muttered.

"So what were you doing with them?" Harper asked. "What did you do last night?"

"Can we talk about this later, please?" Gemma begged. "My head is pounding. My body hurts all over. And I'm so thirsty, it's unbelievable."

"Do you need to go to the hospital?" Harper asked.

Gemma shook her head. "No, I just need to go home."

"If you're fine, then you're going to tell me what's going on." Harper crossed her arms over her chest.

"I was out swimming last night, and . . ." Gemma trailed off and stared at the sun rising over the bay, as if trying to remember exactly what had happened last night. "I went out to the cove, and Penn, Lexi, and Thea were . . . partying out there."

"They were *partying*?" Harper asked, and now she was totally gobsmacked. "You partied with those girls last night?"

"Yeah," Gemma answered uncertainly. "I mean, yes. I think."

"You *think*?" Harper shook her head.

"Yeah, they invited me to join them, and I just had one

drink. But it must've been really strong. It was only one drink, I swear."

"You drank?" Harper's eyes widened. "Gemma! You can get kicked off the swim team for that. And you have practice in an hour, which you clearly can't handle today. What were you thinking?"

"I wasn't!" Gemma yelled. "I honestly don't know what I was thinking! I have no idea how any of it happened last night. I remember having one drink, and then I woke up on the rocks. I don't know what happened, and I'm sorry."

"Get in the car," Harper said through clenched teeth, too pissed off to even yell.

"I really am sorry," Gemma repeated.

"Get in the car!" Harper shouted, and Daniel flinched.

"Thanks for . . . helping," Gemma mumbled to Daniel and stared down at her feet.

"No problem," he said. She tried to open the car door and almost fell over, so he went over and held it open for her. "Get some rest and drink plenty of fluids. Hangovers are a bitch, but you'll survive."

Gemma smiled thinly at him and climbed into the car. Once she was safely inside, he shut the door and turned his attention back to Harper. Her arms were crossed over her chest as she glared down at her sister in anger and disbelief, but when Daniel looked at her, she smiled sheepishly.

"I'm really sorry for dragging you out to help me pick up my drunk sister. I mean, thank you. I appreciate it, but I'm sorry for bothering you."

"No, it was no bother." Daniel grinned. "I was just thinking to myself how tedious it is sleeping in until *after* the sun comes up."

"Sorry," Harper said again. "I should probably let you go back to sleep."

"All right." Daniel nodded and took a step back from the car. "But take it easy on her, okay? She's just a kid. They screw up sometimes."

"*I* didn't." Harper walked around the front of the car to the driver's side.

"Really?" He stopped to arch an eyebrow at her. "You never screwed up?"

"Not like that." She gestured to the car, where Gemma had her forehead resting against the glass. "I never stayed out all night or got drunk. I maybe overslept for school once."

"Oh, wow." Daniel smirked and looked genuinely surprised. "That's actually a little sad. I mean, good for you, not drinking. But a life without *any* mistakes? That doesn't sound like any fun at all."

"I've had fun." Harper bristled, and Gemma groaned in the car, interrupting her argument with Daniel. "I should really get home, though."

"Right, of course." He gave her a small wave and backed away. "I won't keep you from your duty."

"Thanks." Harper smiled at him.

As soon as she got in the car, her smile and any sense of happiness evaporated. Her relief at finding her sister alive had turned into full-blown anger.

"I don't understand how you could do this," Harper said as she put the car in drive and pulled away from the bay. "Dad almost called out of work to look for you. He could've lost his job over this."

"I'm sorry." Gemma squeezed her eyes shut and rubbed her forehead, as if she wished Harper would just stop talking.

"Sorry doesn't cut it, Gemma!" Harper shouted. "You could've died! Do you understand that? You almost *did* die. I don't even know what happened or how you're still alive. How could you do that? How could you put yourself in that situation?"

"I don't know!" Gemma lifted her head. "How many times do I have to tell you that I don't know?"

"As many times as it takes until it starts making sense!" Harper shot back. "This isn't like you. You hate those girls and you hate drinking. Why were you hanging out with them? Why would you risk yourself for people you don't even like?"

"Harper!" Gemma snapped. "I don't remember last night. I don't have any answers, no matter how many times or how many different ways you ask me. I already told you everything I know!"

"You know you are so grounded, right?" Harper asked. "You're *never* going to that bay at night again. You'll be lucky if Dad even lets you go during the day."

"I know." Gemma sighed and rested her head against the window again.

"And I don't know when you'll be able to see Alex again," Harper went on. "He was worried sick about you, too."

"He was?" Gemma looked over at Harper and brightened a little. "How did he know I was missing?"

"I thought you might be with him, so I called and asked if he knew where you were. You're supposed to call him when we get back."

"Hmm." Gemma closed her eyes. "Maybe you should call him. I don't feel much like talking right now."

Harper looked back over at her sister, softening with concern. If Gemma didn't even feel up to talking to Alex, then something definitely had to be wrong.

"Are you sure you're okay?" Harper asked. "I can take you to the hospital right now."

"No, I'm just hungover and have some bruises. I'll be fine."

"Maybe you should get some X-rays," Harper said. "Those bruises might be worse than they look. And I don't even know how you got them."

"I'm fine," Gemma insisted. "Please take me home. I just want to sleep."

Harper still wasn't thrilled about it, but Gemma was probably right. Since Harper'd had the chance to release some of her anger, she decided to let it go. If Gemma was sick, she didn't need Harper yelling at her. So for now Harper would just take care of her.

When they got home, Gemma went into the kitchen and got herself a glass of cold water from the tap. She proceeded to drink glass after glass, gulping it down so fast that water spilled down her chin.

"Are you sure you're okay?" Harper asked, watching her sister uncertainly.

"Yeah." Gemma nodded and wiped her mouth with the back of her hand. "I'm just really thirsty. But I'm better now." She set the glass down in the sink and forced a smile at Harper.

"Sit down, then. You need to get cleaned up."

Gemma pulled out a chair from the kitchen table and eased herself into it. Harper went into the bathroom and got a wet washcloth, antiseptic, and Band-Aids. When she came back, she knelt on the floor in front of Gemma, inspecting her cuts and scrapes.

None of them looked too deep, which was the only good part. When Harper washed off a gash on her thigh, Gemma winced. Harper gave her an apologetic look and dabbed more carefully at it.

"You don't remember how you got any of these?" Harper looked up at Gemma, searching her expression for any clues about what had happened.

"No."

"So you don't know if the girls did this to you?" Harper asked, and Gemma shook her head. "Penn could've beat you up, then? And even if they didn't, they left you to die in the bay, and you don't even know why?"

Just thinking about it made Harper so angry, she didn't realize how hard she was scrubbing at Gemma's cuts.

"Harper!" Gemma grimaced and pulled back her leg.

"Sorry." Harper stopped cleaning the cut, and when she

put a bandage over it, she was much more careful. "Maybe we should call the police on those girls."

"And tell them what? I accidentally drank too much and don't remember what happened?" Gemma asked wearily.

"Well . . ." Harper shrugged. "I don't know. I feel like I should do something."

"You're doing enough," Gemma tried to reassure her. "And right now I just need to get some sleep."

"Don't you want to shower first?" Harper asked as Gemma stood.

"After I wake up."

Gemma gripped the table for support and slowly rose to her feet. Her hair was sticky from salt and dirt, and as Gemma walked past her, Harper plucked a bit of seaweed from the tangles of her hair.

Gemma managed to get up the stairs, but Harper followed close behind, in case she slipped. Gemma changed quickly out of her bathing suit into clean underwear and a T-shirt, then collapsed into her bed.

Once Gemma was tucked in safe and sound, Harper went to her room to make phone calls. She kept both their bedroom doors open, keeping an eye on Gemma, and she spoke softly on the phone so as not to disturb her.

First she had to call her dad and tell him that Gemma was all right. He sounded as excited as Harper had been, and then just as pissed when he found out *why* Gemma had stayed out all night. Brian so rarely got mad at them it was easy to forget how terrifying he could be when he was angry.

The other phone calls went more quickly. She told Alex that Gemma was okay, and she called the coach at the school to tell him that Gemma wouldn't be able to make it in today. After that, Harper decided to call in to work herself. Even though it probably was just a hangover, Harper didn't feel right about leaving Gemma alone.

With the calls out of the way, Harper sat down on the floor in the hallway, right outside Gemma's room. From there she could see her sister sleeping. Gemma had her back to her, and the thin sheet covering her rose and fell with each breath.

Even if Gemma hadn't been sick, Harper didn't know if she'd have gone to work. Facing the possibility of losing Gemma made it hard to be away from her.

Sometimes Harper got so wrapped up in taking care of everything, her father and the house and making sure that Gemma was in line and safe, she forgot that she actually loved her sister. The truth was that Harper would be lost without her.

ELEVEN

Ravenous

Gemma woke up late in the afternoon after her fever finally broke, and her thoughts were a bit clearer. Her dreams had been bizarre and excruciatingly vivid, but the instant she woke up, she forgot them all. All she knew was that they left her feeling gross and terrified.

Harper doted on her, which made Gemma feel even worse. Harper and her dad worried so much, and Gemma never wanted to do anything to betray their trust. Staying out all night would leave her grounded for the summer and banned from Anthemusa Bay, on top of having scared the hell out of the two people she cared about most.

The worst part was that she didn't even know *why* she'd done it.

She couldn't remember anything at all after she'd drunk from the flask. It was all black until the morning, when Harper had found her on the shore. But even before that, before she'd had anything to drink, her memories felt strange and fuzzy.

Gemma remembered going to the cove. In her mind, she could see what she'd done, but it was like watching a show about someone else. All the movements and actions—it was her body doing them, but it wasn't her.

Going to the cove and hanging out with Penn—those weren't her decisions. Gemma would never drink, let alone do it because girls like Lexi pressured her to. She remembered doing it, but it wasn't her. *She* would never do that.

But she had. Or how else would she have ended up washed up on the beach, hungover?

Getting drunk didn't completely explain the night, though. Things were messed up before she drank from the flask, and Gemma had never heard of liquor being thick like that. It had the consistency of honey, but tasted nothing like it.

Maybe it wasn't alcohol, but it was definitely something. It could've been laced with a drug or poison. Or maybe a potion. Gemma wouldn't be surprised at all if Penn turned out to be a witch.

In any event, they had slipped her something. Gemma would probably never know exactly what it was, but it didn't really matter. They had given her something, and she had no idea why.

Worse still, she didn't know what they'd done to her after that. All the scratches were probably from being thrown around in the ocean. After she'd passed out, they must have just tossed her in the bay.

Or had they? If she had been unconscious when she went in the water, wouldn't she have drowned? Or been swept out to sea? How did she end up on the shore with only a few scrapes and bruises? Why wasn't she dead?

"Crap." Harper sighed and walked into Gemma's room, pulling her from her thoughts. "Marcy just called me. There's some kind of meltdown at the library, and I need to go help her out."

Gemma sat up in bed. Her body already felt much better than it had that morning. All the aches had gone away, and even the redness and swelling had gone down around her cuts and bruises. Other than being sticky and dirty, she didn't feel half bad.

"Will you be all right here, alone for an hour or so?" Harper asked.

"Yeah." Gemma nodded. "I'm fine. I think I'll probably take a shower. You go do what you need to do. I don't want to inconvenience you any more than I already have."

"All right." Harper bit her lip and seemed hesitant to leave. "I'll have my cell phone, and you call if you need me. I mean that, okay?"

"Okay." Gemma nodded again. "But I'll be fine."

After Harper left, Gemma felt relief wash over her. Having Harper look out for her like that only worsened her guilt, but more than that, Gemma wanted a chance to clear her head and try to sort things out herself. It was hard to think when Harper kept checking on her and interrogating her about what had happened.

Gemma knew that Harper meant well, and it was actually her own fault that Harper felt the need to be this intensely involved. But sometimes she just needed room to breathe.

It was after Harper and their mom were in the car accident that things had first started getting bad. Even though Harper was the one who had been hurt, she suddenly became ultra-protective of Gemma.

And Gemma hadn't minded, at least not at first. She'd needed it. When her mother was in a coma, Gemma had felt totally lost. In retrospect, she'd been a bit of a mama's girl, and if Harper hadn't stepped up, she didn't know how she would've coped.

Eventually, though, she learned to handle it on her own. That was when she really took to swimming. She'd always loved the water, but after that, she couldn't get enough of it. It was the only place she felt free, and sometimes, when Harper got in a mood, it was the only place that Gemma could really breathe.

Now, because of her stupid mistake with Penn, not only would Harper be way more intense, but Gemma wouldn't be able to go out to the bay to get some release. At least she still had swim practice. And long baths.

Gemma considered taking a bath now, but her skin felt too dirty. It would only take a few seconds before she was swimming in a tub of mud. A shower would be better.

While waiting for the tap water to warm up, she turned on the CD player in the bathroom. Her father's Springsteen album came blasting out, and Gemma sifted through the stack of CDs on the counter, searching for her own music. It was mostly Harper's music in the bathroom, groups like Arcade Fire and Ra Ra Riot.

But for some reason, Gemma's own CDs didn't sound good. She didn't want to hear anything on them. It all felt . . . *wrong,* somehow. Clicking off the stereo, Gemma decided to just forgo music.

Before she got in the shower, she stripped down to her underwear. In front of the mirror, she turned this way and that so she could see all the wounds on her skin.

A large bruise stretched out from the small of her back all way up to her shoulder blades. It was a dark purple color with green around the edges, and Gemma touched it tentatively. It was sore, for sure, but it didn't hurt nearly as badly as she thought it would.

In any event, a hot shower ought to make it feel better, so she finished inspecting herself and hopped in. As soon as the warm water streamed over her, she felt even better. Almost invigorated.

Gemma couldn't help herself, and she began to sing as she washed her hair. At first she was singing the latest Katy Perry song, but a different tune was stuck in her head. It was a song she didn't even know how she knew.

With conditioner in her hair, she paused to think of it. She couldn't quite get it, but it was on the tip of her tongue.

"Come now . . ." Gemma furrowed her brow as she tried to think of the words. "I'll show you the way . . . into my ocean . . ." She shook her head. "No, that's not right."

Sighing, she decided to start singing it, hoping it would come to her as she went along, and almost like magic, it did. The lyrics were on her lips, and she sang them out loudly.

"Come now, weary traveler, I'll lead you through the waves. Worry not, poor voyager, for my voice is the way."

Then this weird sensation came over her. It reminded her of the way it felt when she had butterflies in her stomach, like when Alex kissed her, but it was on her skin. The feeling traveled down her leg, from her thigh to the tips of her toes. She brushed her hand over her leg, following the path of the strange sensation, and she felt her skin ripple underneath her fingers.

She yelped and looked down. She half expected to see something clinging to her leg, like seaweed or maybe even a leech, but there was nothing. Just her skin, looking as ordinary as ever.

In fact, it was a little too normal. The bruises on her skin had faded and the cuts were almost healed. Gemma craned her neck, trying to see her back, but she couldn't.

Her hair was rinsed, and she'd already gone over her skin with a bath sponge, so she decided to end the shower. She had planned to scrub harder, but something weird was going on, and she'd prefer to deal with it when she had clothes on.

When she hung the sponge on the faucet so it could dry, the same way she always did after a shower, she noticed something sticking to it. She picked it out of the sponge and held it up in the light, inspecting it.

It was some kind of large iridescent green scale, too big to belong to the usual small fish she saw in the bay. It had to come from something huge, at least the size of Gemma herself. But it was a color unlike any she'd ever seen on a fish. Admittedly, tropical fish came in all sorts of dazzling colors, but the bay was too far north to get the really pretty fish.

"Gemma?" Alex asked, interrupting her examination of the mysterious scale, and he started knocking on the bathroom door.

"Alex?" Gemma asked in surprise, and she grabbed a towel to wrap around herself, even though Alex was hidden safely on the other side of the door. "What are you doing here?"

"I just . . ." He trailed off, his voice completely lost through the door.

"What?" Gemma asked.

"I needed to see you."

"What? Why? Did something happen?"

"No, I . . ." Alex sighed loudly. "Harper told me you were missing, and I wanted to make sure you were okay. I was giving you time to rest, but I just heard you singing, so I knew you were awake."

Gemma gave an embarrassed look to the open bathroom window. The shades were drawn, but the sash was up; Alex could've easily heard her.

Once she got past her initial shame, she furrowed her brow and turned back to the closed door. "So you just came into my house?" That didn't sound like something Alex would do at all. He was always polite, almost to a fault.

"No, I knocked first, but you didn't answer, and then you

stopped singing," Alex explained. "I heard you yelp, and I thought something might be the matter."

"Oh." She smiled, realizing he was concerned for her well-being. "I just got out of the shower. Let me get dressed, and then I'll come out and talk to you."

Thankfully, Gemma had brought her clothes into the bathroom, and she dressed hurriedly. Alex's surprise visit nearly made her forget about the bruise on her back, but she remembered after she'd gotten dressed.

Gemma turned her back to the mirror and lifted up her shirt. When she looked over her shoulder, her jaw dropped. The massive bruise was nearly gone. It was only a blotch in the center of her back, and the color had even faded from a deep eggplant to a soft gray.

"That cannot be possible." Gemma gaped at the reflection.

"Did you say something?" Alex called from the hallway.

"Uh . . . no." She dropped her shirt, as if he'd be able to see through the door. "I was just talking to myself. I'll be out in a sec."

Hurriedly, she ran her fingers through her hair to comb it out. Even her hair didn't seem as tangled as it usually was. All the salt water and chlorine were harsh on her hair, but it felt silkier than it had in years.

She didn't have time to worry about it, though. Alex was waiting for her, and she wanted to hurry and see him while she still could. When she got home from work Harper would send him away, and Gemma had no idea when she'd get a minute alone with him again.

"It's actually really good that you stopped by," Gemma said as she opened the bathroom door. She'd expected him to be out in the hall waiting for her, but he wasn't.

"Why is that?" Alex asked, his voice coming from her bedroom.

"Because I'm probably going to be grounded from now until the end of time."

She went into her room, trying not to let on how nervous it made her, having him in her room. It wasn't a bad nervous, but this was the first time she'd had a boy she dated in here. This wasn't Alex's first time in her room, but it was different somehow. She hadn't wanted to kiss him before.

She glanced around quickly to make sure she didn't have anything embarrassing out in the open. Her dirty bathing suit was crumpled up on the floor and her bed was unmade, but there wasn't anything too bad. Maybe the poster of Michael Phelps on her wall, but Alex couldn't really fault her for that.

Alex had been standing next to her bed, admiring the picture on her bedside table of her, Harper, and their mother. As soon as Gemma came in the room, he turned to face her, and his brown eyes widened. His mouth opened, but no words came out. He tried to set the picture back on the nightstand, but he wasn't paying attention, and it fell to the floor.

"Sorry." He scrambled to pick it up, and Gemma laughed.

"It's okay."

"No, I'm sorry." He looked back at her, giving her a sheepish smile. "I'm so clumsy. You make me . . ."

"What?" She stepped closer to her bed, and his eyes stayed on her.

"I don't know." He laughed and furrowed his brow in confusion. "It's like . . . I can't think around you sometimes."

"You can't think?" Gemma asked dubiously and sat on the bed. "You're the smartest person I know. How can you stop thinking?"

"I don't know."

He sat down next to her, still staring at her, but something about his stare had shifted from flattering to unnerving. There was something too intense in his gaze, and Gemma tucked her hair behind her ear and looked away from him.

"I'm sorry I didn't call you today," she said.

"It's okay," he said quickly, then shook his head, as if that were not what he meant to say. "I wasn't . . ." He looked away from her, but only for a moment, and then his eyes were locked on her again. "Where were you?"

"You wouldn't believe me if I told you." She shook her head.

"I'd believe anything you said," Alex replied, and the sincerity in his voice made Gemma look at him.

"What's going on with you?"

"What do you mean?"

"I mean . . ." She gestured to him. "This. The way you're looking at me. The way you're talking to me."

"Aren't I talking to you the way I always have?" Alex moved away from her a bit, genuinely taken aback by her observation.

"No. You're all . . ." She shrugged, unable to find the right words to explain it. "Not you."

"I'm sorry." His face pinched as he tried hard to figure out what she meant. "I guess . . . I was scared this morning. Harper wouldn't tell me what was going on, and I was afraid that something had happened to you."

"I truly am sorry about that," Gemma said, deciding that must be what was going on. He'd been worried about her, so he was overcompensating with excessive staring, like Harper did sometimes. "I never meant to scare you. Or anybody."

"But now you'll be grounded?" Alex asked.

She sighed. "Yeah, definitely."

"I won't be able to see you?" he asked, sounding as depressed about it as she felt. "I don't know if I can handle that."

"Hopefully it will only be for a few weeks. Maybe less, with good behavior." She gave him a small smile. "And maybe sometimes you can stop by when Harper and my dad are at work, like now."

"How long do we have until Harper gets home from work?"

Gemma glanced over at the clock and realized sadly that Harper had already been gone for an hour. "Not long."

"Then we have to make the most of this time while we have it," Alex said decisively.

"What do you mean?"

"I mean this." He leaned in to her, pressing his lips to hers.

At first he kissed her in the same sweet way he always did—gentle, restrained, careful. But something changed. An eagerness took over, and he tangled his fingers in her hair, pressing her to him.

When things shifted, when Alex began kissing her with an insistence that was almost forceful, Gemma grew alarmed. She almost pushed him back so she could suggest they slow down, but it was as if he'd awakened something inside of her, a hunger she didn't even know she had.

She pushed him back on the bed, still kissing him. His hands roamed over her body, at first over her clothes, but then sliding underneath her shirt to where her bruise should be. Everywhere his flesh touched hers, that same sensation she'd felt in the shower rippled over her.

Their kisses were getting more frantic, like Alex thought he'd die if he didn't have her. Gemma felt ravenous for him in the most primal way. She wanted him, needed him, couldn't wait to devour him. It surged through her like a fire, and in some dark part of her mind she realized that what she wanted to do with him had nothing to do with passion.

"Ow!" Alex winced and stopped kissing her.

"What?" Gemma asked.

She lay on top of him, both of them gasping for breath. Alex's eyes were clearer now, no longer fogged with passion. His hand had been gripping her side, pulling her to him, but he let go and touched his lip. It came back with a drop of blood on his fingertip.

"You . . . bit me?" Alex said uncertainly.

"I bit you?" She sat up, still straddling Alex.

As she ran her tongue over her teeth, they suddenly felt

sharper to her. Her incisors were so pointed, she nearly pricked her own tongue on them.

"It's okay." Alex rubbed her leg, trying to comfort her. "It was an accident, and I'm fine."

Her stomach growled, audibly rumbling. Gemma put her hand over it, as if that would silence it.

"I'm *starving,*" she said, sounding confused by her admission.

He laughed. "I heard that."

She shook her head and didn't know how to explain it. Kissing him had somehow made her incredibly hungry. And though she didn't remember doing it, she wasn't convinced that biting him had been an accident.

"Harper should be home soon," Gemma said, looking for an excuse to end their encounter. She climbed off of Alex and sat down on the bed.

"Yeah, of course." He sat up quickly and shook his head, as if clearing it of something.

Neither of them said anything for a minute. They both just stared down at the floor, confused by their recent actions.

"Listen, I'm . . . I'm sorry," Alex said.

"What for?"

"I didn't mean to come over and . . . and . . ." He stumbled over his words. "Make out like that, I guess. I mean, it was nice. But . . ." He sighed. "I didn't want to rush you or pressure you, and . . . That's not me. I'm not that guy."

"I know." Gemma nodded. She smiled at him, hoping her

smile didn't look as pained as it felt. "I'm not that girl, either. But you definitely didn't pressure me into anything."

"Okay. Good." He stood up and touched his lip again, checking for blood, then looked back at her. "I guess, um, I'll see you when I can."

"Yeah." She nodded.

"I am really glad that you're okay."

"I know. Thank you."

He paused, thinking for a second, then bent down and kissed her on the cheek. It was a little long for a kiss on the cheek, but it was still over too quickly. Then Alex was gone.

Of all the kisses they'd shared that afternoon, that one before he left was Gemma's favorite. It may have been the most chaste, but it was also the one that felt the most genuine.

TWELVE

Pearl's

The library was slow today, thanks to the pristine weather. The sun shone brightly in the sky, and it was warm without being overly so. It was the kind of day that would make Gemma kill to be out on the bay, and even Harper would've been happy to join her.

Not that Gemma could go anywhere. As predicted, their father had grounded her when he came home from work last night. He'd yelled in a way that almost made Harper stand up for her sister, but she didn't. She hid out on the steps and listened to him rant about how he'd always given Gemma freedom and trusted her, but those days were over.

In the end, Gemma had begun to cry. Brian had apologized then, but Gemma just went up to her room. She spent the whole night up there. Harper had tried to talk to her a couple of times, but Gemma just sent her away.

Harper had hoped to talk to her this morning, but Gemma

had already left for swim practice by the time she got up. On the upside, Brian had remembered to take his lunch to work with him.

Although that was starting to seem like less of a positive now that Harper was sitting at the front desk of the library without much to do. She absently leafed through Judy Blume's *Forever.*

She'd read it before, but that was a couple years ago, so she wanted to refresh herself with the text. It was part of their summer reading program for middle schoolers, and on Mondays Harper met with the ten or so kids in the book club to talk about their weekly reading.

"Did you know that the principal of the high school has had Oprah Winfrey's biography out for the past six weeks?" Marcy asked, clicking on the computer next to Harper.

"Nope, I didn't know that," Harper replied.

Since it was slow, Marcy was going through the computer to search for people who had overdue books, then calling to remind them. Marcy had actually volunteered to do it. Even though she hated interacting with people, she loved calling to tell them that they'd done something wrong.

"That seems weird, doesn't it?" Marcy peered at Harper from behind a pair of black horn-rimmed glasses. Not that she needed corrective lenses—she just thought they made her look academic, so she wore them sometimes.

"I don't know. I heard it's a really good book."

"It's like I always say—you can tell a lot about a person by the books they check out."

"You just like to snoop on people," Harper corrected her.

"You say that like it's a bad thing. It's always good to know what your neighbors are up to. Just ask Poland about that after World War Two."

"There's never a good reason to invade somebody's—"

"Whoa, Harper, isn't that the kid you know?" Marcy interrupted her and pointed to the computer screen.

"Lots of people I know check out books," Harper said without looking up from the Judy Blume book. "It's not all that surprising."

"No, no, I got bored with that so I was just checking out the *Capri Daily Herald*'s Web site to leave angry, anonymous comments on the op-ed piece. But I found this instead." Marcy turned the screen so it faced Harper more.

Harper looked up to see the headline "Local Boy Missing." Below it was a picture of Luke Benfield that Harper recognized as his senior picture from her yearbook. He'd tried to slick back his red curls, but they still stuck out at the sides.

"He's missing?" Harper asked and scooted her chair closer to Marcy's.

In smaller letters the subhead read "Fourth Boy Missing in Two Months." The article went on to give a few basic facts about Luke—that he was an honor-roll student and Stanford-bound in the fall.

The rest of the story told what little they knew about what had happened. Luke had gone to the picnic on Monday, then went home for supper. He seemed normal, and he left after he ate, telling his parents he was meeting a friend, and he'd never returned.

His parents were at a loss as to where he might be. The police had just started their investigation, but they didn't seem to know any more than they did about the other missing boys. Since Luke was eighteen, the police would have ordinarily waited longer to start searching, but with the recent rash of disappearances, the cops were taking this latest one seriously.

The reporter drew parallels between Luke's disappearance and those of the other three boys. They were all teenagers. They had all left to meet some friends. None of them ever came home.

The article went on to mention two teenage girls who had gone missing from nearby coastal towns. All the boys were from Capri, but the girls were from two different towns more than a half hour away.

"Do you think they're going to question us?" Marcy asked.

"Why? We didn't have anything to do with that."

"Because we saw him that day." Marcy pointed to the computer screen, as if to elaborate. "He went missing the night of the picnic."

Harper thought it over. "I don't know. Maybe they will, but the paper said the police just started the investigation. They'll probably talk to Alex, but I don't know if they're going to talk to every person who went to the picnic."

"That's freaky, right?" Marcy asked. "We just saw him, and now he's dead."

"He's not dead. He's *missing,*" Harper corrected her. "He might still be alive."

"I doubt it. They're saying it's a serial killer."

"They who?" Harper asked, leaning back in her chair. "The *Herald* didn't say anything about it."

"I know." Marcy shrugged. " 'They' everybody. The people in town."

"Well, the people in town don't know everything." Harper scooted her chair back to her spot at the desk, away from Marcy and the horrible news story about Luke. "I'm sure he'll turn up all right."

Marcy scoffed. "I highly doubt that. Nobody's found any of these boys. I'm telling you there's some serial killer on the loose picking off—"

"Marcy!" Harper snapped, cutting off her train of thought. "Luke is Alex's friend. He has parents and a life. Let's hope for their sake that he's okay. And we'll leave it at that."

"Okay." Marcy turned the computer screen back toward herself and inched her chair away from Harper. "I didn't know it was such a touchy subject."

"It's not touchy." Harper let out a deep breath and softened her tone. "I just think we should be respectful in times of tragedy."

"Sorry." Marcy was quiet for a moment. "I should probably get back to looking up fines anyway. I have lots of phone calls to make."

Harper tried to go back to reading the book, but she hadn't really been that into it anyway. Her mind wandered back to Luke and his senior picture that tried too hard. She'd never felt anything for Luke, not anything more than friendship, but he was nice. They'd shared a few awkward, strained moments together, and they'd even kissed once. Now he might never come home.

Though she didn't want to admit it, Harper knew that Marcy was probably right. Luke wasn't coming home alive.

"I need a break," Harper said suddenly and stood up.

"What?" Marcy looked up at her from behind her ridiculous eyewear.

"I think I'll just go across the street and grab a Coke or something. But I need to just . . ." Harper shook her head. She didn't know what she needed exactly, but she wanted to stop thinking about Luke.

"So you're gonna leave me here alone?" Marcy asked, sounding frightened at the prospect of having to deal with patrons.

Harper glanced around the empty library. "I think you can handle it. Besides," Harper said as she pushed back her chair, "I abandoned my sick sister yesterday to help out. You can cover for me for like thirty minutes."

"*Thirty* minutes?" Marcy called after Harper as she walked out the door.

Just stepping out in the sun helped alleviate some of her unease. It was too beautiful a day to imagine anything bad happening. She tried to shake off her discomfort as she went across the street to Pearl's Diner.

The diner was run-down and dingy, so it managed to keep away a lot of the tourists, who hung around the beach. It didn't have an over-the-top seafaring theme like most of the places by the bay, aside from one painting over the bar. It was a huge picture of a mermaid sitting on an open clamshell, holding a big pearl.

A few booths lined the large front window, and stools covered in cracked red vinyl ran along the counter. Pearl had a few pieces of pie displayed in a glass case, but she only served two kinds—lemon and blueberry. The tiles on the floor were supposed to be red and white, but the white was more of a beige now.

It was usually only the locals who went there. That was what was so weird about Penn and her friends coming to Pearl's. They frequented it so often, they'd nearly become regulars, and they weren't even from Capri.

At the thought of Penn, Harper immediately looked around the diner. The last thing she needed was to run into them.

Fortunately, Penn, Thea, and Lexi were nowhere in sight. Daniel, however, was sitting at a small table by himself eating a cup of soup when Harper walked in. He smiled when he saw her, so she went over to him.

"I didn't know you ate here."

"I gotta come here for Pearl's famous clam chowder." Daniel grinned, then gestured to the empty seat across from him. "Care to join me?" She chewed her lip, debating whether or not she should, so he said, "You do owe me a rain check after the ice-cream incident."

"I do," she admitted, and, almost reluctantly, she sat down across from him.

"I even got soup, so we're right on track for a meal of equal value."

"That we are."

"So what brings you here?" Daniel asked.

"Lunch," Harper said, and he laughed at the obvious. "Actually, I work across the street at the library. I'm on break now."

"You come here a lot, then?" He'd finished his soup, so he pushed the bowl to the side and leaned forward, resting his elbows on the table.

"Not really, no." She shook her head. "My coworker Marcy hates being left alone at the library, so I usually eat my lunch there."

"Except for when your dad forgets his lunch."

"Yeah, except for that."

"Does he really forget his lunch that often?" He gave her a curious look, his hazel eyes dancing.

Harper returned his curious expression. "Yeah. Why?"

"Really?" Daniel did nothing to mask his disappointment. "Because I was starting to think you were looking for excuses to see me."

"Hardly." She lowered her eyes and laughed.

Daniel smiled, but he looked ready to protest her dismissal of his claims when Pearl came over to take Harper's order.

She was a heavyset woman who used home hair-dye kits in an attempt to cover her gray, but it only left her with blue hair.

"How was the chowder?" Pearl asked, picking up Daniel's bowl.

"Great as always, Pearl."

"You should come in to eat it more, then," Pearl said, then pointed to his slender frame. "You're wasting away. What are you eating out there on the boat?"

"Nothing nearly as good as your food," Daniel admitted.

"Well, I tell you what. My daughter's air conditioner is on the fritz again. Her good-for-nothing husband can't fix it, and she's got those two little babies in that tiny apartment," Pearl said. "They can't handle the heat the way you or I can. If you swing by and check out her A/C tonight, I'll send you home with a big bucket of my chowder."

"You got yourself a deal." He smiled. "Tell your daughter I'll stop by around six."

"Thank you. You're a real sweetheart, Daniel." Pearl winked at him, then turned to Harper. "What can I get for you?"

"Just a Cherry Coke," Harper said.

"One Cherry Coke, coming up."

"You can order more than a Coke if you want," Daniel told Harper once Pearl had left to fill the order. "I was just kidding about you having to pay for something of equal value."

"I know. I'm just not that hungry." In truth, her stomach

was still twisted from thinking about Luke. It had calmed down some since she'd gotten here, but her appetite hadn't returned.

"Are you sure?" Daniel asked again. "You're not one of those girls that won't eat in front of a guy she's trying to impress?"

Harper laughed at his presumption. "First of all, I'm not trying to impress you. And second, I'm definitely not one of those girls. I'm just not hungry."

"Here you go," Pearl said, setting the glass on the table. "Is there anything else I can get you?"

"No, we're fine, thanks." Harper smiled up at her.

"All right. Let me know if you need anything." Pearl touched Daniel's arm gently before she left and gave him another grateful smile.

"What's that about, by the way?" Harper asked in a low voice and leaned across the table so Pearl wouldn't overhear her. "You get paid in chowder?"

"Sometimes." Daniel shrugged. "I'm kind of a handyman, I guess. I do odd jobs. Pearl's daughter doesn't have very much money, and I help out when I can."

Harper appraised him for a minute, trying to get a read on him, before saying, "That's very nice of you."

"Why do you sound so surprised?" Daniel laughed. "I'm a nice guy."

"No, I know that. I didn't mean it like that."

"I know," Daniel said, watching her sip her drink. "So, you don't usually leave for lunch, and you came to a diner even though you're not hungry. What brings you here today?"

"I just needed a break." She didn't look at him directly, instead focusing on the thick black branches of his tattoo, which crept past the sleeve of his T-shirt and down his arm. "A friend of mine is missing."

"What's the deal with you?" Daniel teased. "First your sister goes missing, now your friend." Harper gave him a hard look, and his smile vanished. "Sorry. What happened?"

"I don't know." She shook her head. "He's more of a friend of a friend, but we dated a few times. And he just went missing on Monday."

"Oh, is he that kid from the paper?" Daniel asked.

"Yeah." Harper nodded. "I just read about it before I came here, and I just needed to . . . not think about it anymore."

"I'm sorry for bringing it up, then."

"No, it's okay. You didn't know."

"How is your sister, by the way?" Daniel asked, changing the subject.

"Good, I think," Harper said, then gave him a rueful smile. "I haven't even properly thanked you for helping me find her yesterday."

"You thanked me plenty." He waved off her apology. "I'm just glad she's all right. Gemma seems like a good kid."

"She used to be," Harper agreed. "But I don't know what's going on with her anymore."

"I'm sure she'll turn out all right. You raised her right."

"You make it sound like I'm her mother." Harper laughed somewhat uncomfortably. Daniel just looked at her and shrugged. "You think I act like her mother?"

"I don't think you act like you're eighteen," he clarified.

She bristled as if he'd accused her of something terrible. "I have a lot to worry about."

He nodded. "I can tell."

Harper rubbed the back of her neck and turned away from him. Through the diner window she could see the library across the street, and she wondered how well Marcy was holding up.

"I should probably get back," Harper said, and she reached into her pocket for her money.

"No, no." Daniel waved his hand. "I got this. Don't worry about it."

"But I thought this was my IOU meal for the ice cream."

"I was just kidding. I'll pay."

"Are you sure?" Harper asked.

"Yeah," he said, laughing at her guilt-stricken expression. "If it bothers you so much, I'll let you pay for it some other time."

"What if we don't ever eat together again?" Harper asked, eyeing him skeptically.

"Then we don't." He shrugged. "But I think we will."

"Okay," she said, because she couldn't think of anything else to say. "Thank you for the Coke."

"No problem," Daniel said, watching her as she got up. "And I'll see you around, I guess."

He nodded and gave her a small wave. As she was walking out the door, she heard Pearl ask him if he wanted any pie. Harper went back across the street to the library, and it was very hard for her not to glance back over her shoulder at him.

THIRTEEN

Rebellion

Part of her penance was helping Harper clean. It actually wasn't specifically dictated as part of her punishment, but it helped ease Gemma's guilt over frightening both Harper and her father so badly.

Based on how much Harper complained about it, Gemma thought that cleaning the bathroom was her least favorite chore. So that was the one Gemma had offered to take over. Although, after spending five minutes scrubbing the inside of the toilet, she was really starting to regret it.

When she got to cleaning the tub, she realized that the toilet wasn't even the worst part. The drain in the bathtub was disgusting. Harper always claimed it was mostly Gemma's hair clogging things up, but Gemma hadn't really believed her until now.

Fortunately, she wore thick yellow cleaning gloves, or else there would have been no way she could've handled it. As she pulled out a long wet rope of hair that looked all too much like a drowned rat, Gemma noticed something glinting in the light.

Carefully, she picked it out of the tangles, and when she saw what it was, she dropped the wet mass of hair. It was another one of those weird iridescent scales she'd found in her bath sponge. She'd nearly forgotten about the last one. Or at least she'd tried to.

Gemma sat in the tub, leaning her back against the rim, and stared down at the big scale in the palm of her gloved hand.

Something strange was definitely going on with her. Ever since she'd drunk from the flask, something had felt . . . off.

Not that it was all bad stuff. In fact, Gemma couldn't actually think of anything bad about the changes at all.

Sure, she'd bitten Alex yesterday, but he hadn't really been hurt. And while the making out had been different, it hadn't been bad. Kissing him like that had been fun.

Her body healed crazy fast. All her bruises and cuts had disappeared in just over twenty-four hours.

At swim practice today, she'd had her best times. Coach Levi was totally blown away by her speed. The weirdest part was that she actually had to hold back. She was afraid if she went as fast as she could, he'd think she was on something.

When she was in the pool, that same thing happened to her skin again. That odd sensation that felt like butterflies running from her thighs down to her toes. But it was actually a pleasurable feeling, so she didn't mind it.

So if it was all good, what was she worried about?

Except . . . it wasn't all good. As much as she wanted to brush off biting Alex's lip, she couldn't. She hadn't spoken to him since then, but he'd probably passed it off as a heat-of-the-moment, kinky kind of thing. But it wasn't.

When she'd been kissing him, she'd been so *hungry.* It was unlike any hunger she'd ever felt. It was part lust, like she'd wanted to kiss him and be physical with him. But the other part was actual starvation, and that's why she'd bitten him.

That's what terrified her. The hunger inside of her.

Gemma got out of the tub and flushed the scale down the toilet. Something was seriously wrong with her, and she had to stop it.

"Harper?" Gemma said and poked her head in her sister's room.

"Yeah?" Harper was lounging on her bed with her e-reader.

"Can I talk to you?"

"Yeah, of course you can." Harper set aside her e-reader and sat up straighter. "Wow. Did you do something in the bathroom?"

"Uh . . . why?" Gemma froze in the doorway. "What do you mean?"

"You look . . . *good,*" Harper said, for lack of a better word.

Gemma glanced down, looking herself over, but she knew what Harper meant. She'd already noticed it today. While she'd never been prone to acne, her skin was smoother, and it almost appeared to be glowing. She'd gone beyond her usual scope of pretty into something almost supernatural.

"I've just been using a different moisturizer." Gemma shrugged, trying to play it off.

"Really?" Harper asked.

"No, actually"—Gemma sighed and rubbed her forehead—"that's what I came in here to talk to you about."

"You came to talk to me about moisturizer?" Harper raised an eyebrow.

"No, it's not moisturizer."

Gemma went over and sat down on the bed next to her sister. She didn't know why she found it so hard to tell Harper about what was happening to her, except she knew she'd sound like a crazy person.

"What's wrong?" Harper asked.

"I don't know how to explain it," Gemma said finally. "But . . . there's something wrong with me."

"This is about the other night, right?" Harper asked. "When you went out with Penn and the girls?"

"Yeah, kinda." Gemma furrowed her brow.

"It's perfectly normal to act out," Harper said, trying to keep her tone soothing. "I mean, it's not okay. You shouldn't be out drinking, but it's not uncommon. And I know I can be hard on you sometimes, but—"

"No, Harper, I'm not acting out." Gemma sighed in frustration. "There is actually something *wrong* with me. Like on a cellular level."

Harper leaned back and looked over Gemma again. "Are you sick? You don't look sick."

"No, I feel fine. Better than fine, actually."

"Then I don't understand."

"I know you don't." Gemma shook her head and stared down at her lap. "But something is very wrong."

A loud knocking came from the front door, more of a demanding pound than an actual knock. Harper glanced at her bedroom door, hesitant to leave her conversation with Gemma. But Brian was working late, and the knocking only got more insistent.

"I'm sorry," Harper told her sister as she got up. "I'll be right back. I'll send whoever it is away, and we can talk."

"Okay." Gemma nodded.

As soon as Harper left, running down the stairs and shouting at whoever was at the door to keep their pants on, Gemma flopped back on the bed. She stared up at the ceiling and tried to think of how to phrase it to her sister that she thought she was transforming into some kind of monster.

"What are you doing here?" Harper snapped downstairs, and Gemma listened more closely.

"We're here to talk to your sister," came the reply, and the sultry baby-talk was unmistakable. Penn was at her front door.

Gemma sat straight up, her heart pounding erratically in her chest. Part of her was afraid, the same way Penn always scared her. But the rest of her felt strangely excited. The sound of Penn's voice drew her in, in a way that it hadn't before, almost as if it were calling to her.

"You can't see her," Harper said.

"We just want to talk to her," Penn said sweetly.

"Only for a minute," Lexi chimed in, in her usual singsong way.

"No," Harper said, but her voice had less conviction than it had a moment ago. "You're not her friends, and you can't talk to her anymore."

Gemma got off the bed and raced down the stairs, but she stopped halfway. From her vantage point, she could see them at the front door. It was only Penn and Lexi standing outside, with Harper firmly blocking their path.

Looking at Penn and Lexi just then, Gemma realized she'd begun to look like them. Not *exactly* like them, since Penn and Lexi looked distinctly different. But there was a certain quality to them, a preternatural splendor. Their flawless tanned skin seemed to glow, as if they were illuminated by their own beauty.

"Hi, Gemma," Penn said. Her dark eyes rested on Gemma in a come-hither way that she couldn't deny.

"Gemma, go back upstairs." Harper glanced back at her sister. "I'm sending them away."

"No, don't," Gemma said quickly, but her words were so quiet, she was surprised anyone heard them.

"Gemma, you're grounded," Harper reminded her. "Even if you wanted to see them, you can't. But you don't want to see them."

"Stop telling her what she wants," Penn said with just a trace of venom in her voice. "You have no idea what she wants."

"Right now I don't care what she wants. Get out of my house."

"Harper, stop," Gemma said and descended the stairs. "I need to talk to them."

"No!" Harper shouted, looking totally appalled by the idea. "You are not talking to them."

"I *need* to," Gemma insisted. She swallowed hard and looked again at Penn and Lexi.

They had done something to her. As certain as she was standing there, she knew that they were responsible for whatever was happening to her. That meant they knew how to fix it, or at least how to deal with it. Gemma had to talk with them to find out.

Harper tried to shut the door, but Penn's arm shot out in a flash and pushed the door back open. Penn smiled at Harper, the menacing smile that revealed too many teeth.

"I'm sorry," Gemma said earnestly. "But I have to go." She slid through the gap that Penn had made for her and stepped outside.

"Gemma!" Harper yelled. "You can't go! I forbid you!"

"Forbid me all you want, but I'm going," Gemma said, and Lexi wrapped her arm around her in some kind of camaraderie.

Penn stood between Harper and Gemma, and Gemma could see from her sister's expression that she was considering whether or not to tangle with Penn. Harper turned to Gemma then, and Gemma gave her a pleading look. Harper's gaze went from fierce to torn.

"Gemma," Harper said again, more helplessly this time. "Please come inside."

"I'm sorry." Gemma shook her head and backed up with Lexi toward a car that idled in front of their house. "I'll be home later." She waited a beat before adding, "Don't worry."

"We'll take good care of Gemma," Penn assured Harper, still with her too-wide smile.

"Gemma!" Harper called out as Gemma slid into the backseat with Lexi, and Penn shut the door behind her.

Thea was sitting in the driver's seat, like she was waiting in the getaway car for a bank robbery, and Penn joined her in front a few seconds later.

Gemma stared out the window as they pulled away, watching her sister standing on the front step. She looked up at Alex's house next door, his bedroom window glowing yellow under the darkening sky.

She pulled her gaze away, and her eyes met Penn's in the rearview mirror.

"What are you?" Gemma asked.

"Not yet." Penn smiled. "Wait until we get to the bay. Then we'll show you exactly what we are."

Gemma had always wondered how Penn, Lexi, and Thea got to the cove, and she was eager to find out. Thea drove the car around the bay and headed to the coast on the other side. Once she parked in a gravel lot behind a patch of cypress trees, all the girls got out of the car.

Gemma noticed that they left their shoes in the car, and she would've done the same if she'd even remembered to put them on before she left the house.

Nobody said much of anything as they walked on a beaten path through the trees. The moon was nearly full, shining above them, but other than that there was no light.

Gemma's heart continued racing, and she wasn't completely sure she'd done the right thing by going with them. Part of her knew this was dangerous, especially after what had happened last time she was with them.

But she had a feeling that if they really wanted to kill her, she would already be dead. They were the only ones who knew what was happening to her, and she had to risk going with them to find out what it was.

When they reached a rather steep rocky incline, it took Gemma a minute to realize that they were at the back of the cove on the bay. She'd expected the girls to show her some hidden entrance that allowed them to get into the cove without getting wet, but instead they started climbing up the rocky face.

"You expect me to go up that?" Gemma asked, staring at the sheer climb. She couldn't see anywhere to grip or put her hands, and she'd never been much for climbing anyway.

"You can do it," Lexi assured her as Penn began the ascent to the top of the incline.

"I really don't think I can." Gemma shook her head.

"You'd be surprised what you can do now," Lexi said with a smile. Then, without waiting to see if Gemma followed, she started climbing.

Penn, Lexi, and Thea were all moving nimbly up the rocks. Gemma debated for only a second, then went up after them. It came surprisingly easy to her. It wasn't that she was a better climber exactly, but she was faster, stronger, more deft. She still slipped a few times, but she recovered easily.

When she reached the top, Penn was standing at the edge in front of the bay, so the mouth of the cove was below her. This high up, the wind was stronger, whipping through the girls' hair. A fall from that height, even into water, would be dangerous, and that was assuming she missed the rocks.

"What are we doing up here?" Gemma asked and walked closer to her.

"I wanted to show you what we are," Penn said.

"What are you?"

"The same thing as you." Penn faced her, smiling.

Gemma swallowed hard. "And what's that?"

"You'll see," Penn said, and with that, she reached out and pushed Gemma over the edge.

Gemma tumbled down, screaming and flailing her arms.

When she hit the surface of the water, it felt the same as hitting the ground. It smashed into her back, knocking the wind out of her. She went under the water, and her arm bashed hard against a rock. Blood flowed out from it, and salt stung her wound.

Gemma thrashed toward the surface, trying to swim through the pain overwhelming her body. But the fall had made her disoriented, and it was too dark for her to really tell up from down. She didn't know where to swim, and her lungs burned for oxygen.

But even as she struggled, she felt a change come over her. It was the one she'd felt in the shower and in the pool, only this was more intense. It consumed her legs, fluttering down her skin.

The pain in her arm started to fade, replaced with a tingling sensation not that different from the one she felt going through her lower extremities.

Her body felt good, better than ever, actually, and she would've enjoyed it if she hadn't been drowning. Whatever was happening to her had distracted her, and now she needed to gasp for breath. Her body did it involuntarily, and she expected her lungs to fill with water . . . but instead, when she took a breath, she breathed in air.

She could breathe underwater.

Gemma blinked. She could even see underwater. Her vision was even clearer than when she was on land.

Then she saw the burst of water as Lexi dove into the cove in front of her. Her body was surrounded by white bubbles for a moment. When they cleared, Lexi swam in front of her, her blond hair floating around her like a halo.

She smiled at her, and Gemma saw that Lexi no longer had

legs. She had a long tail, like that of a fish. Her torso was still human, with her chest covered in a brightly colored bikini.

Gemma looked down at herself and realized that she had the same fish's tail, covered in iridescent green scales. Her shorts were ripped and split down the middle from where her legs had converged, and the fabric sat around her waist like a belt.

It was then that Gemma screamed, and Lexi only laughed.

FOURTEEN

Revelations

I'm a mermaid?" Gemma asked once she'd surfaced.

She could probably talk underwater, but she thought the night air might clear her head in case it was all some sort of drug-induced hallucination. After all, this wouldn't have been the first time Penn had slipped her something.

"Not exactly," Penn said, pushing her dark hair back from her face. She and Thea had dived in the water right after Lexi, so all four of them were floating in the bay. "We're sirens."

"What's the difference?" Gemma asked.

"Well, for starters, mermaids don't exist, and we do." Penn smiled.

Thea rolled her eyes, then dove back underwater, presumably swimming off.

"I'll explain it all to you later," Penn said. "For now, why don't you take your new body out for a swim? We'll have plenty of time to talk when you're done."

"I . . ." Gemma wanted to know what she was, *needed* to know, really.

But she could feel her tail below her, swishing through the water. It felt powerful and fast, and it was almost itching to swim.

At least she knew part of the truth now. She knew what they were, and they weren't going anywhere. Without saying anything more, Gemma dove under the water.

It was better than anything she'd ever imagined. She moved faster than she ever thought possible. She darted around the ocean floor and chased fish simply because she could. Outrunning a shark would be a cinch, and she almost hoped she found one so she could try.

It was the most amazing, exhilarating feeling she'd ever had. Her skin felt alive in ways she'd never known possible. Every move, every tremble, every change in the current rippled through her.

She swam as close to the bottom as she could get, then she raced up to the surface and leaped, flipping through the air like a dolphin.

"Easy, there," Penn called. "We don't need to draw attention to ourselves."

Penn sat on the rocky shore of the cove. She'd pulled her tail out so it lay bent on the ground. Right in front of Gemma's eyes, the scales rippled, shifting from iridescent green to the golden tan of Penn's skin. It split into two legs, and Penn stood up. She was completely nude from the waist down, and Gemma quickly averted her eyes.

"Don't be shy." Penn laughed.

She walked away and dug around in a bag that sat by one of the cove walls. From the corner of her eye, Gemma saw Penn pull on a pair of panties and a sundress.

"We have clothes in here for you, too," Lexi said as she pulled herself out of the water. "You don't need to worry."

Thea got out after Lexi, and Gemma waited until all three of them were dressed before she swam over and pulled herself out. She scooted backward up onto the shore, so the rocks scraped her fins. She pulled her tail out, and it flopped on land for a few seconds before the familiar flutter ran through them.

As her tail began to transform back into human legs, she ran her hands over it. She could actually feel the scales shifting beneath her fingertips.

"That's incredible," Gemma breathed, staring in awe at her skin. "How is this possible?"

"It's the salt water," Thea answered and threw a sundress at her.

Gemma caught it and stood up. She half expected her legs to collapse back into a tail beneath her, but they stood strong. Hurriedly, she pulled the dress over her head, putting it on over her tank top, and kicking off her torn up shorts.

"Well, it's not just the salt," Penn corrected her. "You can add salt to freshwater, but it won't really work. It's the sea. You may feel hints of it in ordinary water, but you won't transform unless you're in the ocean."

"But . . . what if I hadn't transformed?" Gemma asked. "I would've died if I hadn't turned into a siren."

"You're fine now," Thea said. She crouched down in the center of the cove and began building a fire.

"Of course, it hurts when you do a back-flop into the ocean." Lexi giggled. "You're supposed to dive, silly."

"I didn't know that, since you pushed me." Gemma glared at Penn. "Why didn't you just tell me what was going on?"

"That would spoil all the fun." Penn winked at her, as if she were referring to a private joke instead of Gemma's near-death.

The fire Thea had been working on suddenly roared into life, filling the dark cove with warm light. Penn sat close to the flames, stretching out her long legs and leaning back on her arms. Lexi sat next to her while Thea seemed content to kneel in front of the pit, stoking the fire.

"You did this to me," Gemma said, but she wasn't accusatory. She wasn't sure what exactly they had done to her, so she couldn't tell if it was a gift or a curse. So far, it felt a lot like a gift, but she still didn't trust Penn. "You turned me into this siren or whatever. Why?"

"Well, that's the crux of the matter, isn't it?" Penn smiled.

"Why don't you have a seat?" Lexi patted the ground next to her. "It's a rather long story."

Gemma stayed where she was, standing by the mouth of the cove. The waves from the bay lapped against the shore, and the engines of boats hummed in the distance. She glanced out at the night, already longing to get back into the ocean.

The last time she'd been out here, Penn had nearly killed her, and it was only a few minutes ago that Penn had pushed her off the top of a cliff. It was hard to juxtapose that with the knowledge that they had given her the most wonderful, exhilarating experience of her life.

Swimming as a siren had been by far the most glorious feeling she'd ever experienced. Even as she stood there, arms crossed over her chest and seawater dripping off her skin, she wanted to get back in the water.

It took all Gemma's energy to force herself to stay on the shore, to hear what they had to tell her. But she couldn't bring herself to step in closer to move farther away from the water that seemed to sing to her.

"Suit yourself." Lexi shrugged when Gemma refused to move.

"It is actually quite a long story," Penn said. "It goes back to when the world was young, when gods and goddesses still lived freely among the mortals."

"Gods and goddesses?" Gemma raised an eyebrow.

"You're skeptical?" Thea laughed, a dry, bitter sound that echoed off the walls. "Your legs just transformed into fins, and you're skeptical?"

Gemma lowered her eyes but said nothing. Thea had a point. After everything she'd seen and felt the last couple of days, she would believe anything they told her. She had no choice, really. Any answer would have to be beyond her scope of reasoning to explain the supernatural things that were happening.

"The gods often lived here on earth, sometimes helping the humans with their lives or merely watching their joys and sorrows for their own amusement," Penn went on. "Achelous was one such god. He ruled over all the freshwater, nourishing all life on Earth. Gods were the rock stars of their times, and they often had many lovers. Achelous was involved with many of the muses."

"Muses?" Gemma asked.

"Yes, muses," Penn explained patiently. "They are the daughters of Zeus, born to inspire and enthrall the mortals."

"So, what does that mean?" Gemma moved closer to the fire and sat down on a large rock. "What does being a muse entail?"

"Have you heard of Horace's Odes?" Penn asked, and Gemma shook her head.

"I'm not in Honors English, but I have heard of Homer's *Odyssey*."

"The Odyssey," Thea scoffed. "Homer is an idiot."

"Ignore her. She's just bitter because she was completely omitted from *The Odyssey*." Penn waved her off. "Back to your question, a muse helped Horace write some of his prose. She didn't write it herself, exactly, but she gave him the inspiration and motivation for his work."

"I think I get it." Gemma's brow remained furrowed, though, as if she didn't completely understand it.

"A muse's job isn't important anyway," Penn said, deciding to move on. "Achelous had a love affair with the muse of song, and together they had two daughters, Thelxiepeia and Aglaope. He then became involved with the muse of dance, and they had a daughter, Peisinoe."

"Those are really ridiculous names," Gemma commented. "Didn't anybody go by Mary or Judy back then?"

"I know, right?" Lexi laughed. "Things are so much easier to spell now."

"Despite the fact that their father was a god, Thelxiepeia, Aglaope, and Peisinoe were the bastard offspring of his affairs with servants, so they grew up without anything," Penn continued.

"Wait. Muses were servants?" Gemma asked. "But their father was Zeus. Wasn't he the most powerful god or whatever? Shouldn't they be queens?"

"You would think that, but no." Penn shook her head. "Muses were created to serve man. Yes, they were beautiful and brilliant, talented beyond all measure. They were revered and worshipped by those they inspired, but in the end, they spent their days working for starving artists and poets. They lived a bohemian lifestyle, feeding into man's desires. When the poets had finished their sonnets, the artists their paintings, the muses were cast aside and forgotten."

"They were glorified prostitutes," Thea summed up.

"Exactly," Penn agreed. "Achelous all but disavowed his daughters, and their mothers were busy servicing men. Thelxiepeia, Aglaope, and Peisinoe were forced to fend for themselves."

"Thelxiepeia tried to take care of her younger sisters," Thea interjected. She gave Penn a hard look, the light from the fire dancing and casting shadows over her lovely features, making her appear almost demonic. "But Peisinoe was never satisfied."

"One cannot be satisfied living on the streets." Penn turned her attention from Gemma to Thea, meeting her gaze evenly. "Thelxiepeia did the best she could, but starvation isn't good enough."

"They weren't starving!" Thea snapped. "They had work! They could've made a life for themselves!"

"Work." Penn rolled her eyes. "They were servants!"

Both Lexi and Gemma watched the exchange between Penn and Thea with fascination. The two girls stared each other down across the fire, and for a moment neither of them said anything. The tension in the air was so thick, Gemma was too afraid to break the silence.

"That was a very long time ago," Lexi said quietly. She stayed close to Penn and gazed up at her, almost adoringly.

"Yes, it was," Penn agreed, finally pulling her death stare from Thea and looking back at Gemma. "They were starving on the streets. Even Thelxiepeia knew it. That's why she went to her father, begging him to find them work.

"They were old enough then that they had started getting the attention of men," Penn went on. "The three sisters had inherited many gifts from their mothers, including their beauty and talent for song and dance."

"Thelxiepeia thought honest work would be the best way to get out of the life," Thea said, joining the conversation in a much more reasonable tone. The anger had gone from her voice, and she was simply telling the same tale as Penn. "Peisinoe, on the other hand, thought marriage was the way to escape."

"It was a different time then," Penn explained. "Women didn't have the choices and the rights they have now. Getting a man to take care of you was the only way out."

"That was only part of it. Thelxiepeia was the oldest, most experienced. But Peisinoe was only fourteen. She was still a romantic and a dreamer. She believed if she fell in love, a prince would sweep her off her feet."

"She was young and stupid," Penn said, almost to herself, then she shook her head quickly. "The job Achelous found for his daughters was working as handmaidens for Persephone. A handmaiden is just a servant, helping to dress and clean up for a spoiled brat."

"Oh, she was not a spoiled brat," Thea chastised her.

"She was, too," Penn insisted. "She was horrible, constantly entertaining suitors, and Achelous's daughters should've had handmaidens of their own. It was an abomination, and Persephone never cared. She just ordered them around like she was married to Zeus."

"Tell Gemma about Ligeia," Lexi suggested, reminding Gemma of a small child who asked to be read the same story every night even though she knew all the words.

"Ligeia was working as a handmaiden for Persephone when Thelxiepeia, Aglaope, and Peisinoe started," Penn said, and Lexi smiled at her. "Ligeia wasn't their sister, but they loved her like she was. And Ligeia had the most beautiful singing voice. It truly was the loveliest sound anyone had ever heard.

"As a servant, Ligeia actually did very little work," Penn said. "She spent most of her days singing for Persephone, but nobody minded because her singing was so enchanting. It made everything seem better.

"But it wasn't all work," Penn went on. "The four girls were only teenagers and needed to have fun. As often as they could, they would escape from their servitude and go out to the ocean to swim and sing."

"It was Ligeia's songs that commanded an audience," Thea said. "She and Aglaope would sit perched in the trees on the shore, singing in perfect harmony, while Thelxiepeia and Peisinoe would swim."

"But it wasn't just swimming," Penn clarified. "It was entrancing, underwater dancing. They put on a show just as much as Ligeia and Aglaope did."

"They did, and travelers would come to see it," Thea agreed. "They even attracted the attention of gods like Poseidon."

"Poseidon was the god of the ocean," Penn explained. "In her naïveté, Peisinoe thought she could entice him with her swimming, and he would fall in love with her and take her away.

"And maybe he did fall in love with her." Penn brushed the sand away from her legs and stared into the fire. "Many men and a few gods have fallen for her over the years. But in the end, it doesn't matter. It wasn't enough."

"Persephone was engaged to be wed," Thea said, taking

back the story. "She had much to do, but instead of helping her, all four of her handmaidens went out to the ocean to swim and sing. Poseidon had invited them out, and Peisinoe was certain that this would be the day he would ask her to marry him. If she could just impress him enough."

"Unfortunately, that also happened to be the day when someone decided to abduct and rape Persephone," Penn said. "The handmaidens were supposed to watch over her, but they weren't even close enough to hear her screams."

"Her mother, Demeter, was a goddess, and she was furious," Thea said. "She told Achelous of his daughters' failure to protect Persephone. But since Achelous was more powerful than Demeter, she had to ask for his permission before she could inflict a punishment on Thelxiepeia, Aglaope, and Peisinoe."

"Peisinoe knew their father wouldn't protect them, as he hadn't cared about them their entire life, so she went to Poseidon, begging him to intervene," Penn said. "She pleaded with him, offering him every part of herself unconditionally if he would only help her and her sisters."

There was a long pause during which nobody said anything. Gemma had leaned forward, her arms resting on her knees as she hung on every word.

"But he didn't," Penn said, so quietly Gemma could barely hear her over the lapping of waves. "Nobody saved them. They only had each other to rely on, the way they always had, the way they always would."

"Demeter cursed them to the life they had chosen instead

of protecting her daughter," Thea explained. "She made them immortal, so they would have to live with their folly every day without end. The things they loved would become the things they despised."

"What things?" Gemma asked.

"They had been too busy flirting, swimming, and singing when Persephone was kidnapped," Thea said. "So that's what they were cursed to become."

"She made them part bird, with a voice so hypnotic no man could deny it," Penn said. "Men would be completely enraptured by it and have to follow it.

"But Demeter also made the girls part fish, so they could never be far from the water. When their suitors came for them, following the sound of their voices, their ships would crash into the shore and they would die."

"That, of course, isn't the worst part of the curse," Thea explained with a wry smile. "Every man would fall in love with their voice, their lovely appearance, but no man would ever get past that. They'd never really know the girls for who they actually were, never really love them. It would be impossible for any of the four girls to ever really fall in love and be genuinely loved in return."

FIFTEEN

Remember Me

Penn and Thea were silent for a time, letting Gemma absorb it all. But it was fairly obvious what the story was about.

"You're the three sisters?" Gemma pointed to them one by one. "Peisinoe, Thelxiepeia, and Aglaope."

"Not exactly." Penn shook her head. "It's true that I was once Peisinoe, and Thea was once Thelxiepeia. But Lexi is a replacement for Ligeia, who died many, many years ago."

"Wait. Lexi *replaced* one of you?" Gemma asked. "Why do you have replacements? And where's your other sister, Aglaope?"

"It's part of Demeter's curse," Thea answered. "We chose our friend and sisters over her daughter, then we must always be with our friends and sisters. There must always be four of us, together. We can never leave or be apart for more than a few weeks at a time."

"If one of us leaves, she will die, and we have to replace her," Penn explained. "We only have until the current moon is full to fill her role."

"I'm Aglaope's replacement." Gemma swallowed hard as the realization struck her. "What if I don't want to be?"

"You have no choice. You are already a siren. If you try to leave instead of joining us, you will die, and we will simply replace you."

"How?" Gemma asked. "How did I turn? That flask?"

"Yes. It was a . . . mixture of a few things." Penn chose her words carefully.

"A mixture of what?" Gemma asked.

Penn shook her head. "It's nothing to concern yourself with now. You wouldn't even understand what they were. In time, it'll all be explained to you."

"Why?" Gemma asked, a new tremor to her voice. "Why me? Why did you want *me* to join you?"

"Isn't it obvious?" Penn asked. "You're beautiful, you love the water, and you're fearless. Aglaope was too afraid, and we needed someone different."

"She wasn't afraid," Thea countered. "She was considerate."

"It doesn't matter what she was," Penn said sharply. "She's gone, and we have Gemma now."

"So . . . you expect me to just join you, leave everything I've ever known, and spend my life singing and swimming?" Gemma asked.

"That doesn't sound so terrible, does it?" Penn asked.

"It really is wonderful," Lexi chimed in. "Once you get used to it. It's a million times better than anything a mortal life could give you."

"But what if I . . ." Gemma trailed off and lowered her eyes, thinking of Harper, her parents, Alex. She lifted her head, meeting Penn's eyes. "I don't want this."

"Then you will die," Penn said. She shrugged as if she couldn't care less, but her voice was hard and her eyes burned. "If that's what you wish, then so be it."

"Penn." Lexi sighed and gave Gemma a softer smile. "It's a lot to take in, I know, and you don't have to decide today. Once you have some time to think, you'll realize that this is the best thing that could have ever happened to you."

"But it's a curse," Gemma said. "Demeter turned you into sirens to punish you."

"Did it really feel like a punishment?" Penn asked slyly. "When you were out in the water, wasn't that the best you ever felt?"

"Yeah, but . . ."

"Demeter was an idiot, and she failed." Abruptly, Penn stood up. "She thought she was giving a penalty, but she set us free. Now her daughter is long since dead, Demeter's all but forgotten, and here we are—as beautiful and powerful as ever, thriving under her 'curse.'

"Now, if you'll excuse me, I think I've made my point," Penn said. "Join us or don't. Live or die. It's up to you, and frankly, I don't care which."

"Wait." Gemma stood up, her mind racing, but Penn ignored her. "Penn, wait. I still have so many questions."

Penn pulled her dress up over head and dove into the water. Thea followed a few steps behind and jumped into the waves after her.

Lexi stayed behind a moment. She went over to Gemma and placed a hand on her arm.

"Go see your friends and family," Lexi told her. "Put your life in order. Say good-bye to the things you need to say good-bye to. Then come join us. You'll never regret it."

After Lexi went into the cove, swimming off into the night with the other two sirens, Gemma considered chasing after them. As fast as she was now, she could probably catch up to them. But to what end? Penn hadn't answered all her questions yet, but Gemma had enough to think about.

She knew Penn and Thea had told the truth, but she didn't necessarily believe it was the whole truth. They'd definitely left something out, and they hadn't told her what became of Aglaope, just that Gemma was needed to replace her.

The curse of the siren that Demeter had supposedly bestowed upon them—it didn't make any sense. Nothing she'd done to them sounded *that* bad. They were granted immortality, eternal beauty, and they could swim and breathe as fish whenever they wanted.

That sounded like a dream come true for Gemma.

She went to the mouth of the cove and sat down at the

water's edge, her legs in the water up to her knees. Her skin fluttered, tingling as scales sprang intermittently from her flesh. Her toes spread out, becoming sheer fins that glided through the water.

Her body wasn't submerged enough in the bay, so she didn't completely transform. Her legs remained legs, only with a few scales, but her feet were more flippers than feet. Gemma swung her legs back and forth, relishing the way the cold water felt running over her scales and flippers.

She closed her eyes, breathing in deeply, and her heart swelled with the pure joy of the moment.

But as amazing as this felt, as unbelievable and impossibly perfect as it all seemed, would it still be worth it? Giving up everything she knew and loved? Leaving behind her sister, her father, Alex?

With her eyes still closed, Gemma slid into the water, still wearing the dress the sirens had given her. She didn't try swimming at all—she just allowed herself to sink, floating down toward the bottom of the bay.

Gemma felt her legs changing, her appendages fusing to form a single tail. It wasn't until she could breathe in the water that she opened her eyes, staring out at the darkness around her.

Just before she hit the bottom, she flipped her tail and began swimming toward the shore. Since she didn't seem to have much of a choice right now, she decided to take Lexi's advice. She'd go home and figure things out from there.

She didn't want people to see her, so she swam to the far end of the bay that was covered in rocks. Because of the tail, she had to pull herself up onto the rocks on her belly, scraping her skin and arms. Once she was far enough out of the sea, she waited and watched with amazement as her scales once again turned back to skin.

Thankfully, she'd kept on the dress, so she didn't have to go home in the nude. She walked the several blocks to her house. Calling Harper or Alex for a ride would've been an option, but Gemma wanted time to clear her head. It was probably almost midnight by now, so she had the streets to herself.

Instead of going straight home, she cut through the alley into Alex's backyard. She snuck as close to his house as she could, afraid that Harper would catch sight of her if she looked out the window. She nearly pressed herself against his house as she knocked on the back door, hoping Alex was still awake.

Her heart pounded in her chest as she waited. She wanted to see him, and yet a part of her was afraid to.

Thea's words hung in her head, the true curse of the siren. No man would ever really be able to love her. Gemma remembered the forceful way Alex had kissed her the other day with the dazed look in his eyes. That wasn't the Alex she was falling for. That was a boy under the spell of a siren, a boy who was incapable of really loving her.

Gemma continued to wait outside Alex's house. She'd nearly decided to go home when the door opened.

"Gemma!" Alex sounded both surprised and relieved.

"Shh!" She held her finger up to her mouth, quieting him before Harper or her father heard.

"What are you doing?" Alex asked. "Are you all right? You're soaking wet."

Gemma glanced down at her dress. It had started to dry on her walk home, but she'd walked fast, so she hadn't given it much time.

"Yeah, I'm fine."

"You look cold. Do you need a coat or something?" Alex started to move back inside the house to get something to warm her, but she grabbed his arm to stop him.

"No, Alex, listen. I just need to ask you something." Gemma glanced around, as if she expected Harper to be lurking around a corner. "Can we talk for a minute?"

"Yeah, sure, of course." He stepped closer to her and put his hands on her arms, feeling strong and warm against her bare skin. "What's going on? You look frantic."

"I've just had the most amazing, terrible night of my life," Gemma admitted, and she was surprised when she felt tears stinging her eyes.

"Why? What happened?" Alex's brown eyes filled with concern.

His worried expression made him look older, more like the man he would someday become, and Gemma's heart ached when she realized that she would probably never see that. Already he was almost painfully handsome, made even more attractive by how oblivious he was to it.

He was much taller than she was, almost towering above her, and his muscled frame only made her feel safer. It was his eyes—a deep mahogany that conveyed so much warmth and kindness—that let her know he'd never do anything to hurt her.

"It doesn't matter." She shook her head. "I needed to know . . . do you like me?"

"Do I like you?" His worry changed to bemused relief, and he smiled crookedly at her. "Come on, Gemma, I think you know the answer to that."

"No, Alex, I'm serious. I need to know."

"Yeah." He brushed back a damp lock from her forehead, and his eyes were solemn. "I like you. A lot, actually."

"Why?" Her voice cracked when she asked that, and she almost wished she hadn't said anything.

His admission had made her stomach swirl with butterflies and her heart soar, but then both her heart and her stomach clenched with fear. She wasn't certain that Alex would know *why* he liked her.

If he was under the spell of the siren, he'd only know that he lusted after her, with no discernible reason for it.

"Why?" Alex laughed at that. "What do you mean, why?"

"It's important to me," she insisted, and something in her expression convinced him how grave this was.

"Um, because." He shrugged, finding it hard to find the words. "You're so . . . so pretty." Her heart dropped at that, but he went on, "And you have a wicked sense of humor. You're sweet, and you're smart. And impossibly driven. I've never met anybody as determined as you. Anything you want, you'll get. You are way, way too cool for me, and you still let me hold your hand, even when we're in public."

"You like me for me?" Gemma asked, staring up at him.

"Yeah, of course. Why else would I like you?" Alex asked. "What? Did I say something wrong? You look like you're going to cry."

"No, you said everything just right." She smiled up at him, tears swimming in her eyes.

She stood on her tiptoes and kissed him. Tentatively, he wrapped his arms around her, and as she kissed him more deeply, he lifted her off the ground. Her arms were around his neck, and she was practically clinging to him.

"Gemma!" Harper shouted from her bedroom window, and Gemma's heart sank when she realized they'd been spotted.

Alex put her back on the ground, but they were slow to untangle from each other. His forehead rested against hers, and she kept her hand on the back of his neck, burying her fingers in his hair.

"Promise me you'll remember this," Gemma whispered.

"What?" Alex asked, confused.

"Me, as I am right now. The real me."

"How could I ever forget you?"

Before Alex could ask anything else, Gemma left, running over to her house without looking back.

SIXTEEN

The Dirty Gull

Harper chewed her lip and stared at *The Dirty Gull*. Her father's crumpled lunch sack in her hand, she'd been pacing the dock in front of Daniel's boat for the past few minutes. This had never happened before, and she didn't know what to do.

Nearly every time she took her father his lunch, Daniel would inevitably be outside in some capacity so she'd run into him. Every other time it had happened, she'd tried to avoid him, but now that she actually wanted to see him, he wasn't out here.

He didn't exactly have a front door, so she couldn't knock, and it seemed too dramatic to stand on the dock shouting his name. Harper supposed she could climb onto the boat, but that seemed awfully presumptuous.

In truth, she didn't even really know *why* she wanted to see him. Part of it was because everything was so messed up with

Gemma, and Harper couldn't talk to her or Alex about it. Those were the people she usually went to with her problems, since Marcy wasn't exactly known for her listening skills.

That sounded so horrible. Harper wanted to see Daniel because she had nobody else to dump her problems on.

But then Harper realized that wasn't exactly true, either. She didn't want to vent to Daniel. That was just an excuse. She wanted to see him just because . . . she wanted to see him.

Her stomach twisted in knots, and she decided to simply move on. She needed to bring her dad his lunch, and she didn't have time for Daniel. It'd be better if she just left.

"So that's it, then?" Daniel asked as soon as Harper started walking away.

"What?" She stopped short and turned back to his boat, but she didn't see him. She spun around, thinking he must be on the dock, but he wasn't anywhere. Confused, she turned to his boat again. "Daniel?"

"Harper." He stepped out from the cabin's shadowy doorway and onto the deck. "I've been standing there watching you go 'round and 'round on the deck, and after all the debate, you're just going to leave?"

"I . . ." Her cheeks flushed with embarrassment when she realized that Daniel must've been standing just inside the door, where she couldn't see him but he could see her. "If you saw me, why didn't you say anything?"

"It was too much fun watching you." He grinned broadly and leaned against the railing, resting his elbows on the bar. "You were like a little windup toy."

"Nobody has windup toys anymore," Harper argued lamely.

"So. What brings you out here?" Daniel propped his chin up on his hand.

"I was bringing my dad his lunch." She held up the crumpled brown paper sack.

As she waited, she had been unrolling and rerolling the bag about a dozen times. By now the sandwich at the bottom had to be completely smashed.

"Yes, I can see that. I hope he didn't have anything in there that he might actually want, because it all has to look like baby food at this point."

"Oh." Harper looked down at the bag and sighed. "I'm sure it's fine. He eats anything."

"Or maybe he can just get something at the dock," Daniel suggested. "They have a hot dog stand right by the boats. Your dad can get a lunch for under three dollars when he forgets his lunch." He paused and tilted his head. "But you already knew that, didn't you?"

"Three dollars here and there adds up, especially as often as he forgets his lunch," Harper explained.

"Not to mention you wouldn't get to see me."

"I wasn't . . ." She trailed off, since she'd obviously been waiting for him today. "That isn't why. I do bring his food out to save him money. Okay, so today, this one time, I was hoping to run into you, but is that so terrible?"

"No. That's not terrible at all." He stood up straighter and gestured to his boat. "Do you want to come up and talk, then?"

"On your boat?" Harper asked.

"Yes. On my boat. It seems much more civil than talking down to you, doesn't it?"

Harper glanced toward the end of the dock where her father worked. She had probably ruined his lunch anyway, and Brian could easily grab a hot dog. But she still wasn't that sure she wanted to hang out on Daniel's boat with him.

Yes, she wanted to see him, but going up on his boat—it felt like admitting something that she didn't want to admit.

"Oh, come on." Daniel leaned over the rail and extended his arm to her.

"Don't you have like a landing plank or anything?" Harper asked, just staring at his hand.

"Yes, but this is quicker." He waved his hand at her. "Take my hand and come on."

Sighing, Harper took his hand. It was strong and rough, the hand of a guy who'd spent his whole life working. He pulled her up easily, as if she weighed nothing. To get her up over the rail, he had to pull her into his arms, and he held her there for a second longer than he needed to.

"Don't you own a shirt?" Harper asked when she pushed herself back from his bare chest.

He wore only a pair of shorts and flip-flops, and Harper purposely wouldn't look at him once she'd stepped away from him. She could still feel his skin on hers, warm from the sun beating down on them.

"My shirts have hit you in the face before, remember?" Daniel asked.

"Yeah. Right." She glanced around the deck, and then,

since she had nothing else to do with it, she held out the lunch sack to him. "Here."

"Thanks?"

He took the bag from her and opened it. He rooted around inside, finding a smooshed ham sandwich, apple slices, and a pickle.

"Apple slices?" Daniel asked, holding them for her to see. "Is your dad a first-grader?"

"He has high cholesterol," Harper said defensively. "The doctor wants him to watch what he eats, so I make his lunch."

Daniel shrugged, as if he either didn't believe her or didn't care. Carefully, he took everything out of their plastic Baggies, which was more difficult for the sandwich, since it had been so severely mashed.

Once he was done, he threw all the food out onto the dock and balled up what was left of the garbage.

"Hey!" Harper yelled. "You didn't need to waste that!"

"I didn't." He gestured to the dock, which was now covered in seagulls fighting over the food. "I fed the birds." Harper still didn't look pleased, so he laughed.

"I guess."

"Let's go belowdecks and talk," Daniel suggested. "It's cooler down there."

He went down without waiting for her protests. She paused for a minute, reluctant to follow him. But it was hot outside, and the sun wasn't making it any better.

When Harper climbed down, she noted that the boat wasn't dirty so much as messy, and that surprised her. He did have stuff strewn all about, but that was in large part because it was such a small space he didn't really have places to put anything.

"Have a seat." He gestured around him.

His bed was the most cleared-off spot, but she didn't want to give him the wrong idea. She leaned against the table instead, preferring to stand.

"I'm fine."

"Suit yourself." Daniel sat on the bed and crossed his arms over his chest. "What did you want to talk about?"

"Uh . . ." Harper was at a loss for words because she didn't really know what she wanted to talk about. All she knew was that she'd wanted to talk to him. It didn't matter what it was about.

"Gemma hasn't been around lately, if that's what you're wondering," Daniel said, and she was grateful that he'd brought up an actual topic so she wasn't left gaping at him.

"Good. She's not supposed to be going anywhere, since she's grounded. But that hasn't really been stopping her." Harper shook her head.

"So she's still sneaking out to the bay?" Daniel asked, but he didn't sound surprised. "You can't keep that girl away from water. If I didn't know any better, I'd say she was part fish."

"I wish she was just going to the bay," she admitted wearily and leaned back. "That I could deal with. But I don't even know what she's doing anymore."

"What do you mean?"

"It's so bizarre. Those girls came over last night to get her, and—"

"What girls?" Daniel asked. "You mean Penn?"

"Yeah." She nodded. "They came to get her, and I told them to get lost. But Gemma insisted on going with them. She pushed right past me, and then they just left."

"She willingly went with them?" His eyes widened. "I thought she was afraid of them."

"I know! So did I!"

"So what happened?" Daniel asked. "Did she come home last night?"

"Yeah, she came back a few hours later." Her face scrunched in confusion, and she shook her head. "But it doesn't make any sense. She'd left the house in shorts and a tank top, and she came back in a dress I'd never seen before, and she was soaking wet. I asked what she'd done, but she wouldn't tell me."

"At least she came home okay," he said.

"Yeah." Harper sighed, thinking. "She didn't come home right away. She stopped at Alex's first—that's the neighbor kid, and he's her sorta boyfriend, I think. I asked him if he knows what's going on, and he says he doesn't. I believe him, but I don't know if I should."

"I'm sorry," Daniel said, and Harper looked up, surprised to see that he meant it. "I know that it's hard having someone you care about doing reckless things. But it's not your fault."

"I know." She lowered her eyes. "And it doesn't feel like my fault, but . . . I have to protect her."

"You can't, though." Daniel leaned forward, resting his arms on his knees. "You can't protect people from themselves."

"But I have to try. She's my sister."

Daniel licked his lips and lowered his eyes. When he wrung his hands together, a thick silver band on his thumb caught the light. He didn't say anything for a moment, and Harper could see he was struggling with something.

"You've seen my tattoo on my back?" Daniel asked finally.

"Yeah. I can't really miss it."

"Do you see what it's covering up?"

"You mean your back?"

"No. The scars." He turned away from her, so his tattooed shoulder and back angled toward her.

Whoever had given him his tattoos had done a very good job. The ink was thick and black, and it wasn't until she looked closely that she saw the branches weren't shadowed to look gnarled and twisted. They had been drawn that way, along the lines of several lengthy scars.

Not all the branches covered scars, and the long, thick trunk that followed his spine didn't appear to have scarring underneath. But there were enough to show he'd been through something.

"And right here." He turned his head to the side and moved his hair. An inch or so into his hair, buried underneath his shaggy haircut, was a thick pink scar.

"Oh, my gosh," Harper gasped. "What happened?"

"When I was fifteen, my older brother John was twenty." Daniel moved so he was sitting normally on the bed again, and he stared out the window. "He was wild and reckless, never looking before he jumped. He would just drive right into everything.

"And I'd follow him. At first because I thought he was cooler and bold and brave. But then, the older I got, I was following him so I could catch him.

"My grandfather had a lot of boats, this being one of them." He motioned around them. "He loved the water and thought kids should be free to roam about it. So anytime we wanted to, we were allowed to take the boats out.

"The night I got these"—Daniel gestured to his scars—"John had gone to a party, and I'd tagged along. He got drunk, I mean totally shitfaced drunk. That wasn't unusual, because John was almost always drunk.

"There were a couple girls at the party he was trying to impress, and he got it in his head that if he took them out on a boat, that would do it. I went with because he was so drunk I knew he couldn't drive. If I was there, I could take control. That would make everything okay.

"So it was John, these two girls, and me on a little speedboat." He sighed and shook his head. "John kept going faster. I told him to slow down. The girls were screaming, and I tried to get the controls from him." He swallowed. "He drove right into the rocks at the end of the bay.

"The boat flipped. I don't know what happened exactly, but I was under the boat, and the propeller got me." He gestured to his scars again. "John got knocked unconscious, and I couldn't find him . . ."

"I'm sorry," Harper said quietly.

"Both of the girls survived, but John . . ." Daniel shook his head. "It was over a week before they found his body washed up on shore two miles down.

"And no, I'm not happy that he died. I never will be. I loved my brother." He looked at Harper then, his eyes deadly serious. "But nothing I did that night stopped him from drinking or getting on that boat. None of my begging or pleading or fighting with him saved him. All it did was nearly get me killed."

"Gemma's not like that." Harper looked away from him. "She's going through something, and she needs my help."

"I'm not saying give up on her or stop loving her. I'd never even suggest that, especially not for Gemma. She seems like a good kid."

"Then what are you saying?"

"It took me years to accept the fact that it wasn't my fault that John died." His shoulders slacked. "I don't know if I'll ever truly forgive myself for what happened. But that doesn't mean you should feel the same way.

"I guess what I'm trying to say is that you can't live somebody else's life for them. They have to make their own choices, and sometimes all we can do is learn to live with them."

"Hmm." Harper let out a long breath. "When I stopped by today, I didn't realize I'd get such a profound life lesson."

"Sorry." Daniel looked embarrassed and laughed a little. "I didn't mean to like go all . . . dark on you."

"No, it's good." She scratched her head and smiled at him. "I think . . . I think I needed to hear that."

"Good. Glad I could help," he said. "So, what did you stop by for anyway?"

"I . . ." She briefly considered lying, but after he'd been so honest with her, she couldn't. "I don't really know."

"You just wanted to see me?" Daniel asked with a small smirk.

"I guess so."

"Are you hungry?" Daniel got up before she could answer.

There wasn't much of a walkway in the boat, so just the act of standing up brought Daniel disconcertingly close. He moved closer so he stood right in front of her, mere inches from touching her.

"You want anything?" Daniel asked as she stared up at him.

"What?" Harper asked, and she had no idea what he'd even asked her. She found herself strangely mesmerized by the flecks of blue in his hazel eyes.

To open his fridge, he had to bend over and lean to the side, and he brushed up against her as he did. Even when he opened the door, he kept his eyes on Harper as he pulled out a couple of cans of soda.

"You want something to drink or eat?" He straightened up, holding out a can to her.

She took it, smiling thinly at him. "Thanks."

Daniel didn't move, though, instead staying right in front of her. When a boat sped by, causing a wave to rock his boat, he fell forward a bit. He caught himself by putting a hand on either side of Harper. As he pressed up against her, she could feel the warmth of his bare chest through the thin fabric of her shirt.

"Sorry," Daniel said, his voice low, but he still didn't move away from her.

His face hovered right above hers, and Harper could feel him leaning in to her, as if she were pulling him into her orbit. His eyes searched hers, and she didn't know how she'd never noticed how beautiful his eyes were before.

He smelled of tanning lotion and shampoo. Somewhere in the back of her mind she'd been expecting him to smell sweatier and muskier. Instead, it was strangely sweet.

Through her shirt, she could feel the smooth muscles of his chest and stomach, and suddenly an intense urge to throw her arms around him took hold of her.

Daniel closed his eyes, and with his lips about to touch hers, Harper finally acted on her impulse. Or at least she tried to.

She moved her hand, meaning to wrap her arm around him. Instead, she only managed to shove the ice-cold can of soda into his side, making him jump back from her.

"Sorry." She grimaced and shook her head. "I forgot I was even holding the soda."

"No, it's okay." Daniel smiled. "It was just cold."

He stepped back toward her, like he meant to go in for the kiss again, but the moment was broken, and Harper once again remembered how stupid it would be to get involved with him.

"I should probably get back to work," she said, moving away from him and toward the door.

"Sure." He put his hands on his hips and nodded. "Of course."

"Sorry," Harper mumbled, feeling apologetic.

"Don't be. You can stop by anytime you want. My door is always open for you."

"I know." Harper smiled. "Thank you."

Harper headed back up on deck. After being in the dim light of the cabin, the sun was blinding. She squinted up at it and walked over to the railing.

Since Daniel refused to use the plank, he had to help her down onto the dock again. He wrapped an arm around her so he could lift her up over the rail, but before he did that, he held her to him for a moment. Harper already had one arm around his shoulder, bracing herself for when he lifted her.

"I'm glad you stopped by."

Then he lifted her up and dropped her gently down on the dock. He stayed out on the deck of his boat, watching her as she walked away.

SEVENTEEN

Falling

For the first time in her entire life, Gemma skipped swim practice.

She wasn't sick, and she didn't call. She simply didn't go. Thanks to her new siren abilities, she was already crazy fast in the water. Besides that, Penn had told her she needed to leave soon, and while Gemma wasn't sure if she'd go along with that or not, it did seem like she'd probably have to quit the swim team.

Despite all that, she felt guilty about it. Gemma had missed practices only when she absolutely had to. Coach Levi would be so disappointed, and she never wanted to let him down.

When she woke up in the morning, she'd gotten ready for practice like she normally would, but instead of going, she rode her bike around to the other side of the block and hid in the small patch of trees there until Harper and her father had both left for work.

Once she was certain they were gone, she went back to her house. She had to see Alex again.

After they'd kissed last night, she'd gone home and had gotten yelled at quite a bit by Harper and Brian. They were both dumbfounded and furious at her recent behavior. Gemma wished that she could explain it all to them, but it would just come off as insanity. Nobody would ever believe that she was a siren, let alone understand it.

Eventually they'd let her go to bed, but she lay awake for a long time. She knew she needed to talk with Penn more before she could really fathom what she was. But that wasn't even what kept her mind spinning late into the night.

They had told her that nobody could love her, that was part of their curse. Maybe Alex didn't love her yet, but he could. If she had enough time with him, Gemma was almost certain that Alex would fall in love with her.

If the sirens were wrong about that, then maybe they were wrong about other things. Like maybe she didn't have to leave her family or her life. Even as much as Harper and her dad had yelled at her the night before, it broke her heart to even think of leaving them. She knew how much they loved her.

Last night, when she'd kissed Alex, she'd been about to give up. But she couldn't. Maybe it didn't mean anything that Alex liked her, but she had to try. He'd told her she was the most determined person he'd ever known, and he was right. She would try everything before she'd go off with the sirens.

Gemma knocked on Alex's back door, but when he didn't answer, she had to take more drastic measures.

His mother had a trellis covered in flowering vines that grew up the side of the house. It probably wasn't strong enough to support her weight, but Gemma climbed up anyway.

One of the boards snapped under her feet, but she regained her footing quickly. A vine gave her a small cut on her finger, but other than that the climb up went surprisingly well. By the time she'd pulled herself up on the roof outside Alex's second-story window, the cut had already healed.

Gemma peered in through his window, and it was just as she'd expected. Alex was sitting in front of his laptop at his desk with his headphones on, bopping along to some song. Based on the state of his hair sticking up all over and his attire of only boxers, she guessed that Alex hadn't been up that long.

For a few minutes she was content to just watch him: the geeky and totally offbeat way he moved, and how every now and again he would spout a few lyrics from what sounded like an old Run-DMC song.

The silliness of his behavior was juxtaposed with how surprisingly sexy he looked shirtless. When he moved, she could see the muscles in his back and his arms beneath his tanned skin.

"Alex." She rapped her knuckles on the glass, and the noise scared Alex so much, he leaped out of his chair.

"Gemma!" he gasped and tore off his headphones. "What are you doing on my roof?"

"You weren't answering the door. Can I come in?"

"Uh . . ." He scratched his eyebrow, staring at her for a moment as if he didn't understand what was happening. "Yeah. Sure."

He came over and opened the window for her, but that wasn't exactly the response she was hoping for. Maybe she'd made a mistake by coming here uninvited.

"Sorry," Gemma said as she climbed into his room. "I didn't mean to disturb you."

"No, you didn't." He shook his head, then rushed around to straighten up his room.

"You don't need to do that because I'm here."

Alex ignored her and continued to pick up the dirty socks and tech magazines that littered his room. It actually wasn't that messy. He was a relatively neat guy. Other than the stack of Xbox games and empty Mountain Dew cans, it was a fairly clean room.

"You know what, Gemma, I'm sorry. I can't do this." Alex abruptly stopped what he was doing, holding an armful of dirty clothes. He rubbed his eye and shook his head. "What are you doing here? What's going on with you?"

"I wanted to see you," she said simply.

"No, I don't mean just right now, but . . ." He set down

his clothes in a pile by the door and turned back to face her with his hands on his hips. "What was last night about? Harper said you just took off with those weird pretty girls, and then you come to my house soaking wet because you need to know if I like you."

"I'm really sorry about that," Gemma said, but he was on a roll.

"And the other night, when you disappeared, *again* with those weird pretty girls! Harper thought you were dead. You know you're scaring the hell out of your sister, and that's not like you.

"And then when I came over on Tuesday and . . ." He lowered his eyes, and his cheeks colored lightly. "And we made out. That was hot and all, but that was . . . not you at all. I don't even know if that was me."

"I know, I know." Gemma sighed. She wanted to tell him everything, but how could she? How could anyone possibly believe what she had to say?

"What's going on?" Alex asked, and the desperation in his voice pulled at her heart.

"Do you trust me?"

"Honestly?" He lifted his head and looked her in the eyes. "A few days ago, I would've said unequivocally yes. But after what's been going on lately, I don't know."

"I've never lied to you." Then she shook her head. "I mean, maybe I did when I was a little kid. But since we started seeing each other, I haven't. And I won't. And I know how crazy everything is, and I don't know how to explain it to you."

"You could at least try," Alex suggested.

"I don't think I can."

"Is it me?" he asked. "Or, I mean, is it us?"

"No, no!" Gemma shook her head emphatically.

"Because that's the only thing that's really changed. You were normal until we started getting involved."

"No." She stepped closer to him, putting her hands on his chest to convince him. "No, it's absolutely not you. You're the only thing that's keeping me sane."

"Why?" He looked down at her, but he didn't reach out and touch her the way she'd hoped he would. "How did I suddenly become your grip on normalcy?"

"Because. I think you're the only person who sees me for who I really am."

"Gemma." He breathed deeply and brushed her hair back, tucking a loose strand behind her ear. Something must have occurred to him then, because he looked around. "Wait. What time is it? Why aren't you at swim practice?"

She smiled sheepishly at him. "I needed to see you."

"Why? It's not that I don't want to spend time with you, but you never skip practice. You love swimming more than you love anything in the world."

"Well, not anything." She lowered her eyes and stepped back so she could sit on his bed. "I know that you're unsure, but can you just trust me?"

He narrowed his eyes, perhaps afraid of what she might be getting at. "How?"

"Let me spend the day with you. Just one day."

"Gemma." He laughed a little and shook his head. "I want to spend every day with you. Why is today so important?"

"I don't know." She shrugged. "Maybe it isn't."

"You're so cryptic lately."

"Sorry."

"All right, then." He scratched the back of his head, then sat down on the bed next to her. "So what do you want to do today?"

"Well . . . you could teach me some of those awesome dance moves you were doing earlier." She tried to imitate some of them.

"Oh, that's just mean." Alex pretended to be offended. "Those were my private dance moves, and you were being a creepy stalker on the roof. I should call the police and report a Peeping Tom."

"Oh, come on." Gemma stood up, doing horribly exaggerated versions of what he'd been doing. "Show me what you got."

"No, never." He laughed at her attempts to copy him.

When she kept going, he grabbed her around the waist and pulled her back on the bed. She started giggling, and he pushed her back down so he was poised over her. His arms were strong around her, and she'd never felt closer to him.

He bent down and kissed her, making her heart skip a beat. It gave her a warm feeling that started out in her belly and spread out through her fingertips.

When she'd been swimming in the bay as a siren, she'd

thought it was the most amazing thing she'd ever felt. But lying there, kissing Alex, she realized she'd been wrong. The way he made her feel was so much better because it wasn't some crazy magic curse. This was real.

"All right," Alex said, still hovering above her. "I guess I can show you a few moves."

Abruptly, he stood up, taking her hands so he could pull her up with him. He busted out some ridiculous moves. Gemma tried to join him, but she was laughing too hard. He put an arm around her waist, pulling her to him and doing an exaggerated waltz.

Eventually they both collapsed back on his bed, laughing. And that was where they spent the rest of the afternoon. Lying in his old twin bed, laughing and talking. Sometimes they kissed, but mostly they just lay together.

The mood got somber when Alex told her how worried he was about his friend Luke. They hadn't been that close, but he'd always liked Luke. Without looking at Gemma, Alex awkwardly admitted that it scared him that somebody could just disappear like that, without a trace.

Gemma had done the best she could to comfort him, holding his hand and reassuring him that everything would turn out okay.

After that, Alex tried to lighten things up. To her disappointment, he'd put on a T-shirt, but it was probably better that way, since she found it hard to focus on much else when he had it off.

He regaled her with tales of his clumsy adolescence, telling stories that made her laugh so hard, her belly hurt. For lunch, he made them peanut butter and potato chip sandwiches, which they also ate in his bed, spilling crumbs all over his Transformers sheets.

At one point, he'd apologized for the sheets, insisting he'd had them since he was eleven, and they were in good shape, so he had no reason to throw them out. Gemma smiled and nodded, but really she thought it was sorta cute how geeky he was.

For a while they just lay there, not saying much of anything. They lay next to each other, looking up at the ceiling but slightly tilted toward each other, so their sides touched. Alex was holding her hand, and sometimes he squeezed so tightly that she could feel their heartbeats between their fingers, pounding in time together.

She rolled over, snuggling closer to him and resting her head on his chest. He put his arm around her, holding her against him. He kissed the top of her head, then breathed in deeply.

"You always smell like the sea," he said, his voice quiet.

"Thanks."

He pulled her even tighter to him, but it was a good tight. It only made her feel safer.

"I don't know what's going on with you, and I don't know why you can't tell me. I wish you could. But whatever it is, I'll be there for you. Whatever you're going through, I'm here. I want you to know that."

Gemma didn't say anything. She just closed her eyes and held on to Alex as tightly as she could. At that moment, she vowed that nothing in the world would take her away from him. Not even sirens or age-old curses.

EIGHTEEN

Discoveries

The wall between them was almost visible. Whenever Harper even tried talking to her sister, Gemma would shut down. It didn't matter what it was about, either. Gemma just didn't want to say anything to her.

After her talk with Daniel on the boat, Harper wanted to approach their relationship from a different angle, but it was as if Gemma didn't want a relationship of any kind.

Even when Brian came home, her attitude didn't get much better. Dinner conversation was stilted and tense. The sad truth was that it was actually a relief when Gemma excused herself and went to her room.

Harper had the next day off, so she drove Gemma to swim practice. Gemma's car still wasn't fixed, and with the way she'd been behaving lately, Brian had no intention of fixing it anytime soon. She didn't seem to care all that much, though. But then again, Gemma didn't seem to care about much of anything anymore.

After she dropped Gemma off, Harper did something she never thought she'd do—she rummaged through Gemma's stuff. In a way, Harper almost hoped she'd find drugs. At least that would explain what was going on.

But other than a weird green fish scale tangled up in her sheets, Harper didn't find anything at all. As far as her room was concerned, Gemma was normal.

Gemma might not have been talking to her anymore, but she had to be talking to someone. Sighing, Harper went next door to talk to the guy whom she still considered one of her best friends.

"Hi," Harper said when Alex opened his front door.

He leaned in the doorway, his T-shirt pulled against his broad chest in a way that Harper still wasn't completely used to. Alex had always been tall and lanky, until the beginning of their senior year when he had a somewhat miraculous growth spurt, and even though Harper didn't care—not the way Gemma or some of the girls at school had started to care—it was still weird to her that Alex was so foxy.

Thankfully, Alex didn't seem to notice. He hadn't figured out that he'd gone from geek to hot, and that was good. Harper didn't think she could've handled being friends with him if he'd given up nights playing video games in pursuit of cheerleaders.

"Hi," he said. "Gemma's not here."

"I know. She's at swim practice." Harper rocked back and forth on the balls of her feet. "Wow. I just realized how sad that is."

"What?" Alex asked.

"The only time we talk anymore is when I'm looking for my sister." She rubbed the back of her neck and looked away from him.

"Yeah, I guess it is," he agreed.

"Can I be honest with you?"

"I always thought you were."

"It's weird to me that you're dating my little sister," Harper admitted, her words coming out in one breath. "I mean, I never liked you, not like that, you know. But . . . you were my friend, and she's my kid sister. And now you're into her." She shook her head. "I don't know. It's strange to me."

"Yeah." He shoved his hands in his pockets and looked down at the steps. "I know. And I felt like I should've talked to you about it first before I asked her out."

"No, no." Harper waved her hands. "You didn't need my permission or anything. I just . . . I feel weird hanging out with you when Gemma's not around. Like I'm betraying her somehow."

"No, I get that." He nodded. "Because you're a girl, even if you're not a girl I was ever interested in."

"Right. Yeah. I'm glad you get it."

"Yeah, me, too."

"But . . . I guess the thing is, you're my friend." Harper

fidgeted with the ring on her finger, twirling it around. "And I want to be friends again."

Alex stared at her, looking confused for a moment. "I didn't know we'd stopped."

"We haven't, not really, but it's been ages since we've hung out," she said. "I think the last time was right after graduation, and that was weeks ago."

"So . . . you're asking to hang out?" Alex asked.

"Yes." She nodded once. "I am."

"Like right now?"

"If you're not busy."

"I'm not." He stepped back. "Did you want to come in or something?"

"Actually, do you wanna take a walk? I could really use the fresh air."

"Uh, sure. Yeah." He glanced around, as if he thought he was forgetting something, then he stepped outside and shut the door behind him. "Let's go."

They walked almost two full blocks before either of them said anything. Harper tried a few times, but she only managed to make sounds and squinted up at the sun. She'd thought a walk would be easier because there would be movement to distract them.

In reality, she didn't understand why things were so awkward between them. She blamed it partially on Alex, since he was uneasy in normal situations. But a big part of it was her, too. She felt nervous around him.

"So," Harper said finally. "How is your summer going?"

"Good, I guess." He shook his head. "I mean, other than what happened to Luke."

"Oh, yeah." She grimaced and looked over at him, trying to get a read on how much it upset him, but he just stared down at the sidewalk. "I heard about that. I'm sorry."

"You don't need to be sorry. It's not your fault." He kicked a rock with his shoe. "I just feel so horrible for his family and everything."

"Yeah, I bet. That has to be really rough."

"His mom called me crying on Tuesday, asking me if I knew anything about it, and then the cops questioned me the next day." Alex didn't say anything for a minute, so Harper reached out and touched his shoulder gently. "I didn't know what to tell them. I don't know where he is."

As he walked with Harper, his dark hair cascading across his forehead, he looked the same as when he'd been twelve and his beloved dog had gotten hit by a car. Underneath his new foxy exterior, he was the same sweet Alex.

A twinge of guilt gripped her heart. As soon she found out Luke had gone missing, Harper should've talked to Alex to find out how he was doing. Instead she'd been too wrapped up in her own drama, and she'd ignored her oldest friend.

"I'm really sorry," Harper said again, but this time she was apologizing for not being there for him.

"It's okay. I'm sure he'll turn up." Alex took a deep breath. Then he glanced over at Harper, forcing a smile. "So what about you? How's your summer going?"

"Uh, pretty good," she said, and she wasn't sure if that was true or not. So far, everything had felt a bit chaotic.

"Are you seeing anyone?" Alex asked.

"What?" The question startled her, and she tripped on a crack in the sidewalk because she wasn't paying attention. "Why would I be seeing anyone?"

"I don't know." He shrugged. "Gemma mentioned something about a guy on a boat."

"What?" Harper quickly looked away, hoping that Alex didn't notice the color on her cheeks. "Daniel? No, he's just . . . he's . . . no. Nope. No way. I mean, I'm leaving in a couple months. And with everything that's been going on with Gemma, I don't have time for that. So. No. I'm not seeing anyone."

"Oh." He paused. "Yeah. That makes sense."

"Yeah." Harper chewed her lip and twisted her ring again. "How . . . um, how are things with you and Gemma?"

"Good." He nodded. "Great."

"Glad to hear it." She let out a deep breath and stared up at the sky, wishing a few clouds would come in and blot out the sun.

"Actually . . ." He stopped walking and looked over at Harper. "Honestly, I have no idea how things are with Gemma."

"Really?" Harper asked, and hoped she didn't sound too eager for information. "Why? How do you mean?"

"I don't know." He ran a hand through his hair and shook his head, then he started walking again. "I probably shouldn't even be talking to you about this."

"No! I mean, of course you can." She hurried to catch up with him. "We're friends."

"You promise you won't say anything to her?" Alex asked.

"I promise. We aren't really talking right now, so it shouldn't be that hard."

"You guys are fighting?" Alex asked, sounding genuinely distressed by it. "I'm sorry to hear that. I didn't know."

"No, we're not fighting, exactly. I think she's just . . ." Harper waved her hand. "Never mind what I think. You were telling me about you and her."

"Oh, yeah, right."

Before Alex could say more, Harper pointed to a trail cutting through the park and leading into the woods. "Let's go that way. It'll be cooler."

It was a thick wooded area filled with cypress trees and maples. The trail that went through it wasn't an official hiking trail, but one that had been worn down by kids making a shortcut to the bay. It actually went right up to the water, so the bugs would be much worse, but it would be worth it to be out of the sun.

"The thing about Gemma is . . ." Alex shook his head and seemed to struggle for the right words. "I like her. I do. Really."

Harper nodded as they walked into the trees. "I know."

"And I think she likes me. Well, I'm pretty sure, anyway."

"No, she definitely likes you."

"Really?" His head shot up, and he smiled a little, looking relieved. "Good."

"You couldn't tell?" Harper smirked.

"That's the thing. Sometimes she's pretty obviously into me. And then other times it's like she's not even there." He looked over at Harper. "Do you know what I mean? She's with you, but her mind is a million miles away."

"Yeah, I know exactly what you mean."

"And now all this stuff with those weird girls." He shook his head. "She won't tell me what she's doing with them or why she keeps hanging out with them."

"She won't tell you?" Harper asked, not bothering to hide the disappointment in her voice.

"No." He looked over at her. "She's not telling you, either?"

"She's not telling me anything, remember?"

"Oh, yeah," Alex said. "And those girls are just so . . . creepy."

"I know," Harper agreed, remembering the way they'd left Gemma on the shore. "I swear, they're evil."

"I wouldn't doubt it. And Gemma's not evil. She really isn't. So I don't know what she's doing."

"I know! It doesn't make any sense at all!" Harper was excited to have somebody to talk about this with, somebody who really knew and understood both her and Gemma. "I just wish this all wasn't happening right now."

"What do you mean?"

"I'm leaving at the end of August for school, and then it'll just be Gemma and my dad. And she's getting all wild and crazy now, and soon I won't be around to deal with it."

Alex didn't say anything to that, probably because Harper

had just reminded him that his time with Gemma was limited, too.

As the trail wound closer to the bay, the bugs got thicker, swarming around them. Harper waved her hand, trying to shoo them away.

"The bugs are ridiculous this year," Alex commented, and Harper had to agree.

The trees had begun to buzz with the sound of them. Then Harper saw them. Big black flies were hovering in a cloud a ways off the trail, where ferns and weeds had overgrown a rocky area near the ocean.

"Ugh." Alex groaned. "What's that smell?"

"I don't know." She wrinkled her nose. "It's like . . . rotten fish, but different."

She'd actually started smelling something faintly as soon as they'd entered the trees, but she hadn't thought much of it. On a hot day like today, it wasn't uncommon to get the scent of bad fish wafting from the docks.

But now the stench was almost overpowering.

Harper stopped walking, but Alex took a few steps ahead of her before he stopped and turned back to her. The flies were getting thicker, and they both swatted at them with their hands.

"This is obscene," Harper said, ducking down to keep from inhaling a bug. "I think I'd much rather take being hot and sweaty over dealing with these insects. Let's go back."

"Okay, good idea." He started walking back to meet her but stopped short.

"What?" she asked.

He stared down at the ground, seemingly frozen. The bugs flocking around him didn't even seem to bother him. Harper was about to ask him what again, but he bent down and picked up something off the ground. It was small and green and on the edge of the path, smashed into the dirt so it had barely been visible.

"What's that?" Harper asked and walked over to him.

Alex brushed the dirt off it, so Harper could see it. She still didn't understand what it was exactly, except that it appeared to be some kind of ring, but Alex's hands had begun to tremble.

"It's a Green Lantern ring." He turned it around in the light. "Luke had his parents get him this instead of a class ring. He never takes it off."

"Maybe it fell off when he was going for a walk or something," Harper offered, trying to ease his fears.

"He *never* takes it off," Alex repeated and started looking around. "He was here. Something bad happened to him here."

"We should get the police." She swatted away another fly, but Alex was oblivious to them now.

His eyes were pinned on the cloud of flies a few feet off the trail. He turned and walked toward them, mindless of the poison ivy and brambles that covered the forest floor.

Despite her reservations—more likely because of them—Harper went after Alex. As soon as he'd found the ring, she'd felt it in the pit of her stomach. A sick tightness. Just like Alex, she'd immediately known that something was wrong, that Luke wasn't okay.

Alex stopped when he saw it, but for reasons she didn't understand, Harper took a few steps forward, as if she wanted a better look. In reality, she didn't want to look at all. She wanted to forget it as soon as she saw it, but it was already etched in her memory, certain to haunt her nightmares for years to come.

Luke lay a few feet away, or at least Harper thought it was Luke based on the shock of red hair on his head. His clothes were stained a dark brown from blood. There'd been so much of it that it clumped in places, looking more like dried jam than blood.

His face and appendages appeared intact, other than the insects that covered him. A thick white grub crawled out of his mouth, and his closed eyelids moved with living creatures beneath them.

From his chest down to his groin, he'd been torn open. Her first thought was that it looked like a grenade had gone off inside him. Because of all the larvae, she couldn't see well enough to be certain, but it looked as though all of his internal organs were missing.

There was another body almost right next to him, but that was in even worse shape, having apparently been there longer. The bugs and animals had really gotten to him, but from what Harper could see, he looked like he'd been left in the same state as Luke—his whole torso torn open down the middle.

A few feet away from that, Harper could only see a leg sticking out of the weeds. If it hadn't been for the old Reebok sneaker on the foot, she actually wouldn't have been sure it was a leg at all. She would've just thought it was a rotting stick.

The disturbing truth was that she might have stayed there all day, staring at the dead bodies, if Alex hadn't turned and bolted back toward the path.

"Alex!" Harper called and ran after him.

As soon as he got to the trail, Alex hunched over and threw up. Her own stomach lurched, but Harper managed to keep her food down. She stood next to Alex and rubbed his back. Even after he'd stopped vomiting, he stayed bent over for a minute.

"Sorry." He wiped his mouth with the back of his arm, then stood up. "I didn't want to contaminate the crime scene."

"That's probably a good idea." She nodded. "We should go get help."

They started out walking on the trail, but before long it had turned into a full-on sprint. They raced all the way to the police station downtown, as if they could outrun death.

NINETEEN

A Way Out

Gemma had gone to swim practice because she'd decided to try at this life. Spending the afternoon with Alex yesterday had cemented her belief that she couldn't walk away from all this yet. She had to at least try to find a way to make it work.

Sleep had been difficult, though. She lay awake, tossing and turning all night. The ocean called to her, almost like a song. The waves beckoned her, and it took all her energy to ignore their pull.

In the morning, Coach Levi had been hard on her about missing practice this week, but her times were so amazing, he couldn't fault her too much. Now, though, swimming in the pool wasn't as much fun as it used to be.

The chlorine irritated her skin. Not that it gave her a rash, but she could almost feel it chafing her flesh, like itchy burlap rubbing against her. She couldn't wait for practice to be over.

Thanks to her fantastic speed, she was actually able to convince the coach to let her go early. Since Harper had dropped her off in the morning, she probably planned on picking Gemma up, too. But Gemma didn't want that. She needed to go see the sirens.

The problem was that she didn't exactly know where the sirens hung out. Gemma imagined that the sea called to them the same way it did to her, so they probably weren't that far from the bay.

Harper was off today, and Gemma had no idea what she might be up to, so she had to sneak around town. It was hard to be inconspicuous, but she tried to avoid Harper's usual haunts, like the library and the docks.

On her way to the water, Gemma stumbled upon the sirens. She'd planned on going by the cypress trees to the rocky coast, where there weren't very many people, so she could swim out to the cove. But she only made it as far as the beach.

It was hot, so the beach was crowded, both with tourists and the locals. Still, the sirens weren't that hard to spot. Gemma was on the grassy hill behind the beach, looking down toward the bay, and she could easily see the three girls in the crowd.

All of them wore bikinis, showing off their ample assets. Penn lay on a beach towel on her belly. Lexi was sitting propped on her elbows, flirting with an older guy standing next to her. In her usual fashion, Thea seemed bored by it all and read a dog-eared copy of *Salem's Lot* while lounging in a beach chair.

Gemma had to push through the people on the beach to get to them, although she realized that she didn't have to push that hard. People actually started parting for her, the way they always seemed to for Penn and her friends.

People were already starting to treat her like one of the sirens, like she belonged with them.

"You're blocking the light," Penn said without looking up. Gemma stood in front of her, casting a shadow across her back.

"I need to talk to you." Gemma crossed her arms and stared down at them.

"Hey, Gemma." Lexi turned to look back at her and used her hand as a visor from the sun. "You look great today."

"Thanks, Lexi," Gemma said offhandedly but kept her focus on Penn. "Did you hear me?"

"Yeah, you need to talk." Penn still hadn't moved on the towel. "So go ahead. Talk."

Gemma glanced around. People were involved in their activities, like tanning or reading or building sand castles, so it wasn't like they were just sitting and staring at the sirens. Yet the people were too close, too crowded together, to ignore the sirens for any amount of time, and they kept looking over.

"Not here," Gemma said, lowering her voice.

"Then I guess we'll talk later," Penn told her.

"No. I need to talk *now*."

"Well, I'm busy *now.*" Penn finally lifted her head to glare at her. "So it will have to wait, won't it?"

"No." Gemma shook her head. "I'm not going anywhere unless you go with me."

Thea sighed loudly. "Penn, just go talk to her. We won't get any rest until you do."

"If I'm going, we're all going." Penn cast a look to Thea, who scoffed and rolled her eyes.

"Fine. I guess we're done here, then." Thea closed her book and shoved it roughly into her beach bag. "Come on, Lexi, let's pack up."

"What?" Lexi looked confused. "Aren't we coming back?" When Thea started to get up, she waved her hand. "No, we'll come back. Somebody can just watch our stuff." She turned to the older man, who was now sitting next to her. "Will you be a sweetheart and watch our stuff until we return? We shouldn't be gone that long."

"Yeah, sure, no problem." He smiled eagerly at Lexi and nodded.

"Thank you." Lexi returned his smile, then stood up and brushed sand off her legs. "Okay. I'm ready."

Penn and Thea got up more slowly than Lexi, and Penn led the way off the beach. Half a dozen guys said hello to them as they walked away, but only Lexi responded. Gemma, who garnered some male attention of her own, wasn't used to quite this much ogling, and she found that she didn't enjoy it.

They went to a rocky area that jutted out into the bay, not

quite to the cypress trees, but far enough to be out of sight of the crowd on the beach.

As soon as they got there, Thea slipped off her bikini bottom and waded out into the water. From where she stood, Gemma couldn't see her legs turn into a tail, but she knew it had happened just the same.

"Shall we go for a swim?" Lexi suggested, slipping down her own bikini bottom.

"No, I don't want to swim," Gemma lied. "I just want to talk."

Lexi's bikini bottom was just below her hips, and she paused, looking from Gemma to Penn. Penn only stared at Gemma for a minute, debating what she planned to do.

"You go ahead and swim," Penn told Lexi without looking at her. "I'll stay here and talk with Gemma."

"Okay." Lexi sounded hesitant, but she took off her bikini bottom and went into the water. Within moments she'd disappeared out in the bay, swimming with Thea.

Gemma watched from the corner of her eye but tried not stare. It was hard to be this close to the ocean and not swim. The waves lapping against the rocks were like music, singing to her.

They were summoning her, seeming to beckon her at a cellular level. Her very being yearned to be in the water, but she needed to talk to Penn. She didn't think she could do that if she were frolicking about in the bay.

"So, what did you want to talk about?" Penn asked, leaning back against a large boulder behind her.

"For starters,. how do you deal with *that*?" Gemma gestured to the ocean beside them and tugged at her earlobe. "It's driving me nuts."

"You mean the watersong?" Penn smirked at Gemma's obvious distress.

"The watersong?"

"That music you're hearing right now, the way the ocean sings to you? That's the watersong. It's calling us back home, and it's why we can never be that far from the ocean."

"So it doesn't ever stop?" Gemma twisted a strand of hair around her finger and glared out at the waves.

"No, it doesn't," Penn admitted somewhat sadly. "But it does get easier to ignore when you're not hungry."

"I'm not hungry," Gemma insisted. "I ate breakfast this morning."

Penn shrugged a shoulder and looked out at the water. "There are different kinds of hunger."

"Listen, I wanted to talk to you about something you said."

"I assumed as much." Penn watched Thea and Lexi splashing around a ways from shore, then turned back to Gemma. "Are you ready to join us?"

"That's the thing." Gemma shook her head. "I don't want to join you."

"So, you want to die, then?" Penn raised an eyebrow coolly.

"No, of course not. But there has to be a way out. There must be something else I can do."

"Nope. There's not," Penn said simply. "Once you take

the drink and transform, you're locked in. You're a siren, and the only way out is death."

"But that's not fair." Gemma clenched her fists because she could do nothing else to ease her frustration. "How could you do this to me? How could you turn me into this without even asking what I wanted? You can't just force me to be this . . . this *thing*."

"Oh, I can, and I did." Penn straightened up and took a step toward Gemma. "It's too late. You're a siren whether you like it or not."

"Why would you even do that?" Gemma asked with angry tears stinging her eyes.

"Because I wanted you." Penn's voice was cold and hard. "And I do whatever the hell I want."

"No." Gemma shook her head. "You can't do this. You can't have me. I'm a person, and you can't just force me to be something because you want me to!"

"Honey"—Penn smiled—"I already did."

Gemma wanted to hit her, but she kept her hands at her sides. She had a feeling that Penn was a lot more dangerous than she looked, and she didn't really want to ignite her wrath. At least not yet.

"I don't think you know as much as you think you know."

"Like what?" Penn laughed drily.

"You said that it wasn't possible for guys to really love a siren," Gemma said. "But Alex cares about me, the *real* me."

Penn's eyes flashed hard and her smile vanished.

"That just shows how young and stupid you are," she hissed. "Alex is what, seventeen? Eighteen? He's a teenage boy with raging hormones. You think he gives a damn about *you*?" She laughed darkly. "Look at you! You're gorgeous, and that's all that matters to him."

"You don't know him, and you don't know *me*." Gemma glared at her. "You picked the wrong girl. I will find a way out of this. I will undo your stupid curse, and I'll set myself free."

"You are so ungrateful!" Penn shook her head, tossing her long black hair around her. "A curse? This is everything you've ever wanted, Gemma. I saw you. The water has been calling to you your whole life." She stepped so close she stood right in front of Gemma. "I gave you everything you wanted. You should be thanking me."

"I didn't ask for this!" Gemma shot back. "And I don't want it!"

"Too frickin' bad." Penn turned away from her, walking back toward the boulder. "You can't undo it! You drank the potion, and now you're a siren until the day you die."

"Potion?" Gemma shook her head. "What potion? What was that?"

"The blood of a siren, the blood of a mortal, and the blood of the ocean," Penn recited.

"The blood of the ocean?"

"It's just water. Demeter always had a flare for the dramatics, especially when it came to composing the rules of the curse."

"So what is the blood of a mortal?" Gemma asked. "Is that like tears?"

"No, that's blood." Penn looked at her like she was a moron. "It was Aglaope's blood and human blood."

"I drank *blood*?" Gemma's stomach clenched, and she put her hand on her belly. "You tricked me into drinking blood? What kind of freaky monster are you?"

"It's called a siren, remember?" Penn rolled her eyes. "You are so much dumber than I thought. Maybe I made a mistake with you. Maybe you're right, and I should let you just go ahead and die."

"Who's blood?" Gemma asked, doing her best not to gag.

"Aglaope's. I already told you that."

"No, the *human* blood."

"Oh, does it even matter?" Penn shrugged. "It was some human."

"How did you get it?" Gemma asked.

"This is so tedious." Penn stared up at the sky and shook her head. "I *hate* turning new sirens. Especially thankless ones like you. This is a waste of my time."

"If you hate it so much, then why did you do it?" Gemma asked.

"I didn't have a choice. We have to have four."

Gemma couldn't take it anymore, and she bent over and started to dry-heave. The thought of drinking blood, together with everything else Penn had been telling her, was too much to handle, not to mention the migraine she was getting from resisting the watersong.

"Oh, my God." Penn sighed, watching Gemma cough and gag. "You already digested the blood, hence the whole siren thing. What do you think you're throwing up?"

"I'm not trying to throw up anything. Just the thought of being like you is making me sick." Gemma stood up straight and wiped her mouth.

Penn narrowed her eyes at her. "You are such a mistake."

"Then tell me how to get out of this! Tell me what to do to change back!"

"I already told you!" Penn growled. "You have to die! That's it! And if you don't stop being such an ungrateful bitch, I'll be happy to put you out of your misery!"

With frustrated tears in her eyes, Gemma shook her head. She pushed her hair back from her forehead and stared out at the ocean. Thea and Lexi's heads occasionally bobbed out of the water as they swam around.

"So then tell me how to live with this." Gemma took a deep breath and looked back at Penn. "You need a fourth, and I don't want to die. So tell me what I need to do."

"First, drop the attitude. Then you leave here and come with us. We'll show you what you need to do."

"Why do I have to leave?" Gemma asked.

"It's better if we don't stay in one place for too long. Things tend to get messy."

"What about my family? And Alex?"

"We're your family now," Penn told her, and her voice bordered on something that resembled kindness. "And Alex doesn't love you, and he never will."

"But . . ." A tear spilled down Gemma's cheek, and she wiped it away.

"It's not his fault, and it's not your fault. He *can't,* Gemma. It's not possible for a mortal to love a siren. I'm sorry." Penn let out a long breath. "But the thing is, when you live long enough, and you see enough things, you realize that it's impossible for mortal men to really love anyone. Knowing this will save you heartbreak."

"How can I believe you?" Gemma asked. "You tricked me and forced me into this. How do I know anything you say is true?"

"You don't," Penn admitted with a shrug of her shoulders. "But who else are you going to believe? Who else knows anything about being a siren?"

Gemma realized bitterly that Penn was right. For better or worse, she'd been put in a situation where she didn't have a lot of options. This hadn't been her choice. This wasn't what she wanted. But she had to make the best of it. She could still do the right thing, even if Penn had backed her into a corner.

A commotion in the nearby cypress trees distracted both of them. Urgent voices echoed through the bay, along with the static sound of a radio. It was far enough away that Gemma couldn't see a lot, but she could see movement and blue uniforms, like those of the police.

"What's going on?" Thea called, drawn closer to the shore by the noise in the woods.

"Are those the police?" Lexi asked, floating next to Thea.

"We should go," Penn snapped and walked toward the ocean. "You should come with us, Gemma."

"Um . . ." Gemma pulled her eyes away from what was happening in the woods and looked back to where Penn had stopped at the edge of the water. "No. At least, not yet."

Penn pursed her lips. "Suit yourself. But we'll only be here a few more days. Then we're gone."

"Come on, Penn," Thea called to her, swimming away from the shore. "We need to get out of here."

" 'Bye, Gemma!" Lexi waved to her.

" 'Bye." Gemma waved back, but Lexi had already ducked under the water.

Gemma watched as Penn waded out into the water. She stopped when it was just about to her waist, and Gemma could see her tan skin changing to iridescent scales glittering up over her hips.

"For what it's worth, I was telling the truth," Penn said, then she dove in the water and swam off.

Gemma stayed on the shore for a little longer, watching the waves, but the sirens didn't surface again. The watersong nearly drowned out the sound of the men in the woods, but she didn't really want to hear them anyway.

Eventually she pulled herself away from the bay and walked back to her house. She still wasn't sure exactly what she should do. Die or join them. Neither option sounded acceptable.

Just as she made it to her house, a police car pulled up in front. Her heart pounded, and she stared wide-eyed as a police officer got out and opened the back door of the car.

Harper and Alex got out of the backseat, and that completely dumbfounded her.

Harper had her arm around Alex, and his face was stark white.

"What happened?" Gemma asked, rushing over to them.

"We found Luke," Harper said quietly.

"He's dead." Alex stepped away from Harper and hugged Gemma. She wrapped her arms around him, holding him tightly to her, and she could feel his tears on her shoulder.

TWENTY

Coping

Harper leaned on the kitchen sink and stared out the window at Alex's house next door. He'd been shaken up since they'd found the dead bodies the day before, and Gemma had spent nearly all her time over at his house.

Both Brian and Harper thought it was better for Gemma to be with him than upstairs in her room grounded. Alex needed her.

"How are you holding up?" Brian asked. He sat at the kitchen table behind Harper, drinking a cup of coffee.

"Fine," Harper lied.

Nightmares had woken her up three times before she gave up on sleep entirely. To busy herself, she'd done all the laundry and rearranged the pantry by the time Brian got up at eight A.M.

"Are you sure?" Brian asked.

"Yeah." She turned back to her dad and forced a smile to reassure him. "I didn't know Luke all that well."

"It doesn't matter. Seeing something like that can get to you."

"I'll be fine." She pulled out a chair across from him and sat down.

Brian had the paper spread out in front of him, the same way he did every Saturday morning. The bodies found in the woods had made the front page, so he had deliberately separated that page from the paper and thrown it away before Harper could see it.

Reaching across the table, Harper grabbed the crossword puzzle. Brian always started filling out the puzzles but gave up after getting only one or two words. He rolled the pen across the table, and she thanked him for it.

"So we're just going to pretend that nothing happened?" Brian asked, and sipped his coffee.

"I'm not pretending anything." Harper pulled her knee to her chest so she could lean on it as she filled out the crossword. "Something horrible happened. I just don't have a lot to say about it."

"Did I ever tell you about how Terry Connelly died?" Brian asked.

"I don't know." She paused, thinking. "I remember when that happened, but I was only five or six at the time. It was some kind of accident at the dock, right?"

"Yeah." He nodded. "A pallet weighing several hundred pounds fell off a forklift and landed on him. It knocked him down and landed on his stomach. I was right next to him when it happened, and he was still alive, so I sat with him until the ambulance came."

"I didn't know that." Harper rested her chin on her knee and watched him talk.

"We weren't friends, but we'd worked together for years, and I didn't want him to be alone," Brian said. "When the rescue team finally came, they had to lift up the pallet to get him out. All his organs had squished out to the sides. You could see his intestines smashed to the bottom of the pallet, dangling off like a dead worm."

"Oh, my gosh, Dad." Harper grimaced. "Why are you telling me this?"

"I'm not telling you to gross you out," he assured her. "The point I'm making is that it was gruesome. Somehow, the pallet sitting on him was keeping him alive, I guess, because as soon as they lifted it, he died."

"I'm sorry," she said, since she didn't know what else to say.

"I had nightmares about it for weeks afterwards. You could have asked your mother about it, if she still remembered." He leaned forward, resting his arms on the table. "I was a grown man when that happened, and it was just a freak accident. Nobody had been murdered or left to rot in the trees, and it still messed me up for a while."

"Dad." She sighed and leaned back in her seat.

"I can't imagine what you're going through, honey," Brian said gently. "But I do know that you are going through something. And it's okay to admit it. It's okay to be hurt and scared sometimes."

"I know. But I'm okay."

"I know you don't always want to talk to me, but I hope you're talking to somebody." He took a sip from his coffee. "Are you going over to Alex's today?"

"No, Gemma's over there."

"So? He's your friend, too. You can be around him when Gemma is."

"I know, but . . ." She shrugged.

"You can still be his friend even though he has a girlfriend." Brian paused. "Is Gemma his girlfriend?"

"I don't know." She shook her head. "Kinda, I think."

"Hmm." He furrowed his brow. "I guess there could be worse boys than Alex."

"Yes, there could," she agreed.

"What about you?"

"What about me what?"

"Are you seeing anybody?"

"Dad," Harper groaned and got up from the table.

"Harper," Brian groaned back.

"Why is everybody so interested in my love life all of a sudden?" She went over to the fridge and grabbed the orange juice. "Not that I have one. Because I don't." Pouring herself a glass of juice, she muttered, "I don't like anybody."

"Everybody's interested in your love life?" Brian asked. "Who's everybody?"

"I don't know. You. Alex." She squirmed and gulped

down the juice so she wouldn't have to say more. "I know it's Saturday, but I don't think I'm going to see Mom today."

"Okay."

"Gemma's pretty tied up today, but maybe tomorrow she'll want to see Mom." Harper glanced back over toward Alex's house. "I don't know. Or maybe she won't. I'll probably still go tomorrow, even if she doesn't want to."

"Okay." Brian nodded. "Good. It's good for you see your mother."

"You know, it would probably be good for you to see her, too," Harper said carefully, and he visibly stiffened at her suggestion.

The doorbell rang, saving them both from another awkward conversation about Nathalie. Neither of them really liked talking about her at all, least of all to each other, but once her name came up, they'd both feel compelled to get into a discussion about her.

"I'll get it," Harper said, even though she was still in her pajamas and Brian was dressed.

She thought it might be the police. They said they would stop by if they had more questions, but she and Alex hadn't really been able to tell them much. They didn't actually know anything, except where the bodies had been found.

Instead of the police she found Daniel standing on her doorstep. He smiled at her, and at first she did nothing but stand there with the door open, gaping at him in surprise.

"Sorry. Did I wake you?" Daniel asked. "If I'm bothering you, I can just go—"

"No, um, it's fine." Harper shook her head, but she suddenly became aware of the fact that she was wearing only a tank top and short girl boxers. She crossed her arms over her chest. "I was awake."

"Good." He scratched at his arm and stared at her. "Can I come in?"

"Oh, right, yeah. Yes. Of course." She stepped back so he could get by, so now they could stare at each other awkwardly in the entryway instead of on the doorstep. Finally she just blurted out, "What are you doing here?"

"Oh, um, I heard about what happened to your friend." Sympathy filled his hazel eyes. "The one that was missing, and I wanted to offer my condolences."

"Oh. Thank you." She smiled thinly at him.

"I stopped by the library to see if you were at work," Daniel explained. "I wanted to check and make sure you were holding up okay, because you seemed pretty distressed when you found out he was missing."

"I have Saturdays off," Harper said, instead of addressing how she was holding up.

"That's what the girl working there told me. It was a surly girl with straight bangs." He held his hand up in front of his forehead to show where her bangs hit just above her eyebrows.

"That's Marcy."

"The coworker you can't leave unattended?" Daniel asked.

"Yeah." She laughed a little, surprised that Daniel had been paying attention and remembered that. "That's her."

"She told me where you lived, and I hope it's not too weird that I'm stopping by. I can go if you want." He motioned to the door beside him.

"No, no. It's good. And I know where you live, so it's only fair, right?"

"I guess." He smiled, looking relieved. "How are you doing?"

"Fine." She shrugged.

"Harper?" Brian asked and came in from the kitchen. "Who's this?"

"Dad, this is, um, Daniel." Harper gestured toward him. "Daniel, this is my dad, Brian."

"Hello, sir." Daniel extended his hand, and Brian eyed him uncertainly as they shook hands.

"You look familiar," Brian said. "Do I know you from somewhere?"

"You've probably seen me at my boat." Daniel put his hands in his back pockets. "*The Dirty Gull.* It's parked down at the docks."

"Oh." Brian stared at him, trying to figure out how he knew him. "Was your grandfather Darryl Morgan?"

Daniel nodded. "That would be my grandpa."

"He was my foreman down at the docks," Brian said. "We lost a good guy when he passed away."

"That we did," Daniel agreed.

"You used to come down to the docks with him, didn't you? But you were just . . ." Brian held his hand up near his hip, but now Daniel was actually a good inch taller than

Brian. "And now you're all grown up." He looked over at Harper. "And you're visiting my daughter."

"Dad," Harper said quietly and gave him a look.

"Okay. Well, it was good to see you again," Brian said. "But I think I'm going to head out to the garage to work on Gemma's car." He walked around them and went to the front door, but paused when he opened it. "But I'll just be right outside if you need me. With heavy tools."

"Dad!" Harper snapped.

"Have fun, kids," Brian said as he disappeared out the front door.

"Sorry about that," Harper said after her father had gone.

"It's okay." Daniel smirked. "I'm guessing you don't have a lot of male suitors."

"Are you implying that *you* are a male suitor?" Harper raised an eyebrow and looked up at him.

"I'm not implying anything," he said, but he smiled at her in a way that made her look away.

"Do you want something to drink?" she asked, walking toward the kitchen. "I just made some coffee a little bit ago."

"Coffee would be great."

Daniel followed her into the kitchen. Harper grabbed two mugs from the cupboard and filled them both with coffee. When she gave Daniel his, he sat down at the kitchen table, but she stayed standing, preferring to lean against the counter and drink her coffee.

"This is really good coffee," Daniel said after taking a sip.

"Thank you. It's Folgers."

"So." He set his mug down on the table. "You never did tell me how you were doing."

"Yeah, I did. I said I was fine."

"Yeah, but that was a lie." He tilted his head, watching her. "How are you really doing?"

Harper scoffed and looked away from him, smiling nervously. "How do you know that's a lie? And why would I lie?" She shook her head. "Why would I not be okay? I mean, I only knew one of them, and I didn't even really know the guy."

"You are a *horrible* liar. Honestly. You're one of the worst I've ever seen. Every time you say something that's not true, you ramble and avoid eye contact."

"I . . ." She started to protest, then sighed.

"Why don't you want to admit how you really feel?" Daniel asked.

"It's not that I don't want to." She stared down at the coffee in her hands. "It's that . . . I don't feel like I have a right to feel bad."

"How do you not have a *right* to feel bad? You're entitled to feel however you feel."

"No, I'm not." She suddenly wanted to cry. "Luke was . . . I barely knew him. His parents lost a son. Alex lost a friend. They loved him. They lost something. They get to feel terrible about it."

She shook her head, as if that wasn't what she wanted to

say at all. "We exchanged a few really awkward, sloppy kisses last fall, and then I kinda blew him off." She chewed her lip, trying not to cry. "I mean, he was a nice guy. I just didn't feel that way about him."

"Because you dated, and it ended, you don't get to feel bad?" Daniel asked.

"Maybe." She shook her head. "I don't know."

"Okay, let's try this. Let's forget how you should feel or shouldn't feel. Why don't you just tell me exactly what you're feeling and thinking right now?"

"It's not . . ." Harper swallowed hard, planning to dismiss Daniel's question, but then she changed her mind. "I can't stop thinking about his face when we found him. He had a maggot crawling on his lip." Unconsciously, she ran a finger over her own lips. "Those were lips that I'd kissed.

"And I can't get the way the bodies smelled out of my nose. No matter how much I shower or how much perfume I spray, I can't stop smelling it." Her voice got thick, and her eyes welled with tears.

"It's his lips and face I keep picturing, but his body was all torn up." She gestured to her own torso. "He'd been ripped open and . . . I just keep thinking how scared he had to be." Tears slid down her cheeks. "He had to be terrified when that happened. They all did."

Daniel got up from the table and walked over to her. He stood in front of her and put his hands on her arms, but she wouldn't look at him. She stared off at a point on the floor, crying.

"We saw him that day," Harper went on. "The day he disappeared, at the picnic. And I just keep thinking, if I'd invited him to hang out with us, he'd still be alive. When I saw him, I was upset because everything was so awkward between us now. And he was a nice guy! If I'd just . . ."

She started sobbing then, her words getting drowned out by her tears. Daniel took the coffee mug from her hands and set it on the counter behind her. Then he reached out, and, almost tentatively, pulled her into his arms, hugging her.

"It's not your fault," Daniel told her as she cried into his shoulder. "You can't save everybody, Harper."

"Why not?" she asked, her words muffled.

"It's just the way the world works."

Harper allowed herself to cry for a little bit longer, feeling both grateful and ashamed at having Daniel's arms around her. When she'd calmed down enough, she pulled away from him and wiped her eyes. He retracted his arms, but he stayed right in front of her, in case she needed him.

"Sorry," she said, pressing her palms to her cheeks to dry the tears.

"Don't be. I'm not."

"Well, you have no reason to be sorry. You're not being a total freak."

"Neither are you." He brushed a lock back from her forehead, and she let him, but she wouldn't look up at him.

"And I know you're right. I mean, that it's not my fault." She sniffled. "But I just can't stop thinking about that day at the picnic. I mean, we saw him that afternoon, and he went missing that night. If I'd just said, *Hey, why don't you hang out with us?* instead of letting him go off with that girl . . ."

"You can't beat yourself up like that. There's no way you could've known."

"Yes, I should've." Her eyes widened as she realized something, and she looked up at him. "The last time I saw Luke alive, he was going off with Lexi."

"Who's Lexi?" Daniel asked.

"One of those really pretty, creepy girls."

"So he left the picnic with this Lexi girl, and then disappeared?" Daniel asked. "Did you tell the cops that?"

"No, I mean, yes." She shook her head. "I told them what I knew, but that didn't seem very important. He went home after the picnic and had supper with his parents. It's after that that he left, then went missing. But he did go off with Lexi, for a little while."

"You think that Lexi and Penn and that other girl are somehow involved with the murders? That's what you're suggesting?"

"I don't know," Harper said, then changed her mind. "Yes. I do. I think they're connected."

"At the risk of being accused of being a sexist pig, I'm going to say something—they're just girls." He took a small step back from Harper, as if he expected her to hit him, but she didn't. "I get that it's the new millennium and equal rights and girls can be serial killers just as well as boys. But those three girls don't really look like they have the upper body strength to, you know, eviscerate somebody."

"I know, but . . ." She furrowed her brow. "They're evil, and they had something to do with it. I may not understand how yet, but I know it."

Daniel watched her for a minute, thinking, then he nodded. "No. I believe you. Now what?"

"I don't know." She sighed. "But I'm not letting Gemma go anywhere near them again. I'll tie her to the bed if I have to."

"That sounds reasonable."

"Desperate times call for desperate measures."

"Where is Gemma?" Daniel asked.

"She's over at Alex's." Harper gestured to his house next door. "She's comforting him."

"So we know she's safe and taken care of?" Daniel asked, and she nodded. "Good. Then why don't we do something that you want to do?"

"Like what?"

"I don't know. What do you like to do?"

"Um . . ." Her stomach rumbled, since crying always made her hungry. "I like eating breakfast."

"That's so weird." Daniel grinned. "Because I like making French toast."

"That works out, doesn't it?"

Together, Harper and Daniel made breakfast. Her dad came in when he smelled it cooking, and the three of them ate together. It could've been a little awkward, but it wasn't. Daniel was respectful and funny, and Brian seemed to like him.

She knew that when Daniel left, her dad would be full of inquiries about the nature of their relationship that she wasn't prepared to answer. But it was still worth it.

TWENTY-ONE

The Island

Being on the island brought back memories. It had been far too long since either Harper or her father had been out to visit Bernie McAllister, so when Brian invited her to tag along with him that afternoon, she happily accepted.

With Gemma still over at Alex's, it was just the two of them, and that was a bit of a shame, since Gemma had always liked Bernie, too. Although, to be fair, Harper had never been that sure if it was the old man or if she really just loved the island.

Brian had borrowed a boat from a friend to get there, and he pulled up to Bernie's dock, which was almost hidden among the bald cypress trees that grew out into the water. There was a narrow path to the boathouse, but otherwise the island was almost overgrown with cypress trees and loblolly pines. The trees towering above them were nearly taller than the island was wide.

"Oy!" Bernie shouted.

Harper shielded her eyes from the bright sunlight that managed to break through the foliage, but she couldn't see Bernie anywhere.

"Bernie?" Brian asked. He climbed off the boat first, onto the dock, then helped his daughter do the same.

"I thought that was you coming 'round there," Bernie said, and Harper finally spotted him trotting down the path and waving his hand. "I wasn't expecting company today, but it's a nice surprise."

"I tried calling," Brian said, "but the number didn't work. Do you still have a phone out here?"

Bernie waved it off. "The storms were always taking it out, so I just got rid of it."

"We aren't intruding, are we?" Harper asked as she and her father walked down the dock to meet Bernie. "We don't want to bother you."

"Bother? Ha," Bernie teased in his cockney English accent, "it's never a bother getting a visit from a pretty girl such as yourself." He winked at her then, making Harper laugh. "And your old man ain't so bad, either."

"So how have things been, Bernie?" Brian asked.

"Can't complain, though I still do." Bernie turned around to start leading them from the dock and gestured widely to the trees around them. "Come on. I'll show you what I've done with the place. Things have changed since you've been here last."

Nothing looked all that different to Harper as she followed

Bernie up the worn path toward his house. Everything still smelled of pine and creeping Charlie, just the way she remembered it. As Bernie and her father talked about all the things they'd been up to over the last year or so, Harper wandered more slowly behind them, admiring the place from her childhood.

Since she'd been about twelve or so—the age at which her father started feeling safer about leaving her home alone in charge of Gemma—they'd come out to stay with Bernie less and less, but before that, it had been a home away from home.

Harper was certain that if she looked, she'd find the fort she and Gemma had built out of branches and old wood in the back, behind Bernie's cabin. They'd secured it with nails and wood, and Bernie had promised to leave it for them always.

When they reached his cabin, she noted that it looked more worn than she remembered it, but it held up remarkably well for its age. Vines covered one side, with Bernie trimming them only around the windows.

As Bernie led them around to the back of the cabin, Harper finally discovered what the "big changes" were—he'd started a vegetable garden. A giant rosebush, covered in large violet blossoms, grew in the center. It was something his wife had planted just before she'd died, and until the vegetable garden, it was the only plant he really took care of.

"Wow, Bernie," Brian said, a little stunned at the sheer numbers of tomatoes, green peppers, cucumbers, carrots, radishes, and lettuce that Bernie had in his yard. The garden plot was nearly the size of his cabin.

"It's a lot, isn't it?" Bernie smiled proudly. "I sell them at the farmers' market. It helps supplement the ol' retirement. You know how extravagant my life can be."

"It is impressive," Brian admitted, "but if you're strapped for cash, you know—"

Bernie held up his hand, stopping him before he could say more. "I know you've got two girls to take care of, and I've never taken charity a day in my life."

"I know." Brian nodded. "But if you do ever need anything, you can always come to me."

"Bah." Bernie shook his head, then stepped into his garden, rubbing his hands together. "How would you like a rutabaga?"

While Brian and Bernie discussed what kinds of vegetables Brian would want to take home, Harper headed out toward the trees, hoping to get a glimpse of her old fort. Coming out here was like stepping into Terabithia.

Some of her best childhood memories involved her and Gemma running through those trees, usually because they were being chased by one make-believe monster or another. Almost always Gemma would be the one who turned around and faced the monster.

Harper would be the one to invent the games, explaining to Gemma in vivid detail what the hideous ogre might look like, and that the ogre wanted two young girls to grind up to make his bread.

But Gemma would always be the one who defeated the ogre, either with a stick that was really a magic sword or by throwing stones at it. She would only run for so long before she would stop and fight back.

As Harper passed through the trees, a breeze picked up, mixing the scent of the ocean with the pines. It also blew up a feather that had been hidden among the trees. When it drifted by Harper, she bent over and picked it up.

The feather was astonishingly large—several inches in width and well over two feet in length. It was a deep black color straight through, even the rachis running down the center.

"Ah, you found a feather!" Bernie said from behind her, and she turned back to look at him.

"You know what this is from?" Harper asked, holding it up so he could better see the peculiar feather.

"From a bloody big bird." Bernie carefully made his way through his garden over to her. "But I don't know what kind of bird it is. It's nothing like I've ever seen."

"What does it look like?" Harper asked.

"I haven't been able to get a real good look at it, but I can assure you, it's huge." He held his arms out as wide as he could to demonstrate. "The wingspan is twice as wide when I've seen it make a pass over the cabin. The sun was setting, and at first I thought it was plane, but the wings were flapping, and a feather came off."

"I didn't know we had birds that big out here," Brian said, watching Bernie as he explained what he'd seen. "That sounds like a condor, maybe."

"My eyesight's not what it once was, I'll admit that, but even the noises they make don't sound right," Bernie said. "I've heard them around the island, making all kinds of weird cackling sounds. At first I thought the seagulls had learned how to laugh, but then I realized that didn't make much sense."

"Maybe you've discovered some new species of bird," Brian said with a smile. "They could name it Bernie's Bird after you."

"I dare to dream." Bernie laughed.

He went back to picking vegetables in the garden, the feather forgotten, and Harper went over to help him. By the time they'd finished, Bernie'd had her fill a wheelbarrow full of produce he could take to the farmers' market.

Brian and Harper stayed on a bit longer, sitting in the backyard and reminiscing about the past. Eventually, though, Bernie seemed to tire, so they excused themselves. Bernie walked them as far as the dock, and when they got on the boat, he stood waving at them for a long time after.

TWENTY-TWO

Confessions

As soon as Alex had told her that Luke was dead, Gemma had known the sirens had something to do with it. The first hour she'd spent with Alex after he'd told her, it had been hard for her to keep from vomiting. It had to have been Luke's blood that she'd drunk, the blood of a mortal that Penn had used in the potion to turn Gemma into a siren.

When Alex explained to her where they'd found the body, it only confirmed her fears. That was why Thea had insisted they get out of there when the police started searching the woods by the bay.

Alex didn't have the same suspicions as Gemma, of course. He tried to speculate on what had happened to Luke and the other boys, but he couldn't even fathom it. Over and over, he'd stare, mystified, and ask, "Why would anyone want to do that to another human being?"

Gemma would just shake her head, because she truly didn't know the answer. Her only hunch was that it hadn't been another human that had done it—it had been a monster. She still didn't understand completely what a siren was, but without a doubt, they were evil.

The one good thing about comforting Alex was that it didn't give her much time to think about herself or worry whether or not she was evil. All her energy went into making sure Alex felt better and making him as happy as she could.

Other than when he'd initially told her about Luke's death, Alex didn't cry. Most of the time he just sat there, his jaw tense, his eyes faraway. Gemma stayed with him until very late on Friday and all day Saturday.

Late Saturday afternoon, his head was in her lap, and she was rubbing his back when he whispered, "I can't stop seeing it. Every time I close my eyes, I see it."

"What?" Gemma asked. "What do you see?"

Other than telling her that he'd found the bodies, Alex actually hadn't said much about it. He refused to tell her any details, instead simply shaking his head whenever she pressed him for more information. Gemma didn't even know how Luke had died or what had happened to him.

"I can't." His voice was tight. "I can't even put it into words. It was most horrific thing I've ever seen."

Alex looked up at her then, his eyes searching her face. Brushing the hair back from her face, he forced a thin smile.

"You don't need to know," he told her. "You don't need to

have that image burned in your mind. You are far too sweet to have to deal with something that awful."

"I'm not."

"You are," he insisted. "And that's part of the reason why I . . ." He licked his lips and stared into her eyes. "It's why I'm falling for you."

Gemma leaned over and kissed him then, partially to keep herself from crying. It was what she'd wanted, what she'd been hoping for, but . . . she couldn't have it now. She didn't deserve it.

The evil that had traumatized Alex like this—Gemma was a part of that. Maybe not completely yet, but she was becoming a monster.

A few times, she had thought of telling Harper or Alex about the sirens. Before she'd found out that was what she was, Gemma had been on the brink of telling Harper about the strange things going on with her.

Now, with the murders and knowing that she was somehow connected to them, Gemma could never tell Harper or Alex or her father.

But there was one person she might be able to talk to, one person whose grasp on reality had become so tenuous, she would never doubt Gemma's story—her mother.

"How are things going with Alex?" Harper asked as she drove them both to see their mother on Sunday morning.

"Do you mean in our relationship, or how he's holding

up in general?" Gemma asked. She was slouched low in the passenger seat, staring through her dark sunglasses out the window.

"Um, both." Harper glanced over at her, as if surprised that her sister had said that much.

They'd barely spoken on the entire twenty-minute ride to Briar Ridge, despite Harper's many attempts at conversation. Now that they were almost to the group home, Gemma started to respond with whole sentences.

"Good, considering. On both counts." Gemma tugged at her ears, trying to alleviate the watersong. It only seemed to get louder, no matter what she tried, and it was maddening.

"Well, I'm glad that you came with me to see Mom today," Harper said. "I know it was hard for you to break away from Alex, but Mom loves to see you."

"About that." Gemma turned to her sister as they pulled in front of the group home. "I want to see Mom by myself today."

"What do you mean?" Harper turned off the car and narrowed her eyes at Gemma.

"I need to talk to her by myself."

"Why? About what?"

"If I wanted to tell you about it, I wouldn't need to see Mom alone," Gemma pointed out.

"Well . . ." Harper sighed and looked out the front window. "Why did you wait until now to tell me that? Why didn't you just come here by yourself?"

"My car's broken, and I knew you'd never let me go anywhere by myself," Gemma said. "At least not in your car. I'm actually a little surprised you let me walk over to Alex's house by myself."

"Don't do that." Harper shook her head. "Don't make me sound like the bad guy. You're the one who has been running around doing God knows what with those awful girls! It's your fault we don't trust you."

"Harper." Gemma groaned and hit her head on the back of the car seat. "I never said it wasn't my fault."

"You're acting totally bananas lately," Harper went on, as if she hadn't heard a thing that Gemma had said. "And there's a serial killer on the loose on top of everything. What else am I supposed to do? Just let you run wild?"

"God! You're not my mom, Harper!" Gemma snapped.

"And she is?" Harper pointed to the group home next to them.

Gemma looked at her like she was an idiot. "Um, yeah, she is."

"Maybe she was, and through no fault of her own, she had to give that up. But who's been raising you the past nine years? Who helps you with your homework? Who worries sick about you all night when you don't come home, and then takes care of you when you're hungover and beat up?" Harper demanded.

"I never asked you to do any of that!" Gemma yelled back. "I never asked for you to take care of me!"

"I know you didn't!" Harper shouted angrily, as if that made some kind of point. She let out a shaky breath, and when she spoke again, her voice was much softer. "How come you can tell her what's going on with you, and not me?"

Gemma stared down at her lap, pulling at the frayed ends of her shorts, and didn't say anything. There was no way she could answer the question without giving something up. She couldn't let Harper know what she'd become.

"Fine." Harper sat back in her seat and turned the car battery on, so she could flip on the radio. "Go on. Tell Mom I say hi. I'll be out here, waiting."

"Thank you," Gemma said quietly and got out of the car.

Often Nathalie would rush out to greet them when she saw their car, but she didn't do that today. That was probably a bad sign, but Gemma needed to talk to someone, and her mother was the only person who would understand.

When Gemma got to the front door, she could already hear the yelling from the inside. Bracing herself, she knocked on the door and waited.

"You never let me do anything!" Nathalie was shouting in the background when one of the staff opened the door. "This is a damn prison!"

"Oh, hi, Gemma." Becky smiled wanly at her. Becky wasn't that much older than Harper, but she'd been working at the group home the past two years, so she'd gotten pretty familiar with the girls and their mother. "I didn't think you were coming this weekend, since you missed yesterday."

"How is she doing today?" Gemma asked, even though she could hear how her mother was doing. From the other room, Nathalie swore and banged something loudly.

"Not so great. But maybe you can cheer her up." Becky stepped back so Gemma could come inside. "Nathalie, your daughter is here. Maybe you should calm down so you can talk to her."

"I don't want to talk to her!" Nathalie snarled.

Gemma flinched, then shook it off. She took off her sunglasses and walked farther into the house. She found Nathalie in the dining room, standing next to the table and glaring at the staff on the other side. Nathalie's stance was wide and her eyes were wild, making her look like an animal about to pounce.

"Nathalie," Becky said, keeping her tone soothing. "Your daughter drove all this way to see you. You should at least say hi to her."

"Hi, Mom." Gemma waved when Nathalie glanced over at her.

"Gemma, get me out of here," Nathalie said, returning her angry glare to the staff opposite her. She grabbed the chair in front of her and shook it so it would bang loudly on the floor. "Get me out of here!"

"Nathalie!" Becky moved closer to her, holding her hands up, palms out. "If you want to visit with your daughter, then you need to calm down. This behavior is not tolerated, and you know it."

Nathalie stepped back from the chair and crossed her arms in front of her chest. Her eyes darted around the room, and she seemed unable to focus on anything as she thought through her next move.

"Fine." She nodded once. "Gemma, let's go to my room."

Nathalie practically ran to her room, and Gemma followed her. Becky was telling Nathalie that she still had to behave, or her daughter would have to leave. As soon as they were in her room, Nathalie slammed the bedroom door shut.

"Bitch," Nathalie muttered at the closed door.

Ordinarily when Gemma visited, her mom's room was pretty clean. Not because Nathalie was clean or organized, but because the staff would get on her if it was too messy. Today it was a total disaster area. Clothes, CDs, jewelry—everything was thrown about her room. Her stereo was smashed in a corner, and her beloved Justin Bieber poster was torn in half.

"Mom, what happened today?" Gemma asked.

"You have to get me out of here." Nathalie grabbed a pink backpack from a pile in the middle of the floor, then flew around the room, grabbing clothes and junk to fill it with. "You have a car, right?"

"My car's broken." She toyed with the sunglasses in her hands and watched her mother trying to shove a Velcro Reebok into her bag, even though the bag was already overflowing. "Mom, I can't take you away from here."

Nathalie instantly stopped what she was doing, half crouched on the floor with the shoe and bag still in her hands, and glared up at her daughter. "Then why did you come here, if you're not taking me away? Did you come here just to rub it in my face?"

"Rub what in your face?" Gemma shook her head. "Mom,

I visit you every week. I just come to see you and talk with you because I miss you and love you. We usually come on Saturdays, but there's been a lot going on at home."

"So I have to stay here?" Nathalie straightened up and dropped her bag and shoe on the floor. "For how long?"

"I don't know. But this is where you live."

"But they don't let me do anything!" Nathalie whined.

"Everywhere you live has rules," Gemma tried to explain to her. "You'll never be allowed to do whatever you want. Nobody can."

"Well, that stinks." She looked around the room in disgust and kicked a teddy bear that Gemma had gotten her for Mother's Day.

"Listen, Mom, can I talk to you?" Gemma asked.

"I guess." Nathalie sighed and went over to the bed so she could flop down on it. "If I can't leave, we might as well talk."

"Thanks." Gemma sat down next to her. "I need your advice."

"About what?" Nathalie looked up at her, intrigued that someone was coming to her for help.

"There's a lot of stuff going on right now, and it's all so crazy." She chewed her lip, then looked at Nathalie. "Do you believe in monsters?"

"You mean like real monsters?" Her eyes widened, and she leaned in closer to Gemma. "Yeah. Of course I do. Why? Did you see one? What was it like?"

"I don't know, actually." Gemma shook her head. "It seemed sorta awesome, but I know it's not right."

"Well, what does the monster look like?" Nathalie asked. She pulled her legs underneath her so she could sit cross-legged, facing Gemma.

"I guess it's like a mermaid."

"A mermaid?" Nathalie gasped and her eyes widened even farther. "Oh, my gosh, Gemma, that's so awesome!"

"I know, but . . ." She rolled her shoulders. "They want me to join them, to be a mermaid like them—"

"Oh, Gemma, you have to!" Nathalie cut her off before she could finish her thought. "You have to be a mermaid! That would be the most amazing thing in the whole world! You could swim on and on forever! Nobody would ever tell you what to do."

"But . . ." She swallowed hard and stared down at her sunglasses in her hands. "But I think they're doing something bad. They hurt people."

"The mermaids hurt people?" Nathalie asked. "How? Why would they do that?"

"I don't know. But I know they are. I think they might be evil."

"Oh, no." Nathalie chewed her thumbnail, considering her daughter's story very seriously.

"So I think if I went with them, I would have to hurt people." Gemma looked up, trying to hold back her tears.

"Then don't go with them. You don't want to hurt people. Do you?"

"No," she admitted. "I really don't. But . . . there's this boy."

"A boy?" Nathalie smiled widely and grabbed Gemma's

arm. "Is he cute? Have you kissed him? Does he look like Justin?"

"He's really cute." Gemma couldn't help smiling with her mother staring so excitedly at her. "And we kissed." Nathalie squealed in delight at that. "And I think we really, really like each other."

"That's wonderful!" Nathalie clapped her hands together.

"Yeah, but if I go with the mermaids, I'd have to leave him behind. I wouldn't be able to see you anymore, either. I'd have to go away forever."

"Oh." She furrowed her brow. "Well. What happens if you stay? If you don't go away with the mermaids?"

"I don't know for sure. But I think . . ." Gemma took a deep breath. She didn't want to tell her mother that she'd die because she had no idea how Nathalie would handle that information. "Something bad would happen to me."

"So . . ." Nathalie's face twisted in confusion as she tried to understand, and she chewed on a long strand of her hair. "If you go with the mermaids, you can swim around forever, but you wouldn't be able to see me anymore, and you might have to do bad things."

"Right."

"But if you don't go with them, something bad happens to you?" Nathalie asked, and Gemma nodded. "If you stay, will you still be able to visit me and see that boy you like?"

"I don't know." Gemma shook her head. "I don't think so."

"Well, then, I think you know what you need to do."

"I do?"

"Yeah." Nathalie nodded. "You have to go with them."

"But I'll have to hurt people," Gemma reminded her.

"It doesn't matter." Nathalie shrugged. "You won't get hurt. Either way, you don't get to see me or your boyfriend anymore. So the choice really breaks down to being a mermaid or getting hurt. And you can't get hurt."

"I don't know." Gemma looked away from her. "I don't think I could hurt people."

"Gemma, listen to me. I'm your mother." Nathalie took her hand and squeezed it emphatically. "I can't take care of you anymore. I wish I could, but I know I can't. So you have to take care of yourself."

Gemma took a deep breath and nodded. "Okay. But I probably won't be able to come around anymore."

"Because you'll be off being a mermaid?" Nathalie asked.

"Yep." Gemma nodded and blinked back tears. She hugged her mother then, knowing this would probably be the last time she ever saw her. "I love you, Mom."

"I love you, too." Nathalie hugged her back, but only for a second, because she couldn't sit still for very long.

When Gemma left, Nathalie told all the staff that her daughter was leaving to become a mermaid.

TWENTY-THREE

Peace

If this was going to be her last night at home, Gemma wanted to make the most of it. She still hadn't decided exactly what she would do, but she knew she couldn't stay here anymore.

Even though she didn't feel it, Gemma did her best to act cheery and happy. She spent the afternoon with her father in the garage, helping him fix her car. They never did manage to get the damn thing running, but that didn't really matter. She'd just wanted to hang out with her dad.

While her dad got cleaned up, Gemma helped Harper make supper. Since she almost never helped with supper, Harper didn't trust her at first. But eventually, when she saw that Gemma wasn't trying to scam time off for good behavior, she warmed to the idea.

Dinner felt like the first family meal they'd had in ages. All three of them talked and laughed. Nobody mentioned

Gemma's recent ill behavior or the serial killer on the loose leaving dead boys in his wake. Those things still hung like dark clouds in the backs of their minds, but for one night, they went ignored.

"Harper, I can get that," Gemma offered as Harper began loading the dishwasher after supper.

Their dad had retired to the living room, too full of the savory pork chops, and Gemma and Harper stayed behind in the kitchen. Gemma had put the leftover pork chops and red potatoes in a Tupperware container while Harper cleared the table.

"No, I got it. You're putting supper away." Harper rinsed off a plate in the sink before putting it in the dishwasher and gave Gemma an odd look. "What is going on with you?"

"What?"

"This." Harper waved her hand at Gemma, accidentally flicking a few drops of water at her. "You've been sulking around the house for the past week, and today you're suddenly happy and helpful?"

"I'm usually happy, aren't I?" Gemma asked as she put the leftovers in the fridge. "And I'm sometimes helpful. It's just lately I've been weird. So today I'm back to normal."

"Okay?" Harper raised an eyebrow, as if she didn't quite believe her sister. "What changed?"

Gemma shrugged and grabbed a wet rag from the sink. She went over to the kitchen table and started wiping it off.

"Was it something Mom said?" Harper pressed when Gemma didn't answer her.

"Not really." Gemma paused, thinking of how she wanted to phrase it. "I guess I realized that I should appreciate what I have."

"Mmm-hmm." Harper had finished loading the dishwasher, so she flipped it on, then turned back to face her sister. "What do you have?"

"What do you mean?" Gemma had wiped the table clean, so she moved on to the counters.

"You said you're appreciating what you have. What exactly do you have?"

"Well, for starters, I have both my parents." Gemma stopped washing the counter and leaned against it. "They're both alive and mostly healthy, which is more than a lot of people can say. I know they both love me a lot, and Dad's even willing to spend his days off futilely working on my piece-of-crap car."

"Yeah, Dad's a great guy. What about your sister?" Harper asked with a playful smile.

"My sister is a bossy, know-it-all control freak," Gemma said, but she smiled at her. "But I know she's just trying to protect me and watch out for me because she loves me so much. Probably too much."

"That is true," Harper admitted, giving Gemma a meaningful look.

"And sometimes it drives me nuts, but deep down I've always known that I was lucky to have someone who cared about me that much." Gemma lowered her eyes. "I've been crazy lucky to have so many people who care about me and to have been blessed with so much . . . just so much of *everything*."

Gemma shook her head and smiled sadly at her. "I just wanted you to know that *I* know that you're awesome."

For a moment they only looked at each other. Harper's eyes were moist, and for a horrible second Gemma was certain she would cry. And if Harper cried, then Gemma would cry, and it would turn into a big blubbery mess, and she didn't want that.

"Anyway." Gemma picked up the rag and started wiping down the counter again.

"Why are you being so weird?" Harper asked, composing herself.

"I'm not trying to be weird." Gemma had actually scrubbed the counter until it was spotless, or at least as clean as old, cracked laminate could be. But she kept doing it because then she could avoid looking at Harper.

"Is this because of what happened to Luke?" Harper asked, and Gemma stiffened.

"I don't want to talk about that. Not tonight." Swallowing hard, she turned back to face her sister and tossed the rag in the sink.

"Okay." Harper leaned back against the counter and crossed her arms over her chest. "What do you want to talk about?"

"Dad told me that Daniel came over for breakfast yesterday."

Harper blushed and looked down, trying to get her dark

hair to fall in her face and cover it up. But she only succeeded in making Gemma laugh.

"He just stopped by, and we happened to eat breakfast," Harper said. "It was nothing."

"Nothing?" Gemma arched a skeptical eyebrow. "Since when has Daniel just stopped by? I didn't think you even liked him."

"I don't," Harper insisted, but she wouldn't even look at Gemma. "Why would I like him? I don't even really know him. And he lives on a boat and doesn't have a real job. And I barely know him. We've barely spoken."

"Oh, my gosh, Harper." Gemma rolled her eyes. "You like him, and from the way I've seen him put up with your crap, I'm guessing he likes you, too. What's the big deal?"

"It isn't a big deal. There's no *deal* at all." Harper squirmed under her sister's accusation. "He's nice, I guess, but I'm going away for college—"

"That's over two months away," Gemma said, cutting her off before Harper could launch into her going-away-for-college routine. "Nobody's suggesting you marry the guy. Just have some fun. Summer romance. Live a little."

"I'm not *not* living." Harper tucked a loose strand of hair behind her ear. "I'm sorry if I don't see the point in fooling around with some guy for a few weeks. If I weren't leaving in the fall, it would be different."

"No, it wouldn't," Gemma corrected her. "Before this, you couldn't date because you had to take care of me or keep your grades up for school. Now it's because you'll be leaving for college, and once you're at college you won't have time for a relationship until after you graduate, and then you won't have time because you're looking for a job, and then it'll be something else."

"Well . . ." Harper twisted her ring on her finger. "All those things are true."

"Not really. Lots of other people somehow manage to go to school and have a life," Gemma said. "Everything I listed there, those are just excuses."

"Concentrating on school is a valid life decision," Harper argued. "We didn't have money for college, and if I hadn't worked my butt off to get that scholarship, I wouldn't have been able to go."

"No, I know." Gemma sighed. "But you've been using both me and school as a shield to keep you from getting close to people. I'm not always gonna be around to act as a buffer. Someday you need to have real relationships with other people or you'll risk ending up alone."

"Wow." Harper laughed darkly. "You make me sound like an old maid."

"No, you're not. I don't think that, even. I just . . . all I'm saying is that maybe spending some time with Daniel this summer wouldn't be such a bad thing."

It wasn't until she'd said it that Gemma realized what she was doing. She was trying to take care of Harper. If Gemma left tonight, she needed to know that her sister wouldn't be alone, that she'd have someone to lean on. Harper didn't think she needed anyone, but she did, and apparently Daniel had seen through her act and knew it, too.

Without thinking, Gemma went over and hugged her sister. Startled and confused, Harper just stood there for a second, then wrapped her arms around Gemma and hugged her back.

"I don't know what's gotten into you," Harper said. "But I think I like it."

After they finished cleaning up the kitchen, Harper went upstairs to read a book, the way she usually did after supper. Gemma stayed down in the living room, watching TV with her dad for a little while. When he got up to go to bed, Gemma hugged him and told him she loved him.

Harper usually stayed up pretty late reading. Gemma had to wait until after she fell asleep to leave, but she pretended to go to bed. Not that she could sleep. The watersong always seemed to get worse at night, and it had kept her awake almost the whole night before.

She kept her bedroom door open, staring at the crack of light coming out from under Harper's door. When it finally clicked off, signifying that Harper was going to bed, Gemma waited another half hour just to be safe.

Without turning on her own light, she crept around her room. Her backpack hung on her closet door, and she started filling it with her personal belongings. It was hard to know what to bring, though.

She wasn't even certain that she would go off with the

sirens. She just knew she couldn't stay here. If she chose to die, she didn't want her family to see that. It would be better if they just thought she'd run away. Then they could imagine she was alive out there somewhere.

The only thing she could really do for her family was leave them with some hope.

In the end, she decided on a few clothes and the picture of herself, Harper, and her mom from next to her bed. She carefully pulled the photo from the frame and tucked it into a plastic bag. Everything else she left behind in her room.

Before going, she paused at her bedroom door and thought of writing a note. But what would she possibly say? What could she tell them?

Gemma stepped outside, closing the back door behind her as quietly as she could. She glanced next door at Alex's house, where his bedroom light glowed. The window was open, and she could hear the faint sounds of whatever music he was listening to.

All day long Gemma had been working on getting her life in order, but she'd purposely avoided seeing Alex. It was hard enough leaving her sister and her dad. She didn't think she could handle talking to Alex.

So she put her head down and walked across the lawn. She cut through his backyard, because it was the quickest way to the bay. The watersong got even louder when she was outside, begging her to swim.

"Gemma!" Alex said from behind her, and she heard his

screen door slam. Gemma just kept walking, though, so he chased after her. "Gemma!"

"Shh!" She whirled around. If she didn't talk to him, he'd make enough noise to wake up her sister. "What are you doing out here?"

"I saw you from the window." He'd stopped a few feet from her. "What are you doing out here?"

"I'm sorry. I have to leave."

"You shouldn't be out here alone, not with the killer on the loose." He took a step back toward his house. "I'll go get my shoes and I'll come with you."

"No, Alex." She shook her head. "I'm leaving for good."

"What?" Even in the dim moonlight, she could see the hurt and confusion on his face. "Where are you going?"

"I don't know, but you can't come with me."

"What?" He stepped toward her, and when he did, she stepped back.

"Alex, I can't do this."

"What?" Alex asked. "What can't you do?"

"Say good-bye to you." She swallowed back tears and tried to ignore the pain in her heart.

"Then don't," he said simply. "Stay here, with me."

"No, I can't." She started to step back, and he followed her, saying her name. "No, Alex. You can't come with. I don't want you to."

"Gemma, if something's wrong I can help."

"No." She shook her head and realized that the only way

she'd stop him was if she hurt him. "You don't get it, Alex. I don't want *you.* I don't even like you. You're boring and lame. I was just using you because you had a car, but . . . I don't want you anymore."

His whole face fell. "You don't mean that."

"I do," she insisted. "So leave me alone. I don't want to see you ever again."

She turned and bolted away from him. With her broken heart pounding in her chest, Gemma pushed herself as fast as she could.

Tears blurred her vision, but it didn't matter. She didn't need to see where she was going anyway. The sea called to her, telling her exactly where she needed to go.

TWENTY-FOUR

Monsters

When Gemma hit the water, the song finally stopped. Her legs turned to a tail, and she breathed in deeply.

Transforming into her mermaid form had silenced the watersong, and she closed her eyes, listening for the sirens. She couldn't hear them, not exactly, but she could feel them. The sirens drew her to them, the same way the ocean did.

If they hadn't had that connection, Gemma probably never would've found the sirens. Instead of going to the cove like she'd thought she would, Gemma found herself pulled out to sea, to Bernie's Island a few miles off Anthemusa Bay.

Before Gemma had even surfaced, she heard the loud music blasting. It was Ke$ha, and that didn't seem like something Bernie would listen to.

Gemma pulled herself up onto the dock, which was more

difficult than it sounded since she couldn't use her fish tail to help her. From that vantage point, she could see Bernie's cabin through the trees, all lit up like a lighthouse.

Once her tail had returned to her usual leggy form, Gemma rummaged through her backpack and pulled on clothes. They were soaking wet, but it was better than being naked.

She walked along the dock to the trail that wound up to Bernie's cabin. The windows were wide open, so the music came blaring out at full volume. Gemma snuck up to them, wanting to see what they were doing before she went in.

Lexi was jumping up and down on the couch, doing some kind of weird dance move. Her mouth moved along with the lyrics, but no words came out.

Rummaging through a cupboard nearby was Thea. The whole cabin looked ransacked, and by the way Thea went through stuff and tossed it around, it was obvious why. Gemma couldn't tell if Thea was looking for anything in particular or not.

Neither Penn nor Bernie was anywhere to be seen, so Gemma crept around the cabin to another window, hoping she could see more from there.

"I'm glad you decided to join us," Penn said, and Gemma jumped back. Penn had somehow come up right beside her, and Gemma hadn't heard her.

Penn smiled at her, and Gemma hurried to compose herself. The last thing in the world she wanted was for Penn to know how much she'd scared her.

"I haven't decided anything yet," Gemma replied coolly, and Penn only smiled wider.

"Oh!" Lexi exclaimed inside the cabin. "Is Gemma here?" The music stopped short, so the only sounds came from the ocean around them and the wind through the trees.

"Come inside." Penn took a step backward, then turned around and went into the cabin. Swallowing hard, Gemma followed her.

Lexi had gotten down off the couch, but Thea continued her searching. She crouched in front of the sink, pulling out containers of Comet and drain cleaner.

"Thea, I think it's safe to assume there's nothing valuable under the sink," Penn said as she carefully stepped over all the things Thea'd tossed on the kitchen floor.

"This is a waste of time anyway." Thea sighed and got to her feet. "Gemma's here. Can we go now?"

"I don't know." Penn faced Gemma and leaned on the back of the couch. "Gemma says she's not sure if she's coming with us or not."

Thea groaned and rolled her eyes. "Oh, please."

"Where's Bernie?" Gemma asked.

"Who?" Lexi asked.

"Bernie." Gemma brushed past them to check out the bedroom in the back. She pushed open the door, but only found more of the mess she'd seen in the rest of the cabin. "Bernie? Mr. McAllister?"

When she didn't see him, she turned back to the sirens.

Penn and Thea just watched her, but Lexi played with her hair and looked at the floor.

"Where is he?" Gemma asked. "What did you do to him? Did you hurt him?"

"He gave us the place." Penn shrugged. "You know how persuasive we can be."

"Where is he?" Gemma repeated, her voice getting harder. "Did you kill him the way you did those other boys?"

"I'd hardly call that old man a 'boy,'" Penn said, her tone teasing.

"Stop it!" Gemma yelled, and Lexi flinched. "You said you told me the truth, but you didn't. I know you've been killing people, and you didn't tell me that."

"I didn't *lie,*" Penn scoffed. "I never said, *We don't kill people, Gemma.*"

Her stomach dropped. "So you admit it."

"Yes. I admit it." As she stepped closer to Gemma, she smiled and tilted her head, her voice silky and sweet. "I'm sorry I didn't tell you. But it's only one little detail."

"One little detail?" Gemma stepped back. "You're murderers!"

"We're not murderers!" Lexi said defensively. "At least, not any more than a hunter is, than you are when you eat a hamburger. We do what we have to do to live."

"You're cannibals?" Gemma's jaw dropped, and she kept stepping back. She wasn't looking where she was going and nearly tripped over a book, but she caught herself on the wall.

"That's why we don't lead with that," Penn explained in a way that sounded so reasonable, so logical that it sent chills down Gemma's spine. "We have eternal youth and unmatched beauty. We can change form into magical, mythical creatures. So we survive on mortal blood. What's that one little thing, when we get so much in return?"

"One little thing?" Gemma asked, laughing darkly. "You're *monsters*!"

"Don't." Penn pursed her lips and shook her head. "I hate the word monster."

Gemma stood straight and moved away from the wall so she wasn't leaning on it anymore. She met Penn's dark eyes. "I just call it like I see it, and right now, standing in front of me, all I see is a monster."

"Gemma," Lexi said, her voice quavering slightly. "Don't push her."

"You really have no idea what you're messing with," Thea agreed.

"It's okay." Penn held up her hand toward Thea and Lexi but kept her eyes locked on Gemma. "She's just forgotten her place. She's forgotten that she is one of us now."

"I'll never be one of you." Gemma shook her head. "I will sooner die than kill anyone."

"I'll be more than happy to arrange that for you."

"Then do it." Gemma raised her chin defiantly. "You said if I don't go with you, then I'll die. And I'm not going with you."

Penn's jaw clenched, and Gemma could see something

happening underneath her skin. Almost like a current running over her face. Penn's eyes even changed color, shifting from dark brown to a yellow-green.

Then all at once the shifting stopped, and her eyes went back to their usual soulless black. When she opened her mouth to speak, her teeth were visibly sharper.

"You've given me no choice. I'm going to have to show you exactly who you are." Penn looked back over at Thea and Lexi. "Call for him."

"Who?" Lexi asked.

"Whoever answers," Penn replied.

Lexi glanced uncertainly at Gemma, then back at Thea. Thea sighed but began singing first. Her voice was beautiful in its own husky way, but it wasn't until Lexi joined in that Gemma felt the full enchanting power of their music.

They were singing the song that Gemma had heard before, the one she herself had sung in the shower. As soon as they opened their mouths, Gemma knew all the words, and she wanted to join in. She actually had to bite her tongue to stop herself.

Thea and Lexi turned and walked out of the cabin, standing on the porch to sing their siren song, calling for someone to come join them on the island.

TWENTY-FIVE

Poor Voyager

Harper!" Alex shouted, and she snuggled deeper into her bed. "Harper!"

"What?" Harper muttered into her pillow, but by then she was awake enough that she heard the panic in his voice. She sat up, looking around her dark bedroom in confusion. "Alex?"

"I'm outside!" Alex yelled, and Harper looked out her window to see him standing there, shouting up at her.

"What are you doing?" Harper asked. "What's going on?"

"Gemma ran away. I tried to stop her . . ." He trailed off for a moment, then continued. "I think she went down to the bay, but I don't know for sure."

"Dammit."

Harper lunged out of bed, scrambling around in the dark to put on her clothes. Alex kept talking outside, but she hadn't really heard much of anything after he said that Gemma was gone. She was pulling on her sweater as she ran out the front door, and Alex was still standing below her now-empty bedroom, talking up to it.

"Alex, come on!" Harper ran around to the side of the house to flag him, then hurried over to her Sable parked in the driveway and got in. As soon as Alex hopped in the car, she asked, "You're sure she went to the bay?"

"No," he admitted. "She wouldn't tell me where she was going. But knowing Gemma, where else would she go?"

Harper put the car in reverse and floored it, making it squeal out of the driveway. Alex didn't say anything, but he put on his seat belt.

"What did she say to you? Are you sure she's running away? Maybe she just went for a swim."

"No, I tried to go with her because the killer's on the loose." He pressed his arm against the window glass, steadying himself as Harper flew around a corner. "But she wouldn't let me go with her."

"Dammit." Harper hit the steering wheel. "I knew she was acting weird today. I knew it, and I didn't . . ." She shook her head, remembering all the things Gemma had told her. "She was saying good-bye."

"But why?" Alex asked, pulling her from her thoughts. "Why is she doing this?"

"I don't know. It's not like Gemma. She never runs from a fight. Whatever she's running from has to be pretty terrible."

Harper got to the bay in record time. She didn't stop soon

enough and actually skidded out onto the dock, making the wooden planks quake under the car. As soon as the car came to a complete halt, she leaped out and started yelling for Daniel.

"Who's Daniel?" Alex asked, chasing after Harper.

"He has a boat," she explained quickly.

The docks were dimly lit, and when she couldn't see his boat, she had this horrible moment of panic, realizing he might be gone. It was a boat. He could leave at any time.

Then the lights flicked on inside the cabin of *The Dirty Gull,* and she ran toward it. He still wasn't on the deck when she reached it, so she slapped her hands against the side of the hull, trying to hurry him.

"Daniel!" Harper yelled.

"First your car wakes me up, now you're hitting my boat." Daniel finally emerged from the cabin, rubbing his eyes. He'd managed to put his jeans on, but they were still unbuttoned. "What's the emergency?"

"Gemma's gone." She leaned over the dock as far as she could, hanging on to the railing of the boat to keep from falling in the water. "She ran away, we think she's out in the bay. I need your help."

"She ran away?" Daniel ran a hand through his hair and shook his head, trying to shake off the sleep. "Why?"

"We don't know, but something's really wrong." She looked up at Daniel, her eyes pleading with him. "Please, Daniel. I need you."

Without missing a beat, he asked, "How can I help?"

"The bay is the only place she really loves. She couldn't have gotten far yet, and with your boat, we could find her."

"The *Gull* isn't as fast as it used to be, but I'll do what I can." He reached over the side of the boat and grabbed Harper to pull her up. "Who's that?"

"What?" Harper asked when Daniel put her down. She glanced back to see Daniel pointing to Alex. "Oh, that's Alex. He's Gemma's boyfriend."

"Oh." Daniel extended his hand to Alex. "Nice to meet you."

"Uh, likewise." He took Daniel's hand uncertainly, and Daniel helped pull him up on the boat. He didn't quite embrace him the way he'd lifted Harper, but he got Alex onto the deck.

"Can you help me unhook the boat?" Daniel asked Alex, gesturing to the ropes that tied it to the dock.

"Yeah, sure." Alex hurried to help Daniel.

Harper went around to the front of the boat. A cold wind whipped over the water, and she wrapped her arms around herself, trying to stay warm against it. She stared out at the bay, hoping against hope that her sister was safe.

"Do you want me to take a pass around the bay?" Daniel asked, coming over to where Harper stood. He'd done up his pants and put on a shirt since untying the boat.

"Maybe." She glanced back at him, then stared out at the water.

"What about the cove?" Alex suggested and pointed to it. "She's running away, which means she needs a place to camp out. The cove would give her shelter but still keep her near the bay."

Daniel looked to Harper for confirmation, and she nodded. Daniel went around to the back of the boat to drive it while Alex went to the very edge, hanging on to the railing, staring out at the night sea. Harper thought about staying with him, but she felt more in control staying with Daniel, telling him where to go.

When Daniel turned the key, the boat chugged but didn't immediately start. Harper cast him a look, and he gave her an apologetic smile.

"I haven't taken her out in a while."

"What's the point of having a boat if you don't take it out?" Harper asked, sounding more hostile than she'd meant to.

"The point is that I get to have a roof over my head. Gas is expensive, and I don't really have anywhere I wanna go." He turned the key, and the motor finally purred into life. "There she goes!"

When they pulled away from the dock, moving toward the cove, Harper relaxed a little bit. Not completely, but she felt better knowing that they were doing something, that they were moving toward something.

"Thank you." She smiled gratefully at Daniel as he steered the boat.

"You're welcome. And thanks to you for waking me up all the time, I'm learning to live without sleep." He smiled at her, and she lowered her eyes.

"I'm sorry for always bothering you, and I really owe you. But I didn't know where else to go."

"Hey, I know." He reached out, touching her arm gently. "It's okay."

"I just hope we find her." Harper breathed in deeply and looked back out at the water.

"The water's pretty choppy," Daniel commented as the boat bobbed erratically. Alex gripped the railing tightly to avoid sliding on the deck.

"The boat can handle it, though, right?" Harper asked.

"Yeah, yeah, but it's just so windy." He bit his lip and watched Harper from the corner of his eye. "It's a cold night for swimming. Are you sure Gemma went out to the bay tonight?"

"Yeah." She nodded. "I know I seem crazy and overzealous, and maybe I am. But I just *know* something's wrong." She put her hand over her stomach, pressing against it. "I can feel it. Gemma's in trouble, and she needs me."

"If you say she's in trouble, then I believe you."

"Thank you." Harper stepped forward, straining her eyes to see in the dark as they got closer to the cove. "Can this thing go any faster?"

"I'm pushing her as fast as she goes," Daniel said. "I knew any slower than that wouldn't be good enough for you."

When they finally got close enough to the cove to really see it, Daniel turned on the boat's spotlight, shining it inside. He had to slow the boat way down to keep it from crashing into the rocks, but even from that distance they could see it was empty.

"No, she has to be there," Harper insisted, shaking her head. "She *has* to."

"Do you want me to pull in closer, so you can check it out?" Daniel asked.

"Yes. Please."

Daniel got the boat as close to the cove's shore as he could, then tied the boat to a cypress tree leaning out over the water. Alex got the landing plank. It barely reached from the boat to the shore, but it just made it. Alex ran down first, with Harper right behind him.

The spotlight on the boat was still shining on the cove, so they could see everything inside it, but there was nothing much to see. A circle of rocks in the center for a fire pit. Footprints in the dirt. That was about it.

"I found something!" Alex yelled and held up a bag.

"Is it her stuff?"

Harper ran over to him and yanked the bag from his hands. She tore through it, but it only took a few slutty tops and thongs for Harper to realize that these weren't her sister's clothes. Still, this bag was the only thing they'd found, so she clutched it to her chest and stared vacantly in front of her.

"It's not hers, is it?" Alex asked, watching a red thong tumble from Harper's grip.

"What'd you find?" Daniel asked. He'd gotten off the boat after them, and he was just coming up behind Harper.

"I think it's those girls'." She turned to face him and held the bag out to Daniel, as if he'd know what to do with it. "Those horrible girls have done something to her."

"You don't know that." Daniel tentatively took the bag from her. "Just because somebody else crashed here doesn't mean that she has anything to do with them."

"But where is she?" Harper asked, tears filling her eyes. "She's not here. Where could she be?"

"Gemma!" Alex resorted to yelling her name since he didn't know what else to do. He stood at the edge of the cove, shouting out at the bay. "Gemma!"

"Maybe we beat her here," Daniel suggested. "We got here pretty fast, right?"

"Do you think?" Harper stared up at him, her frantic eyes searching his.

"Maybe." He shrugged. "Or is there anywhere else you can think of that she might go?"

"No, I . . ." Harper trailed off, her face twisting with confusion, and she tilted her head, listening. He opened his mouth to say something, and she silenced him by putting her hand on his chest. "Do you hear that?"

"What?" Daniel asked, but then he heard it, too.

Very faintly at first, but the wind was carrying music out to the cove. A song unlike anything Harper had ever heard before, but it was one that Alex was all too familiar with.

"It's Gemma," Alex breathed.

"What?" Harper asked, but now without the incessant panic that had been gripping her only seconds before. Her entire expression changed, the tension melting away to a bizarre serenity.

"Harper?" Daniel asked. When she started walking toward Alex at the shore of the cove, he put his hand on her arm to stop her. "Harper? Are you okay? What's wrong?"

"Nothing's wrong." Her brow furrowed momentarily at that, as if she realized that what she was saying wasn't quite right, and she turned to Daniel. "Were we looking for something?"

"Yeah. Your sister." He took both her arms and made her face him. "What the hell is going on with you?"

"She's calling me," Alex said to no one in particular, and then he dove into the water, swimming out of the cove.

"Alex!" Daniel yelled. "Alex! What are you doing? We have a boat!" He ran to the shoreline. Alex was furiously swimming away, and Daniel wasn't about to jump in after him. "Alex! Just get back here in the damn boat!"

"Something's wrong," Harper whimpered, and Daniel turned back to see her looking as if she were about to cry.

"No shit, something's wrong." He went back over to her, apparently deciding that Alex was a lost cause, at least for the time being. "Do you know why Alex just took off?"

"No." She ran her hand through her hair and looked up at him. "Gemma is missing, and I can't . . ." She shook her head and covered her ears with her hands. "It's that song, Daniel! It's trying to make me forget about her, but I won't!"

"The song?" Daniel certainly could still hear it, but he sounded as if he didn't know what Harper was talking about.

"Can't you hear it?" Harper asked, shouting because she'd plugged her ears.

"Yeah, but I'm fine," he assured her.

"We need to go towards the song!" Harper told him. "That's where Gemma is!"

Daniel thought about arguing with her, but something really, really bizarre was happening, and they probably didn't have time to question things anymore. He took Harper's hand, dragging her over to the boat so they could go after Gemma while they still had a chance.

All the while, the song floated through the air. *Come now, weary traveler, I'll lead you through the waves. Worry not, poor voyager, for my voice is the way.*

TWENTY-SIX

True Form

"What are you doing?" Gemma asked, still struggling against her urge to join in the song with Lexi and Thea.

"What needs to be done," Penn told her. "I've tried to reason with you. I've given you everything you wanted. And you still won't see logic. So now I'm going to make you see."

"I don't understand." Gemma glanced through the doorway where the other two sirens sang. "What do you have to make me see? Why can't you just let me go?"

"Because, Gemma, we only had until this full moon to find a new siren, or we all die. And you might be ready to throw in the towel, but I don't give up so easy. I didn't survive the past several millennia just to be finished off by a spoiled little brat."

"Exactly!" Gemma latched on to a point. "I'm horrid. You don't want me. Let me go, and pick someone else."

"I wish it were that simple," Penn said, and she sounded as if she really meant it. "The potion doesn't always take. You're the third girl we've tried, and the first that's turned into a siren."

"What do you mean, the potion doesn't always take?" Gemma asked.

"After you drink it, one of two things will happen. One, you'll turn into a siren, as you did." Penn gestured to her. "Or two, you die."

"What? Why?" Gemma asked. "How come I turned and other girls didn't?"

"We don't know exactly. A siren needs to be strong, beautiful, and connected to the water." Penn shrugged. "Some of the girls we picked just weren't strong enough."

"But . . . you're running out of time. If I died, you would all die?" Gemma narrowed her eyes at Penn. "What's stopping me from killing myself?"

"You don't know how to, for one thing. Sirens aren't mortal. You can't just drown or throw yourself off a building," Penn said. "And the other thing is on its way right now."

Before Gemma could respond, Lexi shouted from the porch, "He's coming! I can see him! He's already on the dock!"

"Good." Penn smiled. "You can stop your singing now, before we summon every man near the bay."

Penn stood in between Gemma and the doorway, but now she stepped to the side, allowing Gemma to get by.

She ran to the doorway, rushing past Lexi and Thea. She didn't know whom they'd called or what exactly they planned to do with him, but Gemma knew whatever it was couldn't be good. She had to send him away before the sirens sank their teeth in him.

When she saw him coming up the trail, walking like he was still asleep, she stopped cold in her tracks. It was worse than she'd feared.

"Alex."

As soon as his name escaped her lips, Lexi was on him, putting her arm around him and leading him up the trail. Thea grabbed Gemma, holding her arms behind her back so she couldn't fight.

"Alex!" Gemma shouted, but he barely glanced over at her. His gaze was too focused on Lexi, who hummed a song in his ear. "Alex! You have to get out of here! Alex, run! It's a trick! They're going to kill you!"

"Shut up," Thea growled and started dragging her up the path to the cabin. "If you would have just come with us, none of this would be happening. It's your fault we're in this mess."

"Please!" Gemma begged. "Please, just leave him alone."

Penn was laughing when they entered the cabin. Gemma fought and kicked at Thea, but it was like fighting against granite. Thea was a three-thousand-year-old demigoddess, and it showed in her strength.

Alex had followed Lexi willingly into the center of the room, and he couldn't take his eyes off her. She circled him slowly, and he turned his head, following her. Lexi stopped in front of him, caressing his face, and he leaned in to kiss her.

"Alex!" Gemma shouted, but he still tried to kiss Lexi. If Lexi hadn't moved her head away at the last second, he would've. "What have you done to him?"

"Actually, *you* did it." Penn stood off to the side of the room, watching Gemma's misery with a look of intense satisfaction. "He wouldn't have gotten here so quickly if you hadn't already put him under a siren spell once before."

"What are you talking about?" Gemma asked. "I never did anything to him."

"Oh, but you did." Penn smiled. "You *sang* to him, calling him. Thanks to that, he's more susceptible to our charms. It'll be harder for him to resist our commands."

"It's our song," Lexi explained. She stayed next to Alex, his arms around her as he stared adoringly at her, but so far she'd avoided all of his attempts at kissing her. "We put men in a trance, make them follow our every order and lust after us. It works a little on women, too, but it's not nearly as powerful."

Gemma wanted to argue that she'd never sung to him, she'd never tried to put a spell on him, but then she remembered. Right after they'd turned her into a siren, she'd been singing in the shower. Alex came over, and that was the day they'd had the intense make-out session that neither of them could explain.

"This really is all my fault," Gemma whispered.

"It's all right," Lexi said, her voice sounding too cheery for the situation. "We all make mistakes. But we can learn from them."

"Lexi makes an excellent point." Penn walked over to Gemma, stopping right in front her. Thea still held her back, but Gemma had stopped fighting. "And you're going to learn a lesson tonight whether you like it or not."

"You don't have to do this," Gemma said. "Penn, please don't do this."

"Lexi, let's see what we're working with," Penn commanded, but she kept her eyes on Gemma.

Lexi slid down low, keeping her body as close to Alex's as she could without touching him. She grabbed the bottom of his wet T-shirt, and in one smooth move she pulled it up over his head, leaving Alex half naked in the center of the room.

"That's better." Lexi smiled at him and admired his shirtless torso. "He's pretty cute, Gemma. You have good taste."

"What are you doing?" Gemma asked. "Why are you doing this to him?"

"You think he loves you?" Penn asked. "He doesn't love you. He's about ready to pounce on Lexi there and have his way with her." She glanced back at him. "Aren't you, Alex?"

"She's the most beautiful thing I've ever seen," Alex said, his voice flat and faraway. Lexi took a step back from him, and he tried to follow her. She held her hand up, keeping him at bay.

"She has a spell on him!" Gemma insisted. "He can't control his actions. He would never act like that."

"But if he really loved you, it would overpower the spell." Penn kept her eyes on Gemma, but motioned to where Lexi and Alex stood. "He would see he loves you. But he doesn't. He can't. He won't." She stepped even closer to Gemma, nearly speaking into her ear. "Mortals are incapable of love."

In front of her, she could see Alex using all his restraint to keep from running to Lexi. She stood a few feet from him, tempting in a way that was driving him mad.

Gemma's stomach twisted, but not with jealousy. The spell that Lexi had over him was making him do this, and that spell had to be hurting him, too.

"Fine, you've made your point." Gemma squirmed against Thea's arms, trying to pull away from her. "He can't love me, and he never will! Now let him go!"

"Don't you see?" Penn crossed her arms and studied Gemma. "Everything he's told you has been a lie. Everything's he's done has been to trick you, because he wants to possess you and sleep with you, the way all men do. He never cared about you. He only cares about himself."

Gemma took a deep breath, and as much as it pained her heart, she realized that what Penn said might be true. Alex hadn't even really looked at her since he'd gotten here, and she was a siren, too. Maybe that meant he didn't care about her.

But he was still the same guy that she was falling for. Even though his hair was dripping wet, a lock of his bangs managed to stick up a little. The way he'd kissed her and held her, that might be all be fake or temporary, but he wasn't. Deep down, Gemma knew without a doubt that he was good and kind and worthy of her love.

"I don't care!" Gemma glared at Penn. "It doesn't matter because *I* love *him*!"

Penn narrowed her eyes at her, and Gemma saw that weird moving thing happening to her face again, like something underneath was shifting. But it stopped just as quickly as it started.

"Let her go," Penn told Thea.

As soon as Thea loosened her grip, Gemma ran away from her, rushing over to Alex. When she ran in front of him, he tried looking around her, because he didn't want to take his eyes off Lexi.

"Alex," Gemma said.

He strained to see past her. She grabbed his face, forcing him to look into her eyes. At first he tried to fight it, but then something changed.

The daze in his mahogany eyes began to clear, and his pupils dilated. He blinked a few times, like a man just waking up, then reached out and touched Gemma's face. His skin was cold and wet, and goose bumps covered his bare flesh.

"Gemma?" Alex asked, sounding confused. "Oh, my God, Gemma, what have I done?"

"You didn't do anything." With tears in her eyes, she laughed a little. "I love you."

She stood on her tiptoes and stretched up to kiss him. His mouth felt cold and wonderful, and the kiss shot through her like lightning, spreading heat all over body. It was real and true, and nothing the sirens could say or do would ever change that.

"Enough of this!" Penn roared, and suddenly Alex flew away from Gemma.

Penn had come up and grabbed him, then threw him so hard into the wall behind them, he fell unconscious on the floor. Gemma wanted to run to him, but Penn stood in front of her. The rage burned so brightly in her eyes that Gemma didn't dare cross her without a serious plan, lest Penn destroy everyone in the cabin.

"You've only seen two forms of the siren," Penn said, and as she spoke, her voice began to change from the silky babytalk to something distorted and monstrous. "I think it's time you see our true form."

Her arms began to change first, growing longer. Her fingers stretched out several inches, ending in sharp hooked talons. The skin on her legs shifted from smooth, tanned flesh to something appearing dull gray and scaly. It wasn't until the feet changed into bird's feet with long claws that Gemma realized Penn had grown the legs of an emu.

Penn arched her back and let out a scream that was more like that of a dying bird than a human. The sound of tearing flesh and rustling feathers filled the room as two wings tore out from her shoulder blades. When they unfurled, they were nearly the length of the room. The feathers were big and black, shimmering in the light.

She flapped them once, and they created a gust so strong it knocked Gemma down. She crawled back on the floor toward the wall, and stared up at Penn as the transformation went from bad to horrid.

Penn's face was still shifting. Her eyes first, from their usual black to the golden yellow of an eagle. Her full mouth lengthened and stretched out, so her lips were pulled back, like a bloodred line around her teeth. Her teeth not only grew but multiplied, going from a single row of flat teeth to row after row of razor-sharp daggers, so her mouth resembled that of an anglerfish.

Her skull seemed to expand, growing larger. The silken black hair remained, billowing out from her head like a dark halo, but it appeared thinner and stringier, since her scalp had gotten bigger.

The only thing about her that remained mostly unchanged was her torso. It lengthened and thinned out, becoming more skeletal, so her ribs and spine protruded grotesquely. But her human breasts remained the same, the bikini top barely concealing them, since the growth of her body had stretched out the fabric.

With the transformation apparently complete, Penn stepped closer to Gemma. She tilted her head back and forth, looking like some sort of human-sparrow hybrid, and blinked at Gemma.

"Now," Penn said, her voice a distorted version of her normal one. "The *real* lesson begins."

TWENTY-SEVEN

Helpless

While Daniel untied the boat, Harper stood at the bow, staring in the direction where the song was coming from. She kept her hands pressed to her ears, afraid of what would happen to her if she listened to the song.

Her hands weren't completely soundproof, though, and some of the music still got in. It would be impossible for her to ever explain the way it made her feel, but the easiest way was that it dulled her senses.

Her panic over Gemma's disappearance or even Alex diving into the choppy water almost completely stopped when she listened to the music. If Daniel hadn't been there, trying to talk sense into her, she might have stayed in the cove forever, or at least as long as the song kept going.

"Oh, shit," Daniel said, loud enough that Harper could hear him clearly, and she turned back to face him. He stood in front of the wheel, his expression grim. "No, come on, baby, please don't do this."

"Daniel?" Harper went closer to the cabin and stared up at him. "What's wrong?"

"The boat." He grimaced. "She won't start."

"What do you mean, she won't start?" Harper asked, her voice getting shrill. "Why did you even turn it off?"

"To conserve gas, but she'll start. She just needs a little loving."

Daniel hopped down and went around the back of the boat. Harper followed him, wondering if she should just dive in the water like Alex had. He flipped open the hatch over the engine, and while she didn't understand what he was doing, she heard a few loud bangs as he attempted to fix something. Based on the expletives he shouted, she didn't think it was going well.

"Daniel!" Harper shouted, her ears still plugged. "I think I should go in after Alex. I can't wait here like this. Gemma needs me."

"Harper!" Daniel stopped what he was doing and looked around.

"No, I need to—"

"No, Harper, listen!" He held up his hand, which was covered with black grease from the engine. "The song stopped."

"It did?" She lowered her hands, and all she could hear was the ocean around her. No more music. "Why? Do you think Alex did something?"

"I don't know." Daniel shut the hatch and stood up. "But hopefully I fixed the problem."

Wiping his hands on his jeans, he ran around to the front of the boat. He climbed up to the captain's seat, and Harper followed right behind. When he turned the ignition, it made the same chugging noise it'd made back at the dock, but it didn't start.

"Daniel—" Harper began, but he held up his hand to silence her.

"Come on," Daniel muttered to the boat. "Just start up one more time. For me." The boat made a loud clanking sound, followed by the engine roaring to life. "Yes!" As they pulled away from the cove, he glanced down at Harper. "I told you she would start."

"I never doubted you for a second," Harper lied.

"Where are we going?" Daniel asked. He steered them in the direction Alex had gone, but that was all he had.

"I don't know." Harper shook her head, straining her eyes to see anything out on the horizon. "The only thing that's out here is Mr. McAllister's place."

"You mean Bernie's Island?" Daniel asked, pointing at the dark shape of the island a ways in front of them.

"Yeah." She nodded. "The song sounded like it was coming from that direction, didn't it?"

"I think so."

"Let's head there, then." She crossed her arms and stared straight ahead. "How come that song didn't make you crazy like it did me and Alex?"

"I don't know." He shook his head and glanced down at her. "How come it made you crazy? It was like it hypnotized you or something."

"I don't know." She let out a deep breath. "Let's just hope it doesn't happen again."

When they got closer to the island, Daniel turned off the spotlight at Harper's suggestion. They had no idea what was going on there, but they both agreed that having the element of surprise would probably work in their favor.

He pulled *The Dirty Gull* up next to the dock, and before it had even come to a complete stop, Harper tried to jump over the railing. Before she could make it onto the dock, Daniel grabbed her arm.

"No," he whispered, his voice low so no one could overhear them. "I'm not letting you go there alone."

"But—" Harper tried to argue with him, but he just shook his head.

Probably knowing she wouldn't give him enough time to tie up the boat, he just tossed the anchor over. Daniel climbed onto the dock first, then helped Harper down.

Her feet had barely touched the planks when she heard Gemma yelling. She couldn't understand completely what she was saying, but it sounded like she was shouting for Alex. Harper wanted to run up to the cabin, but Daniel took her hand, keeping her from running into a dangerous situation like a crazed idiot.

They still hurried along the dock, nearly running, but they slowed when they started up the trail. All the lights in the cabin were on, and they could hear Penn and Gemma talking. The wind blowing through the trees tried to carry their voices away, so they couldn't understand them.

The front door of the cabin was wide open, so Daniel and Harper ducked off the trail before they could be spotted. Under the cover of trees, they crept closer to the cabin.

Both of them were so focused on the cabin, trying to get a glimpse of what was happening inside of it, that they weren't watching enough where they were going. Daniel stepped on something and slipped, falling to his knees in a wet puddle.

He'd caught himself from falling on his face by putting his hand out, and when he lifted it, he had something stuck to his palm. It reminded Harper of a dead worm, but it was too thick.

He looked down, and he noticed it before Harper. Daniel jumped, moving away from the dead body as quickly as he could, and wiped his hand clean on his pants. That was when Harper finally looked down and saw Bernie.

Bernie McAllister lay on his back, his stomach torn open, with some of his intestines hanging out.

A scream started in her throat, but before it could escape completely, Daniel had his hand over her mouth. He pressed her back against the trunk of a large oak tree.

"You can't scream," Daniel whispered, and Harper nodded, so he removed his hand.

The truth was that Harper didn't even want to scream. She wanted to sob and run over to Bernie. This was the same old man who had taken care of her during the worst part of her childhood. He'd been nothing but kind to her, and he'd been gutted like a fish.

Thankfully, between Daniel blocking her line of sight and the darkness underneath the trees, she hadn't been able to get a really good look at Bernie. But she'd seen enough to know he was dead.

Behind them, in the cabin, there was a loud banging, and someone shouting. Harper instantly recognized it as Gemma crying out. That helped her push back the tragedy of Bernie's killing and focus on saving her sister. She turned to run in blindly, but Daniel kept her pinned against the tree.

"We have to get Gemma *now,*" Harper said.

"I promise I won't let her get hurt, but we can't just run in there. They tore open a grown man. We can't go in unarmed."

Harper wanted to disagree with him, but he was right. As much as she wanted to burst through the front door that second and grab Gemma, she knew what those girls were capable of. And if she went in unprepared, she would just end up getting Gemma, Daniel, Alex, and herself killed.

Off to the back of Bernie's cabin was a large shed, and because he lived alone on an island, he never bothered to lock it. Daniel opened it, but it was pitch-dark inside without a light. He felt around for anything he could use as a weapon and nearly stabbed himself with a pitchfork.

He handed that to Harper but continued searching for something for himself. Then Gemma began to scream, and Harper couldn't wait any longer. She bolted toward the front door of the cabin, and Daniel took off after her.

TWENTY-EIGHT

Pact

Penn stepped back from Gemma, and for one brief second Gemma felt some relief. Then Penn turned around, putting her back to Gemma. Her wings almost eclipsed Gemma's view. Gemma was crouched on the floor, and she could see Alex lying across the room from her, completely unconscious.

"Leave him alone!" Gemma scrambled to her feet.

She charged at Penn, but Penn unfurled a wing. It swung back, smacking into Gemma with such force that she went flying and crashed into a wall. Seemingly without even trying, Penn had tossed her aside. She was too powerful for Gemma to fight, at least as a human.

Gemma tried to will herself to turn into the same bird monster as Penn was, but she couldn't. No matter how hard she clenched her fists or strained herself, her form remained the same.

"You have to leave behind your mortal life," Penn said, turning back to look at her. She tilted her head to the side, and her fangs didn't completely come together when she spoke. They were too jagged to ever truly close.

"I'll leave behind anything you want," Gemma said. "Just don't hurt him."

"This is what we do, though. This is part of being a siren." Using one of her long talons, Penn pointed to Alex. "And since you refuse to give him up, what better way to teach you how to be a siren than by eating him?"

"It's really not so bad," Lexi chimed in. She and Thea were standing off to the side of the room, still in their normal human shapes. "It sounds disgusting at first, but it's really amazing once you start."

"It's not about being gross. He's a person," Gemma said, trying to remain calm. "You can't just kill him."

"Yeah, actually, we can," Thea said drily. "We have to, in fact."

"I know, I know." Lexi made a sad face, like she was empathizing with Gemma about a bad haircut instead of how morally reprehensible murder was. "But people die all the time. They're so fragile that we're really doing them a favor. When we kill them, they don't suffer. They welcome death. And Penn's right. Most guys are assholes, and they're asking for it anyway."

"Alex isn't asking for it! He never hurt anybody!" Gemma fought back tears, but she was beginning to realize how futile it was to try reasoning with them. "Okay, you win!"

Penn exchanged a look with Thea, then looked curiously at Gemma.

"We've already won, Gemma," Penn said.

"You're right." Gemma stepped toward her, staring straight up into her reptilian eyes. "I don't know how to kill myself. Or you. Not yet. But if you hurt him, if you lay one claw on his head, I will make it my life's mission to destroy us all."

Penn narrowed her eyes and made a throaty growl.

"*But* if you leave him alone, I will go with you willingly," Gemma promised. "I'll do whatever you ask, whenever you ask, until the end of time. I will join you, and I will be your slave. Just please, leave him."

Penn seemed to consider this for a moment, then turned to Thea and Lexi.

"It would be nice to have a slave." Thea shrugged. "And we just ate, so I'm not that hungry."

Penn let out a deep breath and closed her eyes. "Very well."

"Holy shit!" Harper shouted, and Gemma turned to see her sister standing in the doorway of the cabin.

She had a pitchfork in her hand, as if meaning to stab anyone who stood between her and her sister, but she froze when she saw the monster standing there. Daniel was right behind her, and he stood there gaping until Penn turned toward them.

Penn opened her mouth, letting out a loud squawk, and that spurred Daniel into action. He grabbed the pitchfork from Harper and ran around her. Lexi rushed at him. Before she could tackle him, Daniel hit her in the stomach with the handle of the pitchfork, and she stumbled back.

He charged at Penn, but she was lightning-fast. In the blink of eye, she'd grabbed the pitchfork, ripping it from his hands. With her other hand, she backhanded Daniel, leaving three nasty gashes on his cheek.

Daniel fell backward, and Penn lifted the pitchfork, looking as if she would impale him.

"Penn, don't!" Gemma yelled. She ran in front of her, standing between Daniel and the pitchfork. "I'm going with you! Let's just get out of here! Okay? You've already got everything you wanted from this town. Let's just leave."

"Gemma, no!" Harper tried to run to her sister, but Thea elbowed her in the stomach as she approached. Harper collapsed to the floor, holding her belly and coughing.

"She's right," Thea told Penn. "We're just wasting time. The sun's coming up, and the police are already scouring the bay for more bodies. We should just get out of here."

Lexi had gotten back up, and she kicked Daniel in the arm. "Jerk."

"Lexi, come on." Thea started backing out of the cabin, and Lexi gave Daniel one more disparaging look before she went after Thea. They didn't move past the front porch, where they waited for Penn and Gemma to follow.

Penn rolled her eyes, then snapped the pitchfork in half with her hands. With her considerable strength, she threw both halves through a window, causing the glass to shatter and rain down on the floor.

With that, she started shifting back into her human form. Her wings first, folding into her back, then her legs and arms shortening, and finally her face, until she looked as stunningly gorgeous as she always did.

Harper and Daniel both watched, transfixed, as Penn changed her form. If they hadn't seen it for themselves, they never would've believed it.

Penn cracked her neck and readjusted her bikini strap, but otherwise everything about her looked perfect.

"I spared your family and friends," Penn told Gemma. "You owe me so *huge*."

"I know," Gemma admitted.

"Let's go." Penn grabbed Gemma's arm, in case she decided to change her mind, and started walking toward the door.

"Gemma, don't." Harper got up, still cradling her stomach, and looked plaintively at her sister. "You don't have to go with them. We can fight them."

"Sorry, Harper." Gemma turned around so she could look at Harper and walked backward out of the cabin with Penn. "Take care of Alex for me, okay?"

Thea and Lexi sprinted ahead, running down the trail.

Harper stepped forward, saying her sister's name, but Gemma just shook her head. She turned around, and she and Penn raced down the trail. Harper chased after them, but Gemma was too fast, much faster than she'd ever been before.

"Harper!" Daniel yelled, and he got up and ran after her, meaning to stop her from doing anything stupid.

By the time Harper reached the dock, Penn and Gemma were already at the end of it. Gemma glanced back, then dove into the bay.

The sun had begun to rise, bathing the water in pale pink light, and Harper could see Thea and Lexi swimming away. They'd already transformed, and their mermaid tails splashed out of the water before they dove down.

Just as Harper made it to the end of the dock, she felt Daniel's arms around her, preventing her from leaping into the water after her sister. Her arms were outstretched in front of her, as if she thought she could grasp Gemma with them.

"Gemma!" Harper shouted and tried to push Daniel off her, but he refused to let go.

Gemma surfaced just once, but she never looked back toward the dock. Harper just saw Gemma's head, and then the iridescent scales of her tail shimmering in the sunlight before she submerged.

"Harper, stop." Daniel's voice was firm in her ear. "She's not coming back, and where she's going you can't go after her."

"Why not?" Harper demanded, but she stopped struggling. "Why can't I go after her?"

"Because you can't breathe underwater, and you don't know what you're fighting against."

The fight went out of her, and she went lax in his arms. Daniel lowered her down to the dock, and she knelt on the end of it, still staring out at the ocean. He knelt behind her, his arms still around her.

"What the hell were those things?" Harper asked.

"I have no idea. I've never seen anything like that."

"So I'm just supposed to let her go off with them, and do nothing?" Harper turned to look back at him, her face right next to his.

"No, you won't do nothing." Daniel shook his head. "We'll find out what those things are, figure out how to stop them, and then we'll go get your sister back."

"But she's with them *now*. What if they hurt her? What's to stop them from killing her?"

"Harper," Daniel said as gently as he could. "You saw her swim off with them. She looked like a mermaid." He paused. "She's one of them."

"No, she's not, Daniel. She'd never hurt anybody. She's not like them!"

"I know that, but she can at least pass for one of them. And right now I think that's a good thing. That'll keep her alive."

Tears swam in Harper's eyes, and she wiped at them roughly with the palm of her hand. She turned back toward the water.

"Hello?" Alex shouted from back in the cabin. "Gemma? Is anybody here?" He stumbled out the door.

"Are you okay?" Daniel asked Harper, looking at her seriously. "Will you be fine if I leave you alone for a second to check on Alex?"

"Yeah, I'll be fine." She nodded. When he got up, she turned back to him. "Hurry and get him on the boat. The sooner we leave, the sooner we can figure out how to destroy those bitches."

Daniel smiled wanly at her and nodded. He walked back up the trail to take care of Alex, but Harper stayed where she was, watching the water. She heard Daniel talking to Alex, checking to make sure he was okay, and Alex trying to make sense of what he remembered.

But Harper wasn't really paying attention to any of that. She was focused on making a plan. She would get her sister back, if that was the last thing she ever did.

The Watersong Series Continues with

Lullaby

Available Now

Mariah Paaverud

Amanda Hocking is the author of the *New York Times* bestselling Trylle trilogy and six additional self-published novels. She made international headlines by selling over a million copies of her self-published books, primarily in e-book format. She lives in Minnesota, where she's at work on the next book in the Watersong series.